"WHAT IN THE DEVIL DO YOU THINK YOU'RE DOING?"

Page gave a frightened scream and snatched at her clothing. She was a perfect blend of pink and cream flesh and shimmering honey-gold hair that cascaded about her face and shoulders.

Jeff stormed toward her and without waiting for an answer, he grabbed her wrist. "You doxies all think you can take just about anything you want."

"It's not what you think," Page managed as she clutched her clothes in front of her.

"That's what they all say."

Love's Tormented Flame

Kate MacBride

PINNACLE BOOKS   NEW YORK

Although some of the main characters in this book were real people, and the events herein depicted did take place, in some instances both the people and the events were fictionally intensified to add to the drama of the story.

LOVE'S TORMENTED FLAME

An original Pinnacle Books edition, published for the first time anywhere.

First printing, April 1982

ISBN: 0-523-41465-X

Cover illustration by John Solie

Printed in the United States of America

PINNACLE BOOKS, INC.
1430 Broadway
New York, New York 10018

LOVE'S TORMENTED FLAME

Chapter One

The first gray light of morning was already beginning to turn the sky over Abilene to mother-of-pearl.

"The first morning of the new year," Page Carver said, pausing outside the service entrance to the Drover's Cottage Hotel. "I wonder what 1871 will bring us?"

Her mother, Lily, stretched to relieve the ache in her back, the result of a night spent toiling over the steaming tubs of hot water in the hotel's laundry room.

"I'm afraid it's likely to be much the same as the past year, and the one before that," Lily said, her voice weary with resignation.

The despair in her mother's voice gave Page a momentary pang. In the nearly three years since her father had died, leaving a widow and a daughter of fifteen, Page had watched her mother change from a cheerful, high-spirited woman into a stooped and ever-weary drudge.

It was incredible to think what a change had been made in their lives in that time. Looking back, it hardly seemed possible that she was the same giddy, lighthearted girl her memory pictured, running down the stairs into her father's arms.

His face, at least, was unclouded in her remembrance. She supposed, looking back, that he had been the ne'er-do-well that everyone had since described; to her, he had been warm and loving and generous.

Of course, she knew now that it had been a generosity that he could ill afford. Since that day when his heart had suddenly given up its burden, she and her mother had little to call their own, save debts and memories. The gifts that he had showered upon them without restraint had been snatched from their hands. The house in St. Louis—their home, with its dormers and attic, its bright rooms and spacious, fruited lawns—had gone almost at once, along with all but a very few of its furnishings. The carriages, the horses, the jewelry and furs, all gone, taken by the greedy and the merely acquisitive, who had swarmed down upon them.

After Harry died, leaving mountains of debts and no money with which to pay them, their friends soon abandoned them. Among her husband's papers was a deed for some farmland near Abilene, which brought them to the desolate little town with its stockyard and single line of railroad track. But the farmland proved nonexistent, and they were forced into servitude in the town's only hotel, the only place where work could be found.

Page had watched her mother's eyes pale, from shining to dull. Those lovely hands, of which her mother had once been so proud, had grown gnarled and calloused.

It was hardly surprising if her mother sounded weary or resigned. But even as she thought this, Page caught the sound of New Year's revelers in the distance, some drunken cowhands or farmers wending their way home, and at once her own spirits lifted again.

What did it matter, after all, if they had spent their night toiling in the hotel's laundry room, or if they spent this, the first day of the new year, in exhausted slumber in the run-down shack they now called home? Not only a new day, but a new year was beginning, the eighteenth of her life and who knew what that year might bring? She was young and strong and her high spirits could not be restrained for long.

The revelers were closer. "Happy New Year," a man's voice shouted and another answered in kind, and another after that, until the shouts had become a chorus.

"Happy New Year, Mama," Page said, laughing suddenly for no particular reason.

"It won't be so happy if that bunch finds us, two women alone, and them drunken crazy fools," Lily replied grimly. "You can imagine the type to still be carousing the town with morning practically here. Drovers, sounds like."

They waited, heads cocked, as the voices grew nearer. Page's laughter had faded. Mama was right, it would be dangerous for them to be found alone like this, in a dark alleyway.

Abilene was a cattle town. The cowhands drove the great herds up from Texas and Oklahoma, to the rail lines in Abilene, Wichita and Dodge City. After the long weeks and months on the trail, their only thought once the cattle had been disposed of was to hole up for the winter and whoop it up until their money ran out; then they'd drift back to Texas or wherever there were cattle to be herded. They drank and caroused and sometimes shot it out

3

on the streets and woe to the unfortunate woman who found herself in the wrong place at the wrong time.

"They've gone by," Page said as the voices began to fade into the distance. "We'll go this way."

An icy wind blew against them as they followed the alley and started on their way toward the rail line and stockyard near where they lived.

Lily drew her thin coat tighter about herself. She was sorry she hadn't at least wished her daughter Happy New Year. Since her husband's death, Lily had resolutely and deliberately surrendered her dreams of a brighter, easier future, scrubbing them away in the scalding water with the dirt from the sheets and towels and the clothing sent down from the guests' rooms. To dream, to hope, was to suffer new pain as each dream faded, each hope failed.

And yet, she had not surrendered all her dreams. She still dreamed of a brighter tomorrow for her daughter.

She glanced sideways at Page. How pretty she was, Lily thought, her mother's pride causing a sudden lump in her throat. There had been no money to replace the bonnet that had finally given out the year before, and the honey-blonde hair blew in reckless curls in the crisp wind. The same wind turned the fine, porcelain cheeks to apple-red, and stung the piercing blue eyes with tears beneath their long dark lashes.

For herself, Lily no longer cared, but oh, how she wished that she could provide a decent, comfortable life for her child.

Lily had always loved her husband with passionate abandon, and had left the managing of their elegant life in his hands. Now, though, she had almost come to hate him for what he had done to

4

them, for the pitiful existence that he had forced them to accept afer his death.

I forgave you everything else, Harry, she thought with a suddenly keen bitterness, *but I can't forgive you this. May you burn in hell for leaving our daughter to grow old and stooped from bending over laundry tubs, with no hope of bettering herself, and no prospects but the dull, coarse cattlemen who follow her all the time with their eyes.*

"You need a husband," Lily said aloud.

Page was so surprised by this unexpected declaration that she forgot for a moment about being cold.

"Why, Mama," she started to say, but the sentence was left unfinished.

They had continued along the alley, by unspoken agreement avoiding the street where occasionally they could still hear revelers on their way home from the holiday celebration. Just as they passed a barn doorway, a figure emerged from the shadows, lurching into their path.

"Happy New Year," the man cried, his voice little more than a drunken bleat. "Now here's a fine twosome for a man to start out the new year with."

Lily moved to place herself between the drunken cowhand and her daughter, but the man struck her aside with a blow that sent her crashing to the ground. She lay so still that she appeared to be dead.

Page gave a scream of fright and tried to rush to her, but instead her arm was seized in a fierce grip and she was yanked brutally into the dark doorway from which their attacker had appeared.

His breath, foul with the smell of sour beer and rotting teeth, assaulted her nostrils. Her tender flesh was bruised by the cruel fingers clutching her arm,

5

dragging her into the darkness. Page tried to struggle, slapping at him with her free hand, but he laughed at her futile efforts.

"Damn, looks like I've got me a wildcat," he said, grabbing her other hand as well and yanking her violently against him. "That's fine with me, honey, I like a gal with spirit. Makes the ride better."

Unable to strike him with her hands, Page brought one foot back and kicked him on a shin, causing him to yelp with pain.

Her satisfaction was short-lived, however, for in a moment he had released one of her hands and struck her a sharp blow on the chin.

Her head snapped back, and the darkness seemed to deepen. All but unconscious, she heard the tearing of cloth as he flung aside her thin coat and ripped open the bodice of her dress, making her breasts tingle with the sudden rush of icy air. In the next moment, a huge, hairy paw tore at the silken flesh of one bare breast, making her moan with pain.

She was as helpless as an animal in a trap! There were spots dancing before her eyes, and had he not held her crushed against the rough wood of a door, she would no doubt have fallen to the ground like her mother.

She felt his knees between hers, thrusting them apart, and the hand that had been pawing at her breast moved down between her helpless thighs, tearing aside her skirts. He pressed against her, and she could feel the coarseness of his trousers, and something else hot and rigid, rubbing against her, probing between her trembling thighs.

So occupied was her attacker that he did not hear Lily moan softly as consciousness began to re-

6

turn to her. She lay for a moment without moving, trying to remember where she was, and what had happened. The ground beneath her was hard and frozen cold. How had she . . .

Suddenly she remembered! With a jerk of panic, Lily sat up, looking around. At first her terrified eyes saw nothing, though by now daylight was descending upon the alleyway.

A noise brought her eyes around to the deep recesses of the darkened doorway, and she had a glimpse of a bare leg, pushed wide to the side. At the same moment, Page whimpered a frightened protest.

"Please, don't, I beg you," she said in a mere whisper.

For an answer, the assailant laughed again. "Never you fear, you'll like it good enough once you've got it in you," he said, his voice urgent with passion.

Lily leaped to her feet, frantically searching for a weapon. She found a large rock, and without a moment's hesitation, snatched it up and dashed toward the doorway.

He did not hear her until the last moment, and by then it was too late. He had been about to accomplish his infamy, and before his lust-drugged mind comprehended the danger, Lily had brought the rock crashing down upon the back of his head.

This time it was he who gave a low moan and sank to the ground, his trousers down about his knees.

Sobbing, Page threw herself into her mother's arms. "Oh, Mama," she cried, "He was going to . . ."

"Hush, it's all right now," Lily comforted her, hastily rearranging Page's torn clothes to cover her bare flesh. "Come, let's leave while we can, he won't be glad to see us when he comes around."

Clinging to one another, the two women stepped gingerly over the unconscious figure on the ground and, hand in hand, began to run toward the distant street, already light now with morning. They neither paused nor glanced back, too afraid that they might discover their attacker in pursuit.

In a moment they had gained the street, where a distant cart could be heard creaking slowly in their direction. Safe now from danger, they at last slowed their pace to a brisk walk and hurried toward their tumbledown shack.

Had they looked behind them before quitting the alley, they would have seen yet another shadowy figure emerge from a doorway and approach the man on the ground.

Bull Ramsey had been but a few feet away during the entire incident that had just occurred. On his own way home to the hotel after a night of hard drinking and costly poker, he had just stepped into the alleyway to relieve himself when the two women had come along. Indeed, he had been considering exactly the same sort of action when the other man had jumped out to assault the defenseless women.

Never one to do his own dirty work if it could conveniently be done for him, Bull had waited and watched with interest all that had transpired. It did not occur to him to come to Page's aid.

When the drunken fool who had knocked the old woman out and dragged the young pretty into the doorway was finished with them, if he didn't pass out first, it would be easy enough for someone else to come along and have the same fun with them, with a lot less effort. And if the other one was still around, well, by then he'd be little enough trouble for Bull to get rid of. A knife in the ribs, a well-delivered punch—Bull was a coward in a fair fight, but he knew when a man was too drunk to defend himself well—it was the sort of fight Bull preferred, all the odds in his favor.

The old lady had proved him right, too, by the ease with which she'd knocked the drunken lout out cold; probably it was the liquor as well as the blow that had left him senseless on the ground.

He waited until the two women had rounded the corner onto the street proper before he ran up to the fallen figure and bent down.

Quick as a flash, he emptied the man's pockets of what was there—a bag of Bull Durham cigarette tobacco, and some papers; loose change, a rabbit's foot on a string, his wallet—Bull snatched the bills from this, and tossed the empty wallet to the ground.

"Hey, what's going on?"

With a start, Bull looked and saw the man looking up at him bleary-eyed—he had regained consciousness.

"That's my things," the man started to say, slurring his words. He moved to sit up.

Bull gave him a kick in the chin with his knee, knocking him back to the ground, his head striking with a dull thunk. The red-rimmed eyes snapped shut. Without hesitation, Bull grabbed up the same rock Lily had used earlier and brought it down upon the man's skull with a powerful blow.

There was the sound of bone shattering, and when Bull threw the rock aside, it was crimson with blood. He knelt down, putting his ear to the man's chest.

No doubt about it, this time he wouldn't be waking up. He was dead for sure. Bull's palms turned sweaty, and he looked around nervously to see if there had been any witnesses to the deed. No, the alley was empty. Just after dawn, the morning of New Year's Day, things couldn't be quieter. Even the two women were gone.

The women! Bull suddenly heaved a great sigh of relief, and sat back on his haunches.

Now if that don't all work out just hunky-dory, he said to himself, grinning. Couldn't be better, in fact.

He paused just long enough to check the man's pockets again, in case he had missed anything. Then, jamming his booty into a pocket, Bull jumped up and ran quickly down the alley, to the street where the women had disappeared.

Yes, there they were in the distance, almost out of sight, but not so far away that he couldn't keep up with them to see where they went. Home, he gathered, or off to some job, they looked like working women, sure enough.

He smacked his lips remembering the young one, the glimpse he'd had of a bare breast, ripe and full, and the naked legs he'd seen when she was struggling in the doorway. She'd be a fine prize, she would, and the old one wasn't so bad herself, as far as that went.

And they'd come around, when he talked to them. It would throw a real scare into the pair of them, knowing that there had been a witness to their murdering a man in an alley. They'd even cleaned out his pockets, they had, when they'd killed him off. Why, if he was to go to the coppers with his story, they'd be hanged for sure.

He started off on the trail of the two women, already savoring the bargain he was going to strike with them for his silence.

The old year had ended on a sour note for him. He had left Chicago in a hurry when the boss sent him out of town, after killing that Lafarge character. "Stay out of sight for a while," Danny had ordered, "Go to St. Louis for a vacation, or Abilene, someplace where they don't know you."

Like being exiled, for Christ's sake, and the dullest three weeks of his life—until tonight, that is. Even the whores here were small-time, compared to the women of "the Patch," that section of Chicago that held the gambling and the great saloons, not to mention the liveliest of women.

But these two, especially the young one—he smacked his lips again when he contemplated the fact that the new year was only a few hours old, and he'd be bedding that wench before it was another hour older.

Yes sirree, the new year was starting out just fine for him, he could see that already.

Chapter Two

"What if he was dead?" Lily asked, not for the first time.

"I'm sure he was breathing," Page reassured her, though in truth she hadn't been able even to look at the man after her mother had struck him unconscious.

What if he was dead? The question hovered like an insistent mosquito in Page's consciousness. Would anyone believe their story about how the incident had happened? People would question why they were strolling about in an alleyway instead of on the street, unless it was for some nefarious purpose. She could see that motives that were perfectly sensible at the time could easily look suspect later.

She was sorry now she hadn't taken time to see if the man had been breathing. She supposed she ought to have thought of seeking medical aid for him, but where was she to have found a doctor at such an hour on the first day of the new year? And what would have happened had the man awakened quickly, and as quickly resumed what he had been about before he was knocked unconscious? For all she knew, he might have ended up killing them when he was finished.

13

Still, she could not shake the image of a man lying unconscious on the ground, she knew not how badly hurt.

"Perhaps I'll go back," she started to say, but Lily came to a dead stop, seizing her arm with trembling fingers.

"No!" she all but shouted. "You mustn't."

Page paused to give her mother a comforting hug, but she could not still the shudders that wracked the older woman's body.

"It's all right," Page said comfortingly, "There's nothing to point a finger at us anyway, and besides, you couldn't have harmed him all that much. As drunk as he was, it couldn't have taken much to put him out."

They started on their way again, never noticing the man who had also stopped some distance back, stepping into the shelter of a doorway until they resumed their walk, then following them once more.

They came to the railroad tracks and stepped across them after waiting for an early morning coach train approaching slowly. Page saw faces at a few of the windows, people looking out for this, their first glimpse of Abilene.

What they saw could hardly have been impressive, a single line of track, a switching shed, in the distance a shack that served for a station, and to the left, pens in which in the warmer months cattle—sometimes thousands of them—were kept for shipment. And two women, making their way gingerly over the track once the lonely train had been by.

The whistle of any train gave her a pang. She could not see a train pass without wishing she could be upon it, going somewhere, almost anywhere, it hardly mattered, so long as it was away from here . . . but certainly not back to St. Louis. Here, at least, she could avoid running into people she had known in the past, girls with whom she had gone to Mrs. Andrew's Academy for Young Ladies, friends of her parents in the days when they had entertained and had been entertained by the city's so-called "best families."

She did not mind being poor so much as she disliked being reminded that she had once been like those cruel St. Louis snobs who walked with their noses in the air and never had a worthwhile thought in their selfish, spoiled heads.

"Surely," she told herself as she thought back to her earlier girlhood, "I couldn't have been so shallow and mean when I was among them in St. Louis."

But she knew that she had been, and when she received an act of kindness from one of the other women who worked like slaves in the basement of the Drover's Cottage Hotel or in the maids' quarters or in the stables, she was reminded each time that having more in the past had not made her any more generous.

Lily breathed an audible sigh of relief as they let themselves into the tiny cabin that was their home.

"I'll fix us something to eat," Page said, removing her coat but leaving on her gloves. It was only slightly warmer inside than out, and she knew without looking that the dipper would be frozen solid in the water bucket. She had no pin with which to fasten the torn bodice together; she'd have to sew it later.

"Nothing for me, please, just some coffee," Lily said, not even removing her own coat. She went to

15

the wood box beside the cast-iron stove, but Page came and gently took the sticks from her hands.

"You rest," Page urged. "I'll have the fire going in a minute."

Lily looked as if she meant to argue, then thought better of it. She sank instead into the creaking rocker by the stove and was at once lost in a reverie of her own.

Page glanced at her from time to time as she kindled the fire in the stove—they could not afford to keep a fire burning all night while they were away at work, and winter in this plains town was bitterly cold. She wondered if her mother was still worrying about the man in the alley, or if she had gone back in her memory, as Page knew she did often, to their old way of life.

Was she comparing the Christmas just over to Christmases in the past, with the roast goose and plum puddings, the brightly glowing tree, with mountains of gaily wrapped boxes underneath?

Oddly enough, Page found herself thinking, as she set the water upon the stove to melt and measured coffee into a tin pot, that she had enjoyed this Christmas in a way that she had not enjoyed those others. It had always been so hectic then—so many people, so much activity, perhaps even too many presents.

This year, there had been a gingerbread man for Page, baked in precious spare minutes from carefully hoarded ingredients, and a satin ribbon for Lily, an extravagance for which Page had stubbornly refused to feel guilty, though she could hardly afford the few pennies the ribbon cost.

But there had also been time to sit together, speaking little, and those few phrases filled with

16

their love and concern for one another. They had sung carols without any accompaniment and finished the evening with a reading of the tale from which it had all sprung.

"Please . . ." Lily's voice was heavy with pain and when Page looked she saw her rubbing her wrists gingerly. "My medicine."

The cold and the strain had caused her arthritis to flare up, and Page knew how intense the pain could be. She hurried to the cupboard and got down the little bottle of laudanum, grateful that she had just replenished it a few days before.

Carefully she measured out the dosage, not wanting to be too generous and give her mother too much of the powerful drug, yet wanting also to be certain it was enough to relieve the pain.

Lily sucked the laudanum greedily from the spoon and almost at once sank back into the chair, the drug quickly having its effect. Her eyes closed, and it was hard to tell if she was still awake.

Page went back to the cupboard, peeling potatoes and a carrot and putting them on to cook with some of the now-melted water.

She had the coffee and the stew on the stove when the rapping came at the door. Lily's eyes flew open, the laudanum making them appear liquid with fright.

"Who. . . ?" was all she managed to ask before her voice croaked into a whisper.

It was a moment before Page even realized that the hot stove was burning the back of her hand. She snatched it away, bringing it to her mouth and instinctively sucking at the burn, while she stared in wide-eyed uncertainty at the door.

The knock came again, this time louder and

17

more imperious sounding. Too late, Page remembered that she had not thrown the bolt. She saw the knob turn as someone tested it from without.

The door swung inward, creaking on its hinges, letting an icy blast of air into the room to billow their skirts.

The man standing framed in the doorway was a stranger, though the look with which he swept the room, lingering briefly on Lily and then coming to rest on Page, was all too familiar. He was massively built, like an ox, with thick, powerful shoulders and short, squat legs. His eyes beneath bushy dark brows were narrow and filled with an animal cunning, and his mouth was cruel and sensual.

"What do you want?" Page asked, angry with herself at the tremulousness of her voice. "Who are you?"

"A friend," he said, grinning to reveal blackened and missing teeth. "Come to do you a favor, actually."

To Page's dismay, for she had not missed the blatant lust in his glance when it had raked over her body, he stepped inside, swinging the door shut behind him. Her dress was still torn from the attack in the alley, and without thinking she clutched the bodice closed, though not before she had seen his eyes linger on the exposed flesh of her bosom.

"You can't come in," she said.

Bull laughed and said, "Looks to me like I am in, don't it now?"

He came forward, pausing in the middle of the shabby little room, and taking it in with a sneer. Exactly what he had thought, poor working women—the kind that could be easily crushed into submission.

Page made a movement toward the poker but he saw the motion. With a speed that belied his bulky appearance, he crossed to the stove in two quick strides and snatched the poker from the firebox.

"Now you wouldn't be thinking about using this on me, would you?" he asked, smiling without any warmth. "That's downright inhospitable of you, I'd say. 'Course, maybe you just wanted to stir the fire. How's about if I see to that for you?"

Without waiting for an answer, he lifted the lid of the stove and gave the burning wood a violent poke that sent sparks dancing dangerously into the air.

"I can manage for myself, thank you," Page said, her fear giving way to anger at his arrogance. "Will you tell us what you want, and then leave, or must we call for help?"

"Here?" He laughed again, tossing the poker noisily aside. Outside, the northbound train lumbered by, slowing to stop at the station just ahead. "Who'd hear you over that?" he asked, nodding toward the outside noise. "Or care, if they did hear?"

Despite the fact that she knew he was entirely right, Page darted toward the door. Surely someone would hear if she screamed, and even though he said otherwise, the very act of her screaming might frighten him away.

She had barely reached the door, however, when he said, "I came to save your necks from hanging. Leastways, *her* neck." He made a gesture in Lily's direction.

Page's hand froze on the knob of the door. "What do you mean?" she asked, without looking back at him.

"That's what they do to women who bash men's heads in," he said.

Lily gave a low groan from her chair and sank back into it, her eyes closing again, but she was still listening.

Page turned back to the stranger. One glance at his face told her it was useless to pretend.

"You saw what happened?" she asked.

"Every bit of it," he said, grinning like a man who knows clearly that he has the upper hand.

"Then you know that we were attacked, and only defending ourselves. They can't hang us for that."

The coffee on the stove had begun to boil. Bull glanced at it, then back at Page.

"I could use a cup of that," he said. "It's a mite cold out there. A mite cold in here, too, as far as that goes. How's about putting a bit more wood on that fire?"

It was clearly a command, not a request, but though it rankled, Page went at once to throw some more wood into the fire and fill a mug with the steaming coffee. She handed it to him, shuddering when his fingers brushed hers.

He took a long sip, studying her over the rim of the cup. Finally, holding her eyes with his, he said, "What I saw was this pretty young thing lure some drunk fool into a doorway for some hanky-panky, and then this other woman sneaks up behind him when he's got his mind occupied and cracks his head open with a rock, and they cleans out his pockets before they hightail it."

"But that's not the way it happened," Lily cried, "If you saw the whole thing, you know he attacked us, and I was only trying to save my daughter. Anyway, he couldn't have worse than a headache, no harder than I hit him, and as drunk as he was."

"The man's dead," Bull said, not even bothering to look in her direction. "And his pockets is clean."

"You killed him," Page cried suddenly, the truth flashing before her eyes. "You watched the whole thing, and you waited for us to leave, then you killed him and robbed him and followed us here."

"I followed you here, all right," he said. "Figured it was my duty. But then, I got to feeling sorry for you, seeing as how things don't seem to be going so well for you, and you both seeming like such nice ladies, too nice to be in such big trouble. I figured, maybe we could work us out a deal."

"What kind of deal?" Page asked warily, though she already knew. "We have no money."

"Well, now, I wasn't thinking of money, truly I wasn't. It's just, I'm a stranger here in town, don't know a soul. A man gets lonely in a strange town, gets to missing things—especially having a woman to pleasure him . . ."

He let the sentence finish on a trailing note and cocked one thick eyebrow.

Page's face burned crimson. "I see everything now, you've made up this story to try to force us to . . . to . . ." She made an angry gesture, unable to bring herself to put into words what she saw as his intention. "We'll never do as you want. We'll go to the sheriff ourselves, this very moment, and tell him everything. We'll tell them that it was you who murdered that drunken lout, and that you . . ."

"Who'll believe you?" Bull asked quietly, unmoved by her defiance. I'll tell them what I saw. Nobody saw anything happen the way you say. And they'll ask a lot of questions, won't they? Like, what was you two doing hanging around in that alley anyway, instead of walking down the street, like

21

decent women. And how come your mother's got blood on her coat sleeve, if she didn't hit him with that rock?"

Page saw Lily lift her arm and glance in horror at the spots of blood on her sleeve.

Bull turned suddenly to Lily, his voice angry and threatening. "You did hit him with that rock, didn't you?" he demanded.

"Yes, but . . ." Lily stammered, the laudanum making her sound uncertain.

"So you don't know if you killed him or not, do you? That's what they'll ask you, and you don't know the answer, do you?"

Lily tried to face him, but her own fear and uncertainty confounded her and she let her eyes slide away.

"I'm saying you did kill him," Bull said, a note of triumph in his voice. "And I'm saying, they'll hang you for it, unless you want to see if you can talk me into going along with you and keeping my mouth shut about the whole business. Nobody else knows, just us three—and nobody else has to, either—if you've a mind to be nice to me."

This last was directed at Page, and there was no mistaking his meaning. His eyes moved boldly up and down the ripe contours of her body, his tongue darting out to flick hungrily at the corners of his mouth.

Page shuddered with dread. She knew they were defeated and at his mercy. What he said was true: if he told his story, no one would believe theirs. The worst of it was, neither she nor her mother could be absolutely certain that he wasn't right about the one most important point—they couldn't swear that the blow Lily had struck their assailant with that rock hadn't killed him, no matter how much they wanted to believe otherwise. With him to swear that they had killed him, and no way even to be sure that they hadn't, Lily would surely be hanged, or at the very least, imprisoned.

If it were only herself, Page would never have given in to such blackmail; she would rather be punished for a crime she didn't commit. But she couldn't let her mother be dragged away in chains, to suffer an even more ignominious fate than that she already had to endure. No matter what she might have to suffer at the hands of this monstrous brute, it was better than condemning her poor mother to such an infamous future.

"Very well," she said aloud, tilting her chin proudly upward despite the defeat that she was forced to accept, "I'll do as you ask, but on one condition: that you promise to leave afterward and never bother us again."

"You've got my word of honor on that," he said, gloating.

"No!" Lily fairly shouted.

Bull turned upon her, his hand closing into a threatening fist. "You got no choice," he snarled, "You'll both do as I say, or . . ."

"I do have another choice," Lily said, getting unsteadily to her feet, determination etched upon her face. "I would far rather let them hang me than to allow my daughter to submit to your demands. I will tell them that I did indeed kill that poor fool, and furthermore, I will swear that my daughter had nothing to do with it at all, that she wasn't even there at the time . . ."

"Mama, no," Page cried, running to her mother's side and hugging her tearfully. "I can't let you do that, it would pain me far more than doing what he wants."

"Now that's a sensible way to talk," Bull said, breathing a sigh of relief. For a moment he had been afraid the old lady would do what she threatened; she had looked like she really meant it, but now he could see at a glance that the daughter was already convinced, and of the two of them, she was plainly the stronger. Already the old lady was looking addled and unsure of herself. The daughter would convince her, all right and after he'd had his way with the young one, he'd teach the old bag to show him a little more respect in the future. He glanced around the shack again. It was a dump except for a massive brass bed in the corner, but it was clean, and he'd have the two of them to take care of him for the rest of his stay in this crummy town.

"You mustn't," Lily was saying.

"Please, it's better this way. I don't mind, really," Page insisted, holding her mother's head to her shoulder so that she couldn't see the tears welling in her daughter's eyes.

Page turned her head to give Bull a look, pleading silently with him. "You swear that when it's over, you'll leave and we'll never see you again?"

Not likely, my pretty, Bull thought, but aloud he said, "I swear it." If it made her more agreeable to think that, it was fine with him. There was plenty of time later to spell it out for them.

Page helped her mother back into her chair. After her brief show of defiance, Lily had given in to the hopelessness of the situation. Shoulders slumped in defeat, she buried her face in her hands and began to sob quietly. The last and most cherished of her treasures, her beloved daughter, was to be sullied with the rest, and there was nothing she could do to prevent it.

24

Page turned back to Bull, squaring her shoulders. "Very well," she told him, determined at least that she would not show him the extent of her despair, "I will do what you want."

Chapter Three

Bull grinned broadly, moving as if he would cross the room right then and seize her in his arms. Involuntarily, Page took a step back from him.

"Please," she said, with a quick glance at her weeping mother. "We've just come in from work. I was fixing us a bite to eat. Couldn't we . . . couldn't I just finish preparing my mother's supper?"

Bull hesitated for a moment, eyeing the girl suspiciously for any sign of a trick. She looked like she was beaten, sure enough. And he hadn't eaten anything since the night before, come to think of it. Might even make it a little better, her having to think about it awhile beforehand.

"I could do with a bite to eat myself, now that you mention it," he said. "But be quick about it, you hear, and tell the old lady to stop that sniffling. I'm doing her a favor, ain't I, saving her neck and all?"

Page knelt before her mother and cradled her gently in her arms. "You mustn't cry, Mama," she murmured with all the comfort she could manage, "It will be all right, I promise, in a little while he will be gone and it will be all over with."

"I don't fancy you two doing a lot of jibber-jabbering," Bull roared, dropping heavily into one of the chairs at the battered wooden table. "Where's that food you were rattling on about?"

"Please, my medicine . . ." Lily pleaded without looking at her daughter.

"I'll get it," Page promised, "as soon as I feed our visitor."

She got up and hurried toward the stove, where the stew was now simmering fragrantly.

"That's more like it," Bull said, nodding his approval as she took down a bowl. "And I'll have some more of that coffee, too." He thumped his mug loudly on the tabletop.

Page reached for her mother's medicine bottle. As her fingers touched the cold glass, an idea flashed across her mind:

The laudanum was a powerful drug, even a small dose of it made a patient drowsy and light-headed. In fact, the doctor had warned that it would not take too much to knock her mother out cold.

Would it have the same effect on a big, burly man like the one at the table?

"Coffee," Bull yelled. "And my food, before I lose my patience, girl."

"Coming right away," Page replied without turning. She moved to the stove, her back toward the table, the medicine bottle concealed in her hand. Steam rose from the stew as she ladled it into the waiting bowl. With a deft movement, she had removed the bottle stopper and poured the full contents of the bottle into the stew. She gave it a stir with the spoon, watching the medicine blend with the liquid in the bowl until neither color nor scent gave away its presence.

"I'm afraid this won't be terribly good," she said,

managing an apologetic smile as she carried the stew to the table. "The vegetables were a little old, but they were all we had. Let me just feed my mother first, and . . ."

"To hell with your mother, I'll take that bowl, if you please," he ordered, indicating for Page to set it before him.

With a show of reluctance, she did as he ordered. He took a noisy taste with the spoon and made a face.

"A little old, did you say? Tastes more like they were rotten, if you ask me," he said.

Page's heart skipped a beat. "Maybe some salt," she offered timorously.

"Never mind, I'll eat it as is, being as I'm hungry, but let me give you a piece of friendly advice; if you mean to please a man, learn to cook better than this slop."

To her relief, he began to devour the stew with loud slurping noises, dribbling the juices on his black beard. For a moment Page stared, until he looked up, his eyes narrowing.

"Ain't you never seen a man eat before?" he asked. "Say, where's that coffee? I've a mind to take a belt to you just to teach you some manners, if you ain't a bit more careful."

"I'll get the coffee," she said, hurrying back to the stove. She glanced at her mother as she refilled the mug. Lily appeared to have dozed off, her eyes closed, her chin resting on her bosom.

At that precise moment, Lily opened her eyes and looked directly at her daughter.

"Bring me my medicine, please," she asked.

"In a moment, Mama," Page said, the empty medicine bottle suddenly a staggering weight in the pocket of her dress.

29

"Never mind, I'll get it," Lily said, starting from the chair.

"No," Page almost shouted. Lily paused, giving her a startled look. "I'll bring it," Page added, more calmly, "You just rest."

"But . . ."

"You heard her," Bull said, "Sit down and cut out the jawing, you're giving me a headache."

Page was on the verge of answering hotly, but at the last moment, she bit her tongue. The stew was only half eaten, and for all she knew, that wouldn't be enough. She couldn't even be sure what would happen if he ate the entire serving. What if he got suspicious? What if . . . she gave her head a shake to dislodge these worrisome thoughts, and brought the mug of coffee back to the table, even managing yet another tremulous smile, which he misread.

"Not so high and mighty are you, now that you've thought about it a bit," he said, his eyes glinting with fresh desire.

"If I've got no choice, I may as well get used to the idea," she said, lowering her lashes in an attitude of modesty.

"That's the spirit," he said, resuming his meal. "Things could be a lot worse, you know, there's plenty of women say old Bull is the best there is. You could do a lot worse, anyway, that's for sure."

He paused; then, narrowing his eyes again, he added, "Don't you agree?"

"I—I hardly know about such things," she stammered.

His mouth fell open. "Here, now, you mean to tell I'll be the first?"

"Does that displease you?" she asked.

"Displease. . . ?" He guffawed loudly.

Page saw her mother looking at her strangely,

and before she could speak, Page asked, "Is Bull your name?"

"A little shy of the subject, are you?" he asked, grinning lewdly. "Well, that's all right too, there's nothing like a real virgin for modesty. Bull's my name, sure enough, and don't be thinking you can put anything over on me. I'm a man what knows the difference, from experience, if you want to know."

He pushed the empty bowl away. "But I hope you're better at some things than you are at making a stew, I don't know how that's going to set on my stomach." As if to punctuate the remark, he broke wind noisily.

"Would you like a drink?" Page asked. "There's some whiskey. We keep it for my mother, when her pain gets bad and there's no medicine."

"Well, now, that's downright friendly of you," Bull said, tilting the chair back on its rear legs. "Fetch it for me, like a good girl. And speaking of medicine, get the old crow hers before she busts a gut, why don't you, so I won't have her yapping while I'm having my fun."

Page shuddered, knowing only too well what he intended for his fun. She went to her mother's chair and, kneeling with her back to Bull, brought the medicine bottle from her pocket.

"Your medicine, Mama," she said, showing her the empty bottle so that Bull could not see.

Lily blinked uncomprehendingly. "But . . ." she started to say.

"Yes, I know, there isn't much, but the rest is all gone," Page said quickly. She moved her eyes in the direction of the table.

"What's wrong with her now?" Bull demanded at Lily's quick intake of breath.

31

Lily put a hand to her breast. "The pain," she gasped, trembling visibly. "It comes on sudden-like ..."

"Well, wasn't that medicine supposed to make you shut up about that?" Bull asked. He got up noisily, knocking the chair over. "Here, give me that bottle, I'll give her a dose that'll shut her up."

Lily snatched the empty bottle from Page's hand and made a pretense of draining it. She handed it back, wiping her lips with the back of her hand.

"There," Lily said. "That's better."

"I'm glad to hear it," Bull said. "Now, where's that whiskey?"

He watched the girl bend down at the cupboard, the fabric of her mended dress pulling tight over the luscious fullness of her buttocks.

She was a tasty morsel, all right. The heavy weight in his crotch reminded him of what he had come here for. She straightened and turned, blushing when she saw that he was staring at her.

Page felt a vile taste rise in her mouth as she thought of what he intended to do. Would the laudanum have the hoped-for effect? She had delayed as much as possible, trying to give the drug time to work.

She started toward him with the whiskey. Just then he yawned widely. Her spirits jumped, but, she warned herself grimly, that could be just normal drowsiness from being up all night.

Christ Almighty, Bull thought, yawning again, of all the times to start feeling sleepy. Well, he'd wake up enough to take care of business, no question about that, and there was nothing like a good snooze after you'd finished, to his way of thinking. Yes sir, this was going to be a lot better for him

32

than that stuffy hotel room, and all the service here he wanted, too.

He wet his lips, his swarthy face taking on a reddish hue. Her dress was still torn from the earlier incident in the alley, and she had finally forgotten about trying to hold it closed. As she handed him the jar of whiskey, he reached for her, shoving aside the torn bodice to reveal a rosy-pink nipple. He rubbed it harshly between his fingers, feeling her flesh quiver at his touch.

Page felt sick with disgust and loathing. Would there be an end to it, the degradation, the anger that she was working so hard to suppress?

Bull took a long swig of the whiskey, paused for breath, and finished off what was left in the jar.

"There now," he said, wiping his mouth and handing the jar back. "That ought to wake me up for a bit."

To Page's dismay, it seemed to have done just that. His eyes had taken on a glitter, and with his flushed face and his increasingly rapid breathing, he seemed not to feel the laudanum at all.

He looked around, spying the big brass bed against the far wall. Among the room's furnishings, it stood out, for it had been her parents' bed in the fine home that had been theirs before her father had died. It had head-railing and foot-railing of brass, and a down-filled mattress that was like sleeping on a cloud, it was so soft. It had not been kept out of extravagance or even sentiment. By an act of negligence, it had been overlooked by the auctioneer when the other furnishings had been sold, and afterward, Lily had become attached to it.

"We need something to sleep on, after all," she had always defended keeping it, and in time, even when they had sold off other items because they

33

needed cash, they had stopped talking about selling the bed, accepting it instead as something to keep, the sole reminder of what they once had.

"Now there's a bed fit for a man to sleep on," Bull said, with greedy appreciation. "And more than just sleep, too. How's about getting out of the rest of them clothes, my pretty, and let's see what I'm getting for all my troubles?"

"Couldn't we wait just a bit?" Page asked, her mind darting about frantically. "My mother . . ."

"I'm sick of hearing about your mother," Bull roared, snatching at what remained of her dress. The fabric tore away in his grip, leaving but a few shreds of cloth to conceal her most intimate parts.

Lily sprang from her chair at his outburst and rushed at him, but Bull easily flung her aside. Page made a dash for the door, but he reached there before her and again seized her in his arms, burying his fingers in her hair. He gave a brutal jerk, snapping her head back, and before she could recover, his thick lips were upon hers, his tongue thrusting crudely into her mouth, making her gorge rise.

"I'll say one thing, you've got spirit," he said, taking his mouth from hers. "Now, on to the bed with you, missy, and be quick about it."

He shoved her roughly toward the bed. Page staggered and fell half on, half off the bed, but before he could leap upon her she had slid away from him and gotten to her feet again.

Bull had already half lowered his trousers to reveal dirty long johns underneath that bulged conspicuously outward at the crotch, a reminder, though she needed none, of his intentions.

In other circumstances, it would have been a comic sight to see him trying to hold on to his trousers while chasing her about the room, but

34

Page was too terrified to find any humor in the situation.

For a few minutes she managed to evade him, running to and fro about the room, while Lily huddled helplessly near the stove, the poker in her hand.

Bull stumbled after Page, ignoring Lily, who dared not swing the poker for fear of hitting her daughter. Bull's breath was becoming ragged and his face grew so red that Page actually began to hope he might have a fit of apoplexy.

But she herself was becoming exhausted. She had worked all night long at her backbreaking job, and since then had had neither rest nor food.

At last, to her dismay, he caught hold of one of her wrists, yanking her to a stop with such violence that she feared her arm had been wrenched from its socket.

"Damn you, wench," he yelled, slamming her against the wall and knocking the wind out of her, "Enough of this. You'll do what I want, or I'll see the both of you hanged, I swear it!"

He did not wait for a reply, but slammed a fist into her face, bringing a brief blackness down upon her. She was dimly aware of being lifted in his arms and thrown bodily across the bed.

Damnation, what a sight, Bull thought, all but forgetting his anger at the view she presented. She had fallen upon her back, her legs apart, and her efforts to elude him had resulted in the removal of the few remaining shreds of her clothing. At last he could see her without restriction.

She was a fine-looking wench, the prettiest he'd ever seen. His mouth went dry at the thought that she was at last his to do with as he wished and he was confident that once he'd broken her spirit, there would be no more trouble in getting her to do his will.

Consciousness returned slowly to Page. She felt hands upon her naked flesh, and in the distance she could hear her mother sobbing. She opened her eyes and saw Bull Ramsey leering down at her, actually drooling at the sight. He was about to fall upon her, but at the last minute, he glanced over his shoulder, remembering that Lily was still in the room.

"Oh no you don't," he cried, rushing across the room to wrest the poker from her hands. "I haven't forgotten what you did to the last man that tried to have a little fun with your daughter. In here with you, if you please."

Ignoring her cry of distress, Bull opened the clothes cupboard and shoved Lily into it, slammnig the door upon her and throwing the latch to imprison her inside. She could be heard crying and beating feebly on the door from within, but her frail strength was not enough to force it open.

"That'll take care of her," Bull said, grinning with satisfaction as he turned back to the bed. Page had tried to sit up, to come to her mother's aid, but her head was still throbbing from the blow she had received, and the room began to spin as soon as she stirred.

It was no use; she was helpless. Tears of shame and disgust filled her eyes.

"And now, down to business," he said, starting back to her.

Chapter Four

Halfway across the room, Bull staggered slightly and had to put a hand on the table edge to balance himself.

"Thunderation," he growled, giving his head a shake, "I must be getting old, when a couple of shots of whiskey are enough to make my head spin."

Page lay holding her breath, watching wide-eyed as he came back to the bed. She stared mesmerized as he tugged at his long johns and they fell about his knees, revealing his hardened member jutting out disgustingly before him.

"Regular little wildcat, you are," he said, falling heavily upon her and pinning her to the mattress. "Well, I've tamed 'em before, and when I was done, they was crooning a tune and thanking me for being so good to them. And you'll do the same, I promise . . ."

His voice trailed off. One hairy hand had been thrust between her thighs and for a few seconds more she could feel it moving roughly against the delicate satin of her flesh. Then it too went suddenly still.

It was several seconds more before she realized

that he was not merely pausing in his efforts, but had passed out, as she had been praying he would do since she had given him the laudanum in his stew.

At last, the drug had taken effect.

It took her awhile to move his dead weight from on top of her. It was clear, drenched in his sweat as she was, that Bull Ramsey did not bathe any too often, and when at last she managed to roll him over, she averted her eyes from the red, odious thing that now hung limply between his legs.

Trembling with relief and exhaustion, Page hurried to the clothes cupboard and opened the door. Lily tumbled out into her daughter's arms.

"It's all right, Mama," Page comforted her, holding her close. "He's out cold."

Lily turned her wide eyes in the direction of the bed. "Is he, is he dead?" she asked in a whisper tinged with guilty hope.

"No, Mama, I didn't kill him," Page replied. "The laudanum's knocked him out, that's all."

Lily stared in dismay at the bulky figure flopped ungracefully across the bed. "Even if we drag him outside," she said, "he'll just come back when he's conscious again. And we can't go to the sheriff, it's just our word against his. What on earth are we to do?"

"What we should have done long ago," Page said, stretching on tiptoe to remove a battered portmanteau from the shelf of the cupboard. "If he won't go, then we shall."

"Go?" Lily's face registered her surprise. "But go where? And how?"

"It doesn't really matter where," Page said. A fantastic idea struck her. "That was the north-bound train that pulled up to the station awhile ago. We'll go to Chicago, that's it. It's a growing city, they say, and surely there we'll be far enough away that even if this monster does tell his lies, we'll be safely out of danger."

She was already tossing their things into the portmanteau, speed taking the place of neatness. Lily absentmindedly reached for a gown that Page had thrust into the bag and, taking it out again, folded it neatly before replacing it.

"But we haven't enough money," Lily said at length. "The little we've saved won't take us to Chicago."

Page paused, glancing first at her mother, then at Bull. "He must have some," she said. She got up and went to the bed, fear making her steps cautious as she neared him. She had no idea how long the laudanum would keep him asleep. For all she knew, he might awaken at any moment, and it would hardly do for him to find her at his side.

He groaned once and moved slightly. Page froze in terror, staring wide-eyed at him, but his eyes remained closed, his breathing deep and even.

With shaking hands, Page searched his pockets. She found tobacco, a rabbit's foot on a string, a wallet with some money in it, and a loose wad of bills besides. She remembered that he had said that the man in the alley had been robbed as well as murdered, and she supposed some of this must have been his.

"But it's not right to take his money," Lily said, coming to stand beside her.

"It's no more wrong than what he meant to take from us," Page said, counting out what she figured was enough to get them safely to Chicago, but no more. "Anyway, some of this must have been what he took from that other man, so it isn't rightfully his either."

"But," Lily started to object, but just then Bull groaned again and moved on the bed.

"There isn't time to argue," Page said. "Hurry. Put what we need in the bag and let's get out of here before he comes around."

She found herself thinking that it was fortunate in a way that their personal possessions were now reduced to so few. It took only a moment to pack their things into the portmanteau and her mother's reticule. Bull was still unconscious when they let themselves out.

They paused for a moment in the doorway, glancing around. There was little here that either of them would miss, though Lily felt a pang when her eyes came to rest on the brass bed. She would miss that, she admitted silently, but precious little else. Abilene held few fond memories for her and they had been tainted by unpleasant experiences—such as the one that had just occurred.

Lily found herself unable to move. She knew she had to be strong but the thought that once again she was losing her home was more than she could absorb.

"We've got to go," Page said gently, touching her mother's shoulder. "He'll wake up any minute now."

"I'm ready," Lily said, shaking her head and turning her back on the sordid room and the ugly man whose presence had defiled even this shabby house.

"Well, I've always wondered if there was any advantage to living by the railroad tracks," Page tried to joke as they ambled along toward the station and the train that was getting ready to pull out. "At least we don't have much walking to do to get out of here."

The money Page had taken from Bull's pocket paid for their tickets to Chicago with more than three dollars left over.

"Perhaps we should return the rest of the money," Lily suggested, eyeing the bills left in Page's hand with the rail tickets.

"And walk right back into his arms?" Page replied. "No, let's just think of it as the gentleman's payment for his food and drink, and the exercise thrown in for free makes it a bargain."

Despite her show of bravado, for her mother's sake, Page gave her mother a hug as she saw a vendor selling foodstuffs and poteen to the awaiting passengers. "I'll get you some laudanum from the vendor in case you have another attack of pain."

"Surely a vendor wouldn't have an opiate for sale."

Page smiled. "It's as common as tobacco insofar as train travelers are concerned. The passengers always carry it in order to be able to sleep, I'm told."

Page returned with the small bottle tucked into her coat pocket so she'd be able to find it if the pain came on suddenly. They boarded the train and easily found a seat. Page sat by the aisle, giving Lily the seat by the window, but Lily did not so much as glance out of the coach as the train began to move northward.

They were gathering speed as Page glanced back at the shack in time to see Bull Ramsey stepping out the door and looking around dazedly. He hardly glanced at the train and in a moment they were gone from sight and for the first time since his knock at the door, Page began to breathe easily.

It was a slow journey to Chicago for the train they were on stopped at nearly every town along the way, often for several hours.

To Page, however, their travel was miraculously swift. She dimly remembered their trip from St. Louis to Abilene, but that had been by stagecoach. Now, it all but took her breath away to see the countryside fly by with such blurring speed. It was a countryside of woods and bluffs and hearty winter bluestem grasses, ruggedly beautiful, and largely unspoiled. The twin ribbons of the tracks lay like some primordial scar across the land, often the only evidence of man's encroachment.

There was other evidence too, however. Twice she saw cattlemen driving their herds from one or the other of the winter grazing lands that stretched along the plains.

Once she saw Indians. It was odd, living in the town of Abilene that she'd seen so few Indians. She remembered once in St. Louis seeing an old chief and his squaw walking down the street, in the middle of the street itself, so as not to inconvenience the white folks who were using the boardwalks. She had thought them proud and beautiful and had said so, but the other girls at Mrs. Andrew's Academy had laughed at her, or acted as if they thought her touched in the head for holding such an opinion. Later, she had come to understand more of the Indians' plight, and far from changing her opinions, she had come to feel ashamed at being a part, however innocent, of the westward movement that was robbing them of their lands.

Now, from the window of the train, she saw a straggly file of Indians riding after one of the cattle herds, and realized with an ache in her heart that they were waiting for one of the poor animals to die, or be left behind, so they could have it for food.

As Page watched the Indians she thought with a terrible pain in her heart of their poverty, their once proud way of life being driven away by the white man's advance as the prairie dust was driven by the gusting wind. But the dust would settle and remain while the Indians would never again thunder across the hard earth, crying their freedom and their pride.

Even more fascinating than the sights outside the train were those within. The coach was full of passengers now and at each stop it grew fuller. Page's life had been stifled by her social position, first because she had been cut off from all of her friends and acquaintances when her father died and they were forced to move, and later, ironically, by being cast into poverty which automatically branded her an outsider.

She had had precious little opportunity to mingle with any people other than her mother and the older working women at the hotel. There were no girls in Abilene who'd ever wanted her friendship. They had all grown up there and Page didn't belong.

The passengers on the train were of all classes and Page found it exhilarating to be surrounded by people who accepted her without particular notice.

As the miles between them and Abilene steadily increased, Page began to relax and actually to enjoy the experience. Ahead of them lay a new future, totally severed from all the griefs and humiliations of the past. All of these people, or certainly most of them, were on their way to Chicago too, and she and her mother would be nothing more than a part of that arriving throng, free to make their own way in that strange new city, unknown and unresented.

She was pleased when a middle-aged couple across the aisle struck up a conversation. Lily was asleep in her seat, the strain of recent events finally having its way with her, and Page had been staring out of the windows on both sides of the train, until she realized that the woman across the aisle from her was watching her with friendly amusement.

"Amazing, isn't it," the woman said, in a conversational tone, "When I came out this way, it was in a covered wagon, and here we are, racing with the birds."

"It must be a great deal more comfortable too," Page said, grateful for the opportunity to talk to someone.

"It is," the woman said. At that moment, a puff of black smoke from the engine blew in through an open window, making them both cough. "Except for the smoke and the cinders," the woman added.

"It's the price to be paid for progress, I suppose," Page said, holding a mended handkerchief over her nose.

"I'm Maisie Siddons," the stranger said, giving a warm smile. "This here is my husband, Albert."

Albert leaned forward and tipped his hat in Page's direction. "Pleased to meet you," he said, beaming.

They were, by the standards that had once prevailed in Page's life, rather a coarse sort. Maisie's hair was a shade of red that defied nature, and summer roses had been garishly painted upon her doughy cheeks, but her manner was friendly and encouraging. Her husband was a thin man whose face was unfortunately rodentlike. With his pointed features and sharp, narrow eyes, he might actually have looked menacing were it not for his broad smiles.

"How do you do," Page replied, hesitating for a moment over whether to use her own name; but it hardly seemed likely that the trouble they had just fled would follow them to Chicago, and she felt an instinctive repugnance to beginning a new friendship under a false name. "I'm Page Carver, and this is my mother, Lily, though as you can see she's sound asleep just now."

"She looks tuckered out," Maisie replied, nodding. "I said to Albert when we first saw you, I said, that poor woman looks all done in. I'm glad to see her sleeping, if you want to know, she surely must need it."

"She hasn't been well," Page said, feeling that the safest explanation.

"The poor thing," Maisie said, and Albert, leaning forward and smiling again, added, "It's good to see her getting some rest."

Page found the couple easy to chat with, and almost before she knew it she was telling them about herself—the life she had known as a girl, the sudden change in social and financial status, and the difficulty of adjusting to an entirely different sort of life.

"Got relatives in Chicago?" Maisie asked at one point.

"No, no one," Page answered.

"A big move to make, all the way to Chicago, especially not knowing a soul there," Maisie said. "Got any prospects of a job?"

"No, but we're not afraid of work, and with the way people say Chicago's growing, we're sure to find something quickly."

"Not to be too nosy," Maisie said, leaning across the aisle so that the remark could not be overheard by the other passengers, "But tell me the truth, now, have you got some money on you? Chicago's not a cheap town, you know."

"We've got some," Page said, adding, with a sigh, "Little enough, I suppose, but enough to live on a few days. We've gotten used to being frugal."

Maisie nodded her head knowingly. "A penny saved, as they say. Look, would you like to share a little of our lunch?" She brought a hamper out from under her seat.

"Oh, thank you, I couldn't," Page said. "But—" she hesitated, glancing at Lily. "Perhaps a little something for my mother, when she wakes up. We left without thinking of packing lunch."

"I know just how it is," Maisie said, rummaging in the hamper. "The excitement of a long trip like this one, a body's lucky to remember a thing. Here, here's two nice big apples, one for each of you, now never mind fussing about it, we've got plenty more besides and you've got to eat something too if you're going to look after your mama."

"I—well, thank you so very much," Page said, chastising herself for not having bought food when she bought the laudanum. In her anxiety to be away she'd never thought of food.

She ate the apple slowly; though it made her ravenous she did not want to seem like she was starving and intimidate the Siddonses into sharing more of their food. The second apple she saved for when Lily awoke.

When Lily woke later, however, it was in terrible pain. Her arthritis had flared up. There was the laudanum Page had gotten but propriety prevented her from taking an opiate in public. Lily suffered stoically in silence. Page knew her predicament only too well.

"Looks like she's ailing bad," Maisie said, leaning across the aisle to speak in a low voice. "We're coming into a station now. Why don't you take your mother into the water closet and see if a cold towel won't help a bit? I know about arthritis. My own dear mother died a martyr to it, and that's what I always did for her."

"That's an excellent idea," Page said, smiling gratefully. She waited until the train had come to a stop in the station, before helping Lily from her seat.

"Never mind about your things there," Maisie assured her, "We'll keep an eye on them for you."

"That's very kind of you," Page replied gratefully. "We'll be back in just a few minutes."

She helped her mother from the train, pausing to check with the conductor, who assured her that the train would be in the station for twenty minutes. Then they went into the toilet.

The laudanum helped enormously and although she was still in some pain, Lily walked more easily when they made their way back to the train.

The conductor was calling the "all aboard."

"Looks as if we made it just in time," Lily said as Page helped her into the coach. They made their way along the aisle toward their seats.

"Oh dear, the Siddonses aren't in their seats," Page said, noticing the two empty places. "I hope they haven't gotten off, the train's beginning to move already."

She saw the conductor coming along the aisle just then, and waved for his attention. "I'm afraid these passengers haven't gotten back on yet," she told him, indicating the Siddonses' seats.

"The couple you were chatting with earlier?" the conductor replied. "Why, this is as far as they were going."

"But, they were on their way to Chicago," Page said, "I distinctly recall . . ."

"No, ma'am," the conductor said, in a polite but firm voice. "Their tickets were for Watsonville, and that's Watsonville we just left. See for yourself, they took all their things with them."

"And ours too," Lily said.

Page whirled about, to discover that all of their things were indeed gone, with the Siddonses and their belongings.

The conductor gave an angry grunt. "Swindlers," he said, nodding his head. "I thought they looked fishy."

"But they've taken everything we had," Page cried in anguish. "She promised they'd watch them for us."

"So they did," the conductor replied. "Watched them till you two were out of sight, and then hightailed it—probably got out of you just how much you had, too, and where you were headed. Wouldn't want to risk your getting off in the same town, might run into one another."

"We've got to go back," Lily said angrily. "Before they leave there and go someplace else."

The conductor shook his head, his expression sympathetic while at the same time indicating what he thought of women who allowed themselves to be taken in so easily.

"Next stop's not for forty miles," he said, "And the next train back that way isn't for three hours.

48

I'm afraid by the time you get there, they'll probably have skedaddled. Probably just be a waste of your money."

"But we haven't any money," Page said miserably. "Everything was in our bags."

"Sorry, there's nothing I can do now, except report it to the railroad. Course, we'll keep an eye out for them in the future. People like that get caught sooner or later, have no fears."

"Fat lot of good that'll do us," Lily snapped. "Why didn't you keep an eye on them before?"

"Well, now, there's no crime in riding on a train, providing you pay for a ticket, is there?" the conductor asked, a tone of impatience creeping into his voice. After all, he did have other business to take care of, and it was hardly his fault if these two hadn't had the sense to look after their own things, instead of trusting them to perfect strangers.

"No, of course not," Page said, dropping despondently into her seat. "It wasn't your fault."

"True enough," the conductor said. "Tell you what, I'll be back a bit later to take a full report for the company."

He nodded, and went on with the task of collecting tickets. For a moment Page and Lily sat in gloomy silence.

"What will we do?" Lily asked.

"There's nothing we can do, except go on to Chicago," Page said.

"But we've not a dime," Lily said. "Nothing but the clothes on our backs."

"We'll manage somehow," Page said, with as much confidence as she could muster. Inwardly, however, she could not help but think that their situation looked hopeless. Two women, arriving in

49

Chicago alone and penniless, in the dead of winter. How were they ever to survive?

It was still the first day of the new year—a year, she reflected bitterly, that had not started on an auspicious note!

Chapter Five

As they stepped off the train, Page felt the vastness of the city, the fast pace at which everything moved. The cattle town of Abilene was quickly forgotten as they made their way out of the lofty station with its fancy wrought-iron pillars.

Chicago seemed to teem with an insatiable hunger for the sensational, groaning under an almost unbearable need for precarious living. Everything tingled with the promises of pleasure and drama as Page and Lily moved with the bustling throngs that hurried in every direction.

A man openly ogled Page as he stood shivering in his suede-topped shoes, his muffler tight around his neck, coat collar pulled up as he was buffeted by the wind from the lake. There was something evil in his look that made Page quickly turn away.

She remembered having heard about Chicago, which only sixty-five years ago was a bleak stretch of shoreline, the site of a stockade and trading post, Fort Dearborn, sitting unsteadily on marshy ground. Repeatedly the Indians had whittled away the inhabitants until the small garrison fell. Now here it was the beginning of 1871 and on that very site three hundred thousand people lived and worked and dreamed.

They left the depot and made their way through the clutter of people and carriages outside the station, walking huddled together along the wide, noisy street.

Suddenly the city was different. Her parents had taken her here as a very young girl, but somehow the grandeur of the place she'd seen through those very young eyes was gone. Here in the southwest end of the city there was nothing but wooden, squat buildings crowded together and over it all hung the acrid stench of the cattle lowing in the stockyards that seemed to stretch as far as the eye could see.

Lily stumbled and Page caught her, reminding her that this was no time to gawk about and feel disappointed. They needed food and shelter from the biting wind. However, they were far away from Bull Ramsey, which was all that was really important.

"Here, Mama, sit here," Page said as she led her mother to a barrel sitting inside the doorway of an eating place. "I'll see if we can work for a meal." Without waiting for an answer, Page smoothed her skirts, pulled her coat closer about herself, and went inside.

The place was none too clean but it was warm and she wished she could bring Lily inside if only for a moment, but she was too well aware of how the middle classes looked down upon those poorer than themselves and they would have been sent away before Page could have made her plea.

There was a fat, balding man wiping down the tables and a woman, fat as he, sitting behind a counter near the till. Page knew by the disapproving look the woman gave her that she'd fare better by approaching the man. Though he looked none too encouraging when she came up to him, at least he stopped wiping and straightened up.

He let his eyes move over her and then glanced quickly at the fat woman behind the counter. "What do you want?" he asked in a thick German accent.

"I'm not asking for myself, sir. My mother is outside. She is cold and not well. We just came in on the train from Abilene and scoundrels stole our luggage and our money."

"Out!" the fat woman yelled as she started over. "We'll have no vagrants here."

"But I'll work for our meal. Please, sir," Page said turning back to the man. "Only some soup perhaps and a crust of stale bread. Anything."

The man hesitated.

"Out, I say!" the fat woman said, pointing to the door. "Work indeed." She looked Page up and down. "I know well enough the kind of work your kind's good at and it don't require standing up on your feet."

Page felt her cheeks burn. "You judge me unfairly, madame," she said coldly. "We are poor, yes, and hungry, but we are good decent women who only ask for a bowl of soup."

"Hilda," the man said as he hunched his shoulders. "What can it hurt to be charitable? We were poor strangers here once ourselves."

The woman fixed a bitter scowl on her face and laid a stubby finger alongside her sagging jowl. "All right," she said finally, irritably. "But she and the mother will eat in the kitchen and then they can scrub all the floors."

"Thank you, ma'am," Page said as she hurried to bring Lily in out of the bitter cold.

"And go around to the back door," the proprietress ordered.

The kitchen was a large, warm room with a blazing fire burning in a large fireplace. From the rough beams hung pots and every conceivable kind of cooking utensil. A sizzling side of beef roasted on a spit over the glowing coals, the very sight of which made both their mouths water.

Page helped her mother into a chair beside the fire, then slipped out of her thin coat as she looked about.

The door opened and the fat woman waddled in, still looking unfriendly. "My stupid husband would give away everything we have," she grumbled as she took down two tin plates from the shelf and ladled some soup into them from a large cauldron sitting on a cast-iron stove. She tore off two hunks of bread from a hard loaf and plunked them down on the table. "Eat. Go then," she said sharply and started to leave.

"But we will be only too happy to scrub the floors," Page said.

"I don't want you two here any longer than necessary. My husband says feed you, I feed you. Then go!"

"But please understand," Lily said as the warmth of the fire began to revive her. "Madame, we are not beggars. We will gladly work for whatever you give us."

"There's enough of you doxy-types coming in on the train every day. My man is blind but I can tell your kind from a mile off."

"Doxies!" Lily said aghast. "You are mistaken," she added indignantly.

The fat proprietress shook her finger at Lily. "If

54

you are indeed this girl's mother, which I very much doubt, you should be ashamed of yourself for bringing her here."

"I am indeed the girl's mother and we are here only through an unfortunate circumstance. We look for work and a place to live. No more."

"There's plenty of that in the Patch with the rest of your kind," the woman sneered. "Now eat and get out." She lumbered out of the room, slamming the door.

Page and Lily stared after her.

"Why was she so angry?" Page asked as they settled themselves at the table and began to eat.

"She mistook us for dance hall girls," Lily said but knew doxies were a lower lot than that. She made a face. "Which doesn't say much for Chicago's reputation. It was once a very nice, quiet place as I recall. Your father took us here once. Of course, you were too young to remember."

"No," Page said, thinking back. "I remember a coach with matched grays and a big white hotel where everything sparkled. We had a balcony outside our rooms and we ate our breakfast there and I fed the pigeons."

"It seems so long ago." Lily sighed as she finished eating. "Progress can sometimes be very destructive. And Chicago is a very progressive city from all I hear."

"What is this *Patch* she spoke of?"

The fat man quietly slipped into the kitchen, looking behind him, obviously sneaking away from his wife. "A most sinful place," he said, answering Page's question. Then he rolled his twinkling eyes and said, "But it is where all the fun takes place. Music and dancing and gambling and oh, so many

55

pretty, pretty girls are found in the Patch." He ogled Page and laid his hand on her shoulder.

Page instinctively cringed away but the man didn't seem to take any notice. He said. "You'd be very appreciated there, a lovely young girl like you. You'd have no trouble at all finding work and a place to live."

Lily said coolly, "It is not the type of place we are likely to go and not the kind of work we are looking for."

He moved his flabby shoulders and put his hand on Page's arm, letting his fingers play lightly over her lovely, satiny skin. Page pulled quickly away but again the fat man persisted. He winked at her and said, "Of course I could arrange for you to . . ."

The door burst open and his wife barged into the kitchen, her eyes wild with rage, her fists clenched. "I can't leave you for a minute without you're chasing after some young tramp." She picked up a pot and flung it at his head. A pan followed the pot, then a kettle and a mixing bowl that shattered against the far wall.

The man covered his head with his hands and darted about the room dodging the flying missiles. Somehow he managed to make it to the rear door, pulled it open and fled, coatless, out into the cold. He slammed the door behind him just as a large piece of crockery smashed against it.

"And you two get out too!" the woman yelled, picking up a pot and threatening them.

Page and Lily hurriedly struggled into their light coats and scurried out the door, keeping their eyes on the woman lest she fling something at them.

As they hurried away from the place they saw

the husband hiding behind the door to a barn, motioning for them to follow him inside. Page started toward him but Lily grabbed her arm and pulled her in the opposite direction.

"Page, you are too trusting," her mother admonished. "One day your blind innocence will get you into trouble."

"He only wants to help us," Page pointed out.

"Surely you must know he'd expect payment for his help, and I am not referring to money."

Page suddenly thought of the odious Bull Ramsey and shuddered. "Are all men like that, Mama?"

Lily thought back to her days as a girl when she'd first met Harry Carver and of how beautiful their love affair had been. "No, there are some very fine, wonderful men in the world, Page. None of them are perfect, of course," she added as she remembered her husband's extravagance, his lack of responsibility that had caused their present state. "But one day you will find a man who you believe to be perfect and if you truly love him he will be perfect, in your heart, despite all his faults."

They turned the corner of the building and a cold, biting wind lashed at them, carrying with it a threat of snow.

"We must find shelter," Lily said as she clutched Page's arm and hurried along the wooden sidewalk. "It's going to snow."

The first gusts of snow began to blow before they'd gone a mile down the road which a sign told them was named Jefferson Street. One-story wooden stores and houses skirted both sides of the dirt road, deep-rutted from the heavy wagon traffic but frozen solid from the cold. They turned off the main street onto DeKoven Street, feeling that they would have a better chance finding shelter along a less commercial thoroughfare.

"A stable, a barn, anything," Lily said as she shivered with cold and thanked God for the hot soup they'd been given. The pains were starting again in her bones and joints but she refused to think about them.

"There!" Page pointed as they saw a large, sagging barn sitting a short distance apart from a clapboard house built on one level with a wide porch and shingled roof. "And look at all that wash hanging on the lines," she said. "Why would anyone who could afford such expensive linens and cottons live in such a poor-looking house?" she asked as they went nearer and saw the fineness of the laundered clothes.

"The barn door's unlocked," Lily said as she pulled it wider and slipped inside, tugging Page behind her. She looked around. In a far corner a stove was burning wood, giving warmth to the place. There were six cows in separate stalls and at the other end were two horses and a goat. One of the brown cows turned its head and lowed as they shut the door, cutting off the cold blast of air, and moved toward the heat of the stove.

Lily noticed the cow's swollen udder. "The poor thing needs milking. It looks as if she hasn't been milked for a day or more." Warm milk laced with laudanum was what she craved suddenly, yet milking the cow, she convinced herself, would be more for the cow's benefit than her own. She searched out a stool and a pail and set them beside the beast. "There, there, girl," Lily said as the cow grew skittish when she patted her rump.

"Perhaps we shouldn't, Mama. There must be a

reason why she hasn't been milked." She looked at the other cows. "All the others have been."

When Lily reached for the teat the brown cow suddenly bucked and viciously kicked out its back foot. Lily went to its head and smoothed her hand over its muzzle until it settled down. "She's skittish today, that's why she wasn't milked. I can settle her," she assured Page. She spoke softly to the beast until it was quieted then casually worked her way back to the stool and reached for the teat. The cow stayed calm and Lily began to milk her.

"Poor, dumb thing," Lily said as she worked. "I'll take the milk to the house later as repayment for their letting us shelter ourselves here in the barn."

Page watched her mother, wondering idly where she'd learned how to handle a skittish cow. She went to the cow's head and started to pet it as her mother had done but the cow suddenly kicked back and skidded away from Lily, knocking Lily off her stool into a pile of straw.

Page gave a little squeal and rushed to help her mother, but finding her unhurt they both began to laugh.

"Temperamental lady," Lily chortled as she hugged her daughter. She glanced at the milk in the pail. "Some warm milk is what we both need," she said, rubbing the growing stiffness in her hands and arms. "I'm afraid I'll need some laudanum too, Page. The pains are getting worse."

When she saw Page frown Lily added, "We'll repay the nice people by working for them. With a big laundry as we saw on the lines, they must have an awfully big wash and that's our trade, isn't it?" She gave Page a little push. "Put more wood on the fire. I'm sure it will be all right, darling."

Jeff O'Leary sat at the kitchen window watching the gray curl of smoke rising from the barn chimney. He was feeling too sorry for himself to notice that the smoke got thicker, heavier, but when he did become aware that someone was building up the barn-stove fire it didn't bother him much. He was used to vagrants warming themselves in the shelter of the barn, particularly on hard winter days like this and especially in this section of town where there were always plenty of unfortunates in need of a place to sleep out of the weather.

As he watched the snow coming down he didn't much care who was burning their wood in the stove. He didn't much care about anything but the large pile of money he'd lost in the all-night poker game at Danny O'Shea's Scarlet Lady. Jeff reached for the whiskey bottle, then slammed it down on the kitchen table. He was getting a little drunk, he knew, but it helped ease some of his loss.

Mooning over his depleted pocketbook wouldn't bring back his hard-earned money, he kept telling himself, and the worse pain of all was that they'd cheated him out of it. It hadn't been an honest game and it made him really angry at both himself and at O'Shea. They'd taken him for a sucker and he hadn't been smart enough to see it. He'd had too much New Year's celebrating in him when he got into the game, but that was no excuse for having been so stupid.

"One day," he said to the whiskey bottle, "I'm going to get even with you, Danny O'Shea. I'm going to rid the Patch of you and your kind if it takes everything I've got."

Jeff felt like kicking himself every time he

60

thought about how he'd let those doxies set him up. It was the old con game that Danny had pulled. They'd sat on his lap, stood behind him rubbing his shoulders, they served him liquor and all the while they were pretending to pay him so much attention they were giving O'Shea and his goons signals as to what kind of cards Jeff had.

"Stupid," Jeff called himself, slapping his forehead. "Just like some greenhorn from Mick-town."

He told himself that he certainly should have known better. He and Danny O'Shea went back a long way. He hated the man even though he did odd jobs for him now and again, jobs he needed to do to pay his mother's bills and keep his father at the California desert place which was supposed to be so good for his bad lungs.

As he took another swig from the whiskey bottle Jeff thought about the futility of his life. All he did was help out delivering the laundry to his mother's customers. His brother's law practice wasn't off the ground yet and there was feed to buy for the cows that Jeff milked and his mother sold. But the milk and the laundry didn't take in all that much money and the big money that Jeff made from working about the Patch went almost completely to that place in California and his father.

He wasn't proud of what he did in the Patch, jobs that weren't always on the up-and-up. But then what in hell *was* on the up-and-up in the Patch, Jeff asked himself as he took another swig from the bottle.

He closed his eyes and felt the dull ache in his head. Other than the loss of his money and the fact that he had a hangover, the three-day New Year's party had been terrific. He decided on a New

Year's resolution, however. No more women! He was finished with them. He never wanted anything more to do with women, especially doxies. They were bad luck from start to finish. In all his twenty-four years he still hadn't met a single one he could trust. His mother was the only exception, but hell, mothers didn't count. Mothers weren't women in the way he thought about women.

He stared at the whiskey bottle and grinned, knowing he'd never be able to keep such a resolution. Women were as much in his veins as the blood that was there. He could never resist looking at the tantalizing loveliness of firm, round breasts, the sensual curves of a woman's hips, the lush, deep red of female lips, the silky softness, the scent of a woman's hair.

No, Jeff told himself, he could never keep such a ridiculous resolution, no more than he could keep his eyes off the lovely young girl who was taking the two pairs of woolens down from the wash lines.

When he realized what he was watching he jumped to his feet. "Women!" he shouted staring in disbelief at the brazenness of the girl with the honey-colored hair who was stealing some of his mother's wash in broad daylight. "Hey!" he called but she couldn't possibly hear him from inside the kitchen. Jeff banged on the glass but the girl went back inside the barn.

"Damn!" he swore, pounding his fist on the table. "You brazen doxy," he said as he shook his fist at the closed barn door. Now that he thought about it the girl looked like one of the tramps who'd helped empty his pockets at The Scarlet Lady last night. She was most likely some extra girl O'Shea had brought in for the big party and now that it was over Danny was finished with her and had kicked her out.

Still, Jeff didn't feel a bit sorry for her, convinced as he was through his drunken haze that she was one of the trollops who'd set him up.

"Damn your pretty hide," he said. "You're not going to steal my money and my mother's wash as well."

Kicking aside the chair he stomped to the back door, his face screwed up in anger, his fists clenched. He went out into the yard, staggering slightly, and made his way toward the barn.

Inside the barn Page had heated a large bucket of water on top of the stove and had found a cake of hard soap which she'd shaved into slivers and had added to the water. She laid the heavy woolens she'd taken from the line near the stove for warmth and began to unhook the back of her dress. The corner of the barn was toasty and snug and she took an old horse blanket from a peg, shook it and tucked it around her mother, who lay fast asleep in a mound of hay in the corner.

Jeff stepped inside the barn just as Page, not having heard him, let her underclothes drop to the floor and began sponging herself with a washrag. He stood there gazing at her naked beauty as the cloth smeared the soapy water over her loveliness. The golden hair glistened in folds around her shoulders and the texture of her skin was like white satin. Never in his life had he ever seen such beauty.

Somewhere he found his voice. "What in the devil do you think you're doing?"

Page gave a frightened scream and snatched up her clothing, covering her front.

Jeff stormed toward her and, without waiting for

63

an answer, grabbed her wrist. "I asked you a question."

Page was too frightened to speak.

Jeff saw Lily lying asleep a short distance away. "So there are two of you." Remembering the poker game he added, "I should have known your kind always works in pairs."

"My kind?" Page managed, shivering both from fear and cold as she clutched her clothes in front of her. She felt the pain of his grip and tried to pry herself free without exposing her nakedness. "Let me go!"

"I'm turning you in for stealing and trespassing."

"No, please," Page begged. "We meant to pay for what I took. And there are so many pairs of woolens and flannels; surely you won't miss two. I took the most worn, the oldest. They've been mended once already so it isn't like I was taking something brand-new."

"You doxies all think you can take just about anything you want."

"It's not what you think," Page argued as she struggled to get away from him.

"That's what they all say."

"Please. Let me go!"

To keep her from struggling free he pulled her against him and wrapped his arms around her. "A regular little wildcat," he said. Suddenly he was conscious of her soft flesh pressed against the hardness of his body. A warm delicious feeling started to stir deep inside him. The girl in his arms smelled sweet and fresh and clean and her eyes flashed with a fire that matched the one that was beginning to ignite his loins.

This was one of the girls who'd stolen from him,

he convinced himself, and a voice inside him told him that the least she could do was to pay back some of what he'd lost—and he didn't want payment in money.

Chapter Six

Jeff tightened his arms around her and brought her face close to his. Page smelled the liquor on his breath, saw the lust in his eyes, felt the hardness of him against her thigh.

"Let me go," she said as she twisted and turned in an effort to get free if his embrace.

"I know what you are, pretty miss, and I intend taking some of what you make other men pay for."

"Please," Page said as she felt herself being forced toward a bale of hay. "I'm not what you think."

"You lie as beautifully as you look."

"It's the truth. My mother and I . . ."

Jeff cut her off with a laugh. "Mother? If that one passed out over there is your mother, I'm your Uncle Sam."

"Please," Page begged as she felt him pulling away the clothing that was between them. "I'll scream," she threatened and opened her mouth to do so.

Jeff clamped his hand over her mouth and reached into his back pocket for his handkerchief. His whiskey-fogged mind blinded him to everything now but the need for release from the frustrations that he harbored. He held her hands behind her back and lowered her onto the bale of hay. Keeping her captive by the weight of his body atop her, he fitted a gag across her mouth.

Page twisted her head back and forth, preventing him. "Don't do this, please," she begged. "I've never had a man. I'm a virgin."

"Sure you are, sweet thing . . . about as virgin as I am."

When she found herself unable to speak through the gag she started to kick and scratch but to no avail. He easily used her underpinnings to tie her wrists and ankles to either side of the bindings of the hay bale, leaving her spread-eagled and vulnerable to whatever he wanted to do to her.

Ignoring the pleading in her eyes, the tears that rolled down her cheeks, Jeff stood and feasted his eyes on the most beautiful of sights he'd ever seen. She was a perfect blend of pink and cream flesh, shimmering honey-gold hair that cascaded about her face and shoulders, flesh that seemed to radiate from within, like ivory under the soft glow of firelight.

He tested her bindings to make sure the cloth was holding her, not harming her in any way, and looked longingly at the ripe firm breasts, the dark nipples pointing temptingly. His eyes devoured the creaminess of her thighs, spread so invitingly, the copper mass curling where the thighs parted.

The heaviness in his loins became unbearable though a touch of conscience told him that it was wrong to take advantage of her in this way.

Then he scowled more at his thought than at Page and began stripping himself of his clothes. It wasn't as if he would be the first to lie with her. She was a damned tart, he reminded himself as he threw aside his shirt and vest and began taking off his boots, then his trousers.

She was far from innocent, he told himself, seeing the way she was looking at him, and Jeff smiled to himself, feeling that she was watching him with admiration as he stood naked and aroused over her.

It wasn't with admiration that Page's eyes grew wide but rather with curiosity. She had never seen a man completely naked before, never one so young and handsome. His body was like sculptured marble, his arms curved with muscles, his chest broad and matted with dark hair, his stomach hard and rippled. Page moved her eyes lower and when she saw the awesome sight of his erect manhood she tore her gaze away and bit down on her lower lip as the trembling began deep inside her.

Like a falling sapling he came down on her, forcing her surrender. He pulled down the gag and immediately replaced it with his mouth. He took hold of himself and aimed his throbbing erection at the very center of her being. With one quick, hard thrust he was inside her, gaining easy access by the wetness of her unconscious excitement.

Page cried out under his mouth as a searing stab of pain shot up through her. She tried to fight him off but she found herself helpless as she tugged against her silken bindings.

Deeper and deeper Jeff thrust himself into her body, the scent of her hair driving him mad with lust.

The hurt started to ebb away as Page felt a strange heat building up from the depths of her very core, spreading out like soft, warm hands, caressing, soothing. A new feeling took the place of her resistance to his assault as the heat grew and grew, enveloping every part of her lower body. She found herself tugging against the bonds but welcoming the feel of their restraint as it helped relieve the guilt for the pleasure she was beginning to experience. Jeff was pounding unmercifully into her and she found herself beginning to relax and move, meeting his thrusts with thrusts of her own.

Page knew she should remain still and fight against this cruel onslaught with every fiber of her being, but she could not help herself. Some involuntary force had taken control of her body and was demanding that she obey its will rather than her own.

He interpreted her thrusts and bucking as passion and drove at her with renewed fury, his teeth clenched, his eyes shut, his muscles taut.

With a shattering moan he drove deep into her and then, as every ounce of strength bolted from his body, he fell on her, pressing her deeper into the hay bale. He lay quite still for a moment, then with a sigh he relaxed and slid his mouth from hers.

Rather than scream, Page knew it was finished and a scream would accomplish nothing now that the damage had been done. "Will you unfasten me now?" she said through tight, angry lips.

"What?" He stirred, his senses coming back. "Yes, of course." He undid the silk bindings and started to get into his clothes. "I'm sorry, miss, but you deserved the treatment."

"Deflowering a virgin is hardly what I call just retribution for borrowing two woolen articles of clothing."

"A virgin," Jeff scoffed. "Are you going to insist on that old saw?"

"The evidence is here, sir, if you care to examine it."

Jeff moved his eyes without much interest toward her parted thighs. His eyes widened when he saw the spots of blood on the hay bale. "Good Lord!" he breathed. "You were a virgin!"

"Good Lord, indeed," Page said indignantly. "And you are quite correct: I *was* a virgin."

"But . . . you reacted to me. You enjoyed it as much as I. You didn't fight me."

"And how was I to fight you with my wrists and ankles fastened? I was as vulnerable as new-fallen snow to a footprint."

Jeff slapped his forehead. "It isn't possible," he said with a stricken look.

"The evidence speaks for itself. Did you take me for a liar when I told you I'd never lain with a man before?"

"You're a doxy."

"That was your assumption. Obviously you were wrong. You would have known if you'd believed me. My mother and I . . ."

Jeff looked toward the corner. "Your mother? That other . . . that woman is your mother?"

Page glowered at him. "Have you lived your entire life among liars?"

"Where women are concerned, yes," he snapped.

"Then I would suggest a change in the company you choose for yourself." Page finished pulling herself into her clothes. "My mother and I came here from Abilene to get away from men like you. All we want is a humble job and a place to live. If that isn't possible in Chicago, then obviously we made a mistake by coming here." She saw the hurt and shame in his eyes and had a strong need for vindication. "Naturally finding an honorable husband was something I had hoped for, but after this, my dreams and hopes are ruined. I'd prized my

71

maidenhood; unfortunately, you stole that along with my dignity."

Jeff bristled. All right, he'd made an error in judgment but he'd be damned if he was going to permit this lass to make him grovel. "Look," he said, squaring his jaw. "I made a mistake. But, damn it, how long do you think a beautiful, innocent young girl like you would be able to scrounge about this section of Chicago before someone far worse than me would take advantage of you? So kindly stop being so blasted dramatic."

"Dramatic, am I? I suppose by saying that, it helps remove your guilt? My mother and I have thus far been able to ward off the lecherous attentions of men and we can continue to do so."

"Your mother is well over the hill and you've become ripe; that's all that's saved you thus far. How long do you think you'd last out there? It's winter, damn it, and Chicago can be pretty disagreeable if you have no job, no place out of the cold. You'd settle soon enough for a man who'd provide."

"We'll manage, I assure you."

Jeff saw her determination and smiled in spite of himself. "Yes, I imagine you will." He hunkered down beside her as she sat on the bale picking straw out of her hair. "Look, maybe I can help. I have a few connections in town. There's always someone looking for help."

"In one of the bawdy houses you obviously enjoy?"

"No. Believe it or not, I know quite a few respectable people." He touched her hand. Page pulled it rudely away.

"I don't even know your name," Jeff said.

She hesitated, but seeing the pain in his eyes, the

deep feeling of guilt, her compassion took hold of her. "Page," she said. "Page Carver."

"Jeff O'Leary." He jabbed his thumb toward the house outside. "I live here with my mother and my brother, Allan. They are real respectable." He looked at her with what Page took to be a kind of pleading. "I've been partying for the last few days, since before New Year's, and I lost a bit of money. I was trying to drown my loss in whiskey when I saw you take the woolens off the line. You resembled one of the girls who'd set me up in a card game. I came looking for revenge. Please, forgive me. I really am truly sorry for what I did."

Page huffed for a moment but the damage was irreparable so she saw little reason to dwell on it. She shrugged her pretty shoulders. "It was a mistake, then." She thought suddenly of the warm feeling that had spread throughout her body when he was inside her. "I suppose everyone makes mistakes."

He touched her hand. "Thank you. And if there is any way I can help you, I'm at your service, Miss Carver." He found he could not stop looking at her. She was the most enchanting creature he had ever laid eyes on. "Tell me, what brought you and your mother to Chicago at this time of year? Usually people move about when the temperatures are a bit warmer."

"We came from Abilene, as I said." She told him about the couple on the train who'd conned them out of their money and traveling bags. "So we got off the train without a cent and nothing to wear but the clothes on our backs."

"But why come here?"

Page felt she couldn't tell him about Bull Ramsey and about the murdered man in the alley. "We

73

lost our jobs," she lied. But it was only a little lie, she convinced herself.

"And what kind of work do you do?"

"We worked in the hotel laundry."

"Laundry!" Jeff put back his head and began to laugh.

"I see nothing funny about being a laundress. It is very hard, but honest work."

"Oh, forgive me, Page Carver. I wasn't laughing at your occupation, it's just . . ." He laughed again and when he'd collected himself he said, "Haven't you any idea of what's hanging on the lines out there?"

"Of course. Your washing."

"My mother's washing," he clarified. "Surely you didn't think all of those clothes belonged to us? Have you taken a good look at our house? It's no more than an exaggerated cottage with rooms built on. The clothes are those of rich people, not the likes of the O'Learys."

"Then . . ."

"Yes. My mother takes in laundry." He looked down the line of cows. "And sells milk. That's how she makes a living. And so far as the laundry is concerned, she turns away new business every day for the lack of help. But this is perfect," Jeff said, rubbing his hands together. "There's an extra room off the kitchen large enough for two beds."

Page's mind suddenly drifted back and her heart began to ache as she thought of the beautiful big brass bed they'd been forced to abandon in Abilene.

Seeing her far-off expression he mistook it for uncertainty. "It's a nice, large room. You wouldn't be cramped. And being next to the kitchen, it is always warm in the wintertime. My mother would be only too glad to hire you, I'm sure of it. Of course, she wouldn't be able to pay much until the new business started to pay off, but you'd have room and board and a few pennies to spend. What do you say?"

In the far corner Lily stirred and a soft moan escaped her lips. Page's eyes widened when she remembered only too vividly what had happened to her while her mother slept. She said, "You will have to make your offer to my mother. I'm sure she'll be happy to accept, but you must promise me one thing."

"Anything," Jeff said, suddenly overjoyed there was a possibility that he'd be seeing this lovely creature every day.

"My mother must never know why you are making this offer to us. She must never learn of what you did to me."

Jeff nodded as he felt his cheeks get hot. "I promise, of course. And the same goes for my mother and for Allan, my brother. It'll be our secret, Page. I promise you on my life, no one will ever know."

Lily called Page's name.

In a whisper Jeff said, "As far as anyone is concerned, Page, you are as pure as the snow that is falling outside."

Page no longer felt pure, yet she knew that for the sake of keeping peace between her mother and Jeff's, she had to content herself with their secret.

"Page!"

She went quickly toward the corner as Lily came out of her laudanum sleep. She got to her feet with an effort, wrapping the old horse blanket around her. When she saw her daughter's hair in disarray and the handsome young man standing beside her, Lily's indignation rose.

"This is Jeff O'Leary," Page said quickly. "His mother runs a laundry. He's offered us work."

Lily narrowed her eyes. "What price did you have to pay for the offer?"

"Oh, Mama," Page said self-consciously. "You mustn't be so suspicious." She hoped that her mother would let it go at that.

Jeff bowed. "Permit me, Mrs. Carver." He offered her his arm. "Come inside and let me introduce you to my family."

Lily hesitated.

Page linked her arm in her mother's. "You said you wanted to repay the family for the milk we drank."

Lily hesitated, then took Jeff's arm as he walked them toward the house.

Chapter Seven

Mrs. O'Leary was a short, hearty woman with apple cheeks and an Irish face all bright and laughing, who took an immediate liking to Lily and Page, especially when they seemed so eager for work in payment for room and board and little salary.

"Just enough money for my mother's medicine. She suffers something terrible from arthritis at times."

"Saints preserve us, I know how painful that can be," Mrs. O'Leary said to Lily. "I get the rheumatism something awful meself when the weather gets cold and wet like this, but I found meself a good remedy," she added going to the kitchen cupboard and taking down a bottle.

"Laudanum," Lily admitted slightly embarrassed, "seems to be the only thing that helps me."

"Laudanum eats away the insides," Mrs. O'Leary insisted. "Here. Just rub some of this on your aching joints, Lily. It's oil of wintergreen and menthol. It'll knock out the pain just like that," she said, snapping her fat fingers. "And to keep the pain from coming back, don't drink any water at

77

mealtimes. Instead, drink cod liver oil with lemon or orange juice."

Lily took the bottle and gave the other woman a wry smile. "Oranges and lemons," she said wistfully. "It's been a very long time since Page or I have seen the likes of them."

"Don't you fret none, Lily," Mrs. O'Leary said. "My boys will find them if they're to be found." She turned to Jeff who was standing quietly inside the kitchen door gazing at Page. "Speaking of which, where is your older brother? Allan should be home by now. He said he'd be finished at the courthouse by three o'clock and it's almost five."

As if on cue, the door opened and in walked one of the most handsome men Page had ever seen. Allan O'Leary was a tall, slender man with hair of a sandy brown color, eyes the color of emeralds and a smile so wide and sincere she felt her heart give a little tug. The tiny lines at the corners of his eyes told her he was several years older than Jeff but they only accentuated his good looks. He was very agreeably dressed in a conservative suit, tight-fitting, which was the height of fashion, and wearing a bowler, which he hung on the hook behind the door alongside his beaver-collared coat.

"Well," Allan said smiling appreciatively at Page and Lily. "I thought I got my Christmas presents last week."

"Begone with your Irish blarney," his mother said, laughing. "These two dear things are going to be living and working here so you behave yourself, both of you."

She introduced Page and Lily to her oldest son and Jeff filled him in on the details of how they'd come to be here. Mrs. O'Leary put on a pot of tea and the five of them settled around the kitchen table.

"You're an attorney-at-law, Jeff tells me," Page said looking into his handsome face.

Jeff saw the admiration in her eyes and said, "Don't let that impress you, Page. Allan's just another big dumb Irishman."

"Speak for yourself," Allan shot back. With a tolerant smile he said to Page, "Forgive my little brother, Miss Carver, he isn't accustomed to being in the company of ladies."

Jeff jumped up ready to fight, but his mother only laughed and grabbed his arm, tugging him back into his chair. She shook her head and said to Lily, "Thanks be to God you had a girl and not sons, Lily. Show these two hot-Irish-heads a pretty ankle and they're like two fools after leprechaun gold." To her sons she said, "Behave yourselves, both of you. Your father would thrash you good if he were here seeing the way you're tearing at each other all the time."

Lily, to relieve the tension between the two men, asked Allan, "Do you have your own practice here in Chicago, Mr. O'Leary?"

He nodded. "I'm just small potatoes as compared to some in Chicago, but I have one thing most of the others don't have and that's an honest desire to clean up the corruption in this city."

Page leaned forward, interested. "What kind of corruption, Mr. O'Leary?"

"It would please me if you both called me Allan." Then he said. "You name it, Miss Carver. We have it all here, starting from the very top on down to the Patch."

"Yes," Lily offered, "we've already heard of the Patch. Just what is it, Mr.—Allan?"

"Not a decent place to be talking about," Mrs. O'Leary said. "A whole section of nothing but dance halls, pool parlors, gambling palaces, and far worse."

"Worse?" Page said innocently.

Jeff ventured a wink that no one else saw. "Doxies on every corner and in every barroom."

"Jeffrey!" his mother said sternly. "We may all be working women here, but we are decent and I won't have that kind of person even mentioned in my house."

Allan looked very sober. "The vice and corruption that flourishes isn't confined to the Patch, but that's where it's most visible. Chicago is in the grip of dishonest politicians who corrupt everything they touch, from the grain trade markets to the price of a bottle of milk." He leaned back in his chair, balancing it on two legs. "I dream one day of seeing this city white and tall and shining like a piece of polished ivory gleaming in the sun, with buildings so high you won't be able to see the tops of them, and rail cars that carry you across town over the tops of the streets, free food for those who can't afford it, low-priced housing for the needy, great hospitals—not the wooden, clapboard lean-tos they put up these days. I see a city that will withstand any catastrophe."

Jeff watched Page's eyes go soft and limpid as she listened and watched his brother. He too wanted to see the city free from vice and crime but he resented the way Allan was dramatizing. There was no question that he'd captured Page and Lily, even his mother sat enraptured, listening to his idealistic speech. Just looking at them all told Jeff he was outranked by his brother's polish and education, an education he'd helped pay for.

Quietly Jeff got out of his chair and left the room.

"Chicago was always a wild place," Allan continued, holding his captured audience. "Some say its name alone means *wild onion*, but there's another version which I'll have to tell you about one day." He grinned then grew serious again. "It started as a trading post, you know, about a hundred years ago. A Frenchman by the name of Point du Sable started doing business with the Indians right where the middle of town is now, on the north bank of the Chicago River, just a short ways away from the new water tower on Michigan Avenue. They called the river the Chicago Creek back then. There were always squabbles with the various tribes. I know both you ladies are too young to remember the Black Hawk Wars about forty years ago but old Black Hawk put a curse on the city when he felt the government had cheated his people out of this land on which the city's built. Old Black Hawk claimed the governor, who was the agent for Andy Jackson, got all his Indian braves drunk, then had them agree to ridiculous terms, giving them more whiskey and some silver half-dollars for their land. Black Hawk said that the settlement of Chicago would one day suffer the same fate as his bones."

"Dry up and blow away?" Mrs. O'Leary ventured.

"That's what everyone thought he meant, so a group of historians—to play it safe—brought his bones to the Historical Society Building in Burlington, Iowa. The structure burned to the ground and absolutely nothing remained but ashes."

Page felt herself shiver as Lily gave a little gasp.

Mrs. O'Leary slapped the table and laughed.

81

"Ha, the nerve of the likes of that Indian putting a curse on Chicago. Now if it had been an Irish curse then there'd be something to be worried about."

They laughed and the tension of the moment was broken.

Lily asked, "You mentioned a new water tower. What is it?"

"It was built about a year or so ago. I'll have to give you ladies a tour of the city. The tower's a beautiful structure, about one hundred eighty-five feet high and made of pale yellow limestone. It houses a standpipe that absorbs the pulsations caused by pumps across the street in the water-works, which keeps a steady stream of water flowing through the city water mains."

"Dear me," his mother said. "Will you look at the time and me with no dinner ready and wash still to be taken in and ironed."

"Here," Page said jumping up. "I'll fetch the wash."

"And I'll start on the ironing," Lily volunteered quickly.

By the time the dinner was ready and on the table it was as if Page and Lily had been with the O'Learys most of their lives, though Page did notice that Jeff never came into the kitchen while Allan sat and talked and even helped out by showing them where to find things, where to put things, telling them the names of the customers and which articles belonged to who.

"You seem to know an awful lot about your mother's customers," Page said.

"I used to do all the deliveries after Pa had to go away. He had bad lungs. He had to go to a drier climate . . . a place someone recommended out in California."

"Ah, that's too bad. And what does Jeff do?" Page asked innocently, never imagining that she was prying.

She turned sharply when the younger brother came up behind her. "I do what my big brother used to do so he can finish his schooling."

"Jeff means getting me through law school," Allan said. "I'm a certified lawyer, but according to my little brother I'm still in need of learning."

Jeff said, "You're blind to everything that's going on, is all. You think you can clean up Chicago with speeches and good intentions. Well, you're dead wrong, my friend."

His mother hit him with a wooden spoon. "And how would you go about it? With your rough Irish fists, like your father used to?"

"It's the only way to get rid of Danny O'Shea and the rest of that trash," Jeff said stubbornly.

As they sat down around the table Page's mouth watered at the sight of the food. She and her mother looked hungrily at the large roast of beef, the bowls of boiled potatoes and green beans, the thick brown gravy and fresh bread warm from the oven.

"Now don't be shy with your appetites," Mrs. O'Leary told them. "All the food that goes on this table is to be eaten. If you leave the table hungry it's your own fault." Her eyes twinkled. "And it wouldn't be a good idea to insult my cooking by not eating it." She took it upon herself to heap their plates, then settled down with a heaped plate of her own. "First time at my table I'll treat you like guests; the second time, you're on your own."

"Your husband has tuberculosis?" Lily asked.

"Not exactly. He was shot during a brawl in one of those barrooms in the Patch. It affected his lungs." She tapped her chest. "He can't breathe unless it's dry as dust outside."

"It must make it difficult for you having to keep him in California."

Mrs. O'Leary shook her head. "You and Page have enough of your own troubles without having to listen to ours."

The conversation turned back to brighter things as Jeff started to talk about some of the funny stories his father was fond of telling. By the time they'd finished eating they were all in a very jovial mood.

Allan was the first to get up from the table. "If you'll all excuse me, I have some paperwork to take care of."

"And we have ironing to finish," Lily said to Page.

Mrs. O'Leary said, "I'll have a hand in the ironing, Lily. Page, you and Jeff clean up the table and attend to the dirty dishes.

As Page washed and Jeff dried, she said, "I like the way you spoke of your father. You were obviously fond of him."

"He was a dumb Mick."

She chuckled. "I don't think you believe that."

"There's a lot more behind that story of why he's in California."

"You mean it wasn't because of his bad lungs?"

"Oh, he got shot in the lung, all right. My father and a man named Tom O'Shea were partners in a very thriving business on Market Street. Being two bad-tempered Irishmen, they were always fighting over the money. Tom O'Shea shot Pa in the chest. I honestly don't think he meant to kill Pa and he claimed afterwards that it was an accident, but the bullet punctured a lung and Pa was laid up. After

Pa could get around, Tom's body was found floating in the lake. His son, Danny O'Shea, convinced everybody that it was Pa who did his old man in. Things got bad and Pa's health got worse, so Ma managed to scrape money together and we got Pa to California."

She handed him another plate to dry. "Is there still bad blood between the O'Learys and the O'Sheas?"

"We don't like each other much. Danny O'Shea now runs a very notorious saloon in the Patch and Allan's always after him. In fact, Allan's against all the businesses in the Patch. I don't blame him, mind you, but my brother is going about it all wrong. He's a dreamer, all ideals and no common sense. Now I'm a mixer and a bit of a conniver. There's only two possible ways of fighting O'Shea and his crowd and the first is from the inside. And if that doesn't work, then the only other way the Patch and the O'Sheas will be put out of business is by burning their places to the ground. For two cents I'd put the match to it myself."

She handed him another plate and when their fingers touched Page felt a spark, remembering the touch of him earlier. She pulled away and the plate dropped, but Jeff caught it neatly before it hit the floor. He smiled at her and saw the crimson rise in her cheeks.

"Funny," he said as he leered at her, "we were both obviously thinking the same thing."

She looked around to make certain no one heard him. "I forbid you ever to mention that again, do you understand?"

"Only if you'll let it happen again."

"Never!"

"Oh, stop it, Page. You enjoyed it as much as I did."

She glowered at him, her face a mask of outrage. "If our mothers weren't in the next room, I'd slap your face so hard it would slide off your shoulders."

"I like the way your eyes dance when you're mad."

Just then Allan put his head in the door. "Any coffee left?"

"In the pot," Page said. "But go back to your work, Allan. I'll bring it to you."

When his brother was gone Jeff said, "Why are you so nice to him and so snappy with me?"

"Because, Jeff O'Leary, I have a very good memory and I firmly believe your brother is not the kind of man who drinks too much, loses money in poker games and ravages innocent girls in a cow barn." She slammed down the dishrag and went to fix a cup of coffee for Allan.

Begrudgingly Jeff said, "He takes two sugars, no cream, and you'll find him in the little alcove off the living room, through that door."

"Thank you," she said haughtily as she flounced out.

Jeff wiped the saucer so vigorously it fell from his hand and broke on the floor. When his mother appeared in the doorway, hands on hips, Jeff shrugged. She shook her head and went back to helping Lily with the ironing.

It was about two weeks later when Lily and Mrs. O'Leary were finishing up folding and sorting the laundry that Catherine O'Leary said, "I can't get over the changes around here since you and Page came, Lily. Already the money's almost twice what

86

it used to be, so I won't hear tell of you not taking your right share."

"Oh, you've been too generous already, Catherine. Page and I don't need any more than we have, unless you'd prefer we start looking for our own place to live."

"What?" Mrs. O'Leary said with false indignity. "And break up the family? I won't hear tell of it. Besides, who'd keep my boys in line if you two lived separate? Why, I've never seen such a change in them these past weeks."

Lily laughed. "I think you can blame that on Page. Between us, Catherine, I think they both have taken a shine to my girl. And two better men she couldn't find."

Modestly Mrs. O'Leary said, "Allan was always a good boy; it's Jeffrey I'm bowled over by. Why, he's actually drinking less and he hasn't been in a card game or a gambling house since you both came here, Allan tells me. Jeff's even more responsible about the deliveries and about keeping his records of accounts." She poked Lily with her elbow and leaned close. "He's even getting to bed at a decent hour every night. I almost don't know he's my same boy."

She folded the last of the linens into the basket and closed the lid. "That finishes the Harringtons' wash for a week. I'll put it out on the porch with the others so Jeff can start his deliveries." She trudged out, leaving Lily alone.

Lily turned back to the rinse tub and began running the clothes through the rubber rollers that squeezed out the water. She didn't much mind working here for Catherine O'Leary. It was a cozier sort of job, not backbreaking like the laundry room at the hotel in Abilene. There they had no modern equipment, just tubs and washboards. The wringing was done by hand with Page twisting at one end of the sheets and her at the other.

Turning toward the contraption in the center of the room, Lily carried over the boiling kettle of water from the wood burner. She filled the tub of the mechanism. Mrs. O'Leary had told her the machine had come all the way from Philadelphia, thanks to a friend of Jeff's, and was the first mechanical washing machine of its kind, complete with a drum that held the dirty clothes and revolving paddles that turned the clothes over and over when a crank on the side of the tub was turned by hand.

Yes, there were so many comforts here in Chicago. Lily was glad now that they'd been forced to come. Still, lingering far back in her mind was this friction that was developing between the O'Leary boys over Page. It was as plain as day that they were both smitten with her and though Catherine thought it wonderful to see her sons compete, Lily sensed a feeling of foreboding. Jeff's temperament ran too hot and Allan's too smoothly . . . a bad mix, like fire and water, which always created steam and pressure when combined.

Page came in. "I've finished hanging that last batch on the lines. The sun's out high and warm so they should be dry in no time."

"I'll have another batch ready in half an hour."

Page rubbed her shoulders. "Allan asked if I'd walk out with him for a few minutes. The snow's all melted and it's very nice out. Will that be all right, Mama?"

"I'm sure that is up to Mrs. O'Leary, not me. It's her time you'll be stealing."

Page frowned, wondering why her mother sounded so disapproving. "I've already asked Mrs. O'Leary and she told me to take all the time I liked."

Lily started to turn the crank of the washing tub. "You had better start keeping an eye on those two fires you've set."

Page cocked her head, not understanding.

"I'm talking about the ones inside Allan and Jeff O'Leary. Mark my word, Page, you might start a blaze that you won't be able to control."

"Oh, Mama. It's nothing like you think. We're just good friends, like brothers and sister." She shifted uncomfortably under her mother's look of cynicism.

"You know better than that, Page. They're both taken with you and you're playing one against the other. Just watch you don't overplay your part, young lady."

It was true, Page admitted to herself as she hurried along to meet Allan who was waiting on the porch. They both were attracted to her and she was attracted to them. No, that wasn't quite true, she told herself. She didn't like Jeff at all. He was no gentleman like Allan was. Jeff was always trying to kiss her and touch her. Still, he had softer eyes than Allan and a broader smile.

When she saw Allan she shrugged off the image of Jeff and reminded herself that Allan was taller and better-looking, smoother and more refined. She decidedly preferred that to Jeff's lustful looks and constant eyeing of her.

"I thought we'd take the buggy today and I'd give you a brief tour. You really haven't seen much of Chicago since you got here," Allan said.

"I'd like that." Page took the arm he offered and let him help her into the buggy hitched to the dappled mare he called Maureen. He switched her rump with the buggy whip and reined her left toward the lakeshore.

"Believe it or not, Page, not more than twenty years ago this whole city was nothing but squalor. Houses were very few, the streets so bad they became quagmires whenever it rained and everywhere you looked, streets, squares, parks, you'd see public hog pens."

"Hog pens?" Page laughed.

"Yes. The hog nuisance was the main issue of the day back then. The city had no public utilities until a group of progressives took matters in their own hands and started installing water and gas systems."

He looked proudly about at the thriving avenue of stores and houses. "One day Chicago will be the finest city in the nation." Then, with a little less bravura he added, "Well, perhaps at least one of the finest."

Page found it difficult to share his dream as she saw the endless row of wooden-frame buildings with their shingled roofs and sagging clapboard sidings, all built right up against each other and the narrow thoroughfare that was too clogged with people and carts and animals.

They drove for about fifteen minutes and Page had to admit that the downtown area, with its stone buildings, showed some promise of fulfilling Allan's dream.

A wind came up and Page pulled her shawl tighter about herself. "It's time I got back to the washing," she said.

Allan switched Maureen into a slow trot. He drove in silence for a while, then said, "I trust I do you no affront, Page, when I say that I'm quite attracted to you."

Page laid her hand on his arm. "Please, Allan, I would so appreciate it if you didn't speak to me of anything but friendship."

Allan felt a deep scowl cut into his forehead. "It's Jeff you prefer then," he said bitterly.

Page saw his anger and tried to keep her tone as casual as possible. "I don't prefer any one to the other, Allan. I'm fond of you both in equal measure, though I do admit," she said with a sweet smile, "Jeff is more difficult to like than you are."

She saw his expression brighten and quickly changed the subject.

Mrs. O'Leary was standing on the porch scanning the street, her arms folded angrily across her ample bosom. "Thank goodness you two are back," she said, looking worried and upset.

"What's the matter?" Allan asked.

"It's Jeff. He's been in a fight." She wrung her hands. "And he's been so good lately. I was sure he'd reformed his ways."

"Where is he?"

"At Barney Hogan's place on the lakefront."

"Not in the Patch?" Allan said, amused. "Well, Mama, at least he's in a classier saloon." He helped Page out of the buggy, then started toward his horse hitched near the gate. "I'll go fetch him home. Be back in an hour."

But he wasn't back in an hour. The sun was down and their dinner was still in the warming oven when Mrs. O'Leary stopped pacing the kitchen floor and glanced at the baskets of laundry still to be delivered. "Glory be to God," she breathed to Lily. "All our new customers who live near the Patch are lost to us already. The first loads of laundry and we can't deliver them as promised." She shook her head. "It says poorly about the O'Leary laundry."

"I'll deliver them," Page offered.

"Oh, no, child," Mrs. O'Leary said. "It's the families skirting the Patch. You'd have to cross right through an edge of that heathen area. I wouldn't hear tell of it, especially at this time of the night."

"It's still early, Mrs. O'Leary. Nobody will bother me so early in the evening." She smiled. "Why, they won't have had time to get fired up yet, so there's nothing for me to fear. Besides, if we lose the new customers and the business falls off, Mother and I will be out of our jobs. Please," she implored, "let me deliver the baskets. I'll be back quick as a flash. The buggy's already hitched."

Neither Lily nor Mrs. O'Leary liked the idea but they all had their selfish reasons for making light of the dangers of a young girl venturing alone into so disreputable an area. In the end they decided to let Page go.

"Use the buggy whip if you have to," Mrs. O'Leary told her. "And I don't only mean on old Maureen."

Chapter Eight

Experiencing some difficulty finding the various houses, Page finally finished with her business and turned Maureen in the direction of DeKoven Street and home.

"You've earned yourself some extra feed tonight," she told the horse. "And I personally will see that there's a warmer fire in the barn wood-burner. But don't you get fidgety like you did last night. You got that old brown cow so upset she practically kicked out the boards in her stall. I really think, Maureen, that you purposely get pleasure out of annoying that old cow."

Suddenly, just as Page turned onto one of the narrow streets that led out of the Patch, a horse and rider raced passed her, frightening both Page and Maureen, sending the horse rearing up on her hind legs and almost upsetting the buggy. A man ran out from the shadows of a saloon and grabbed the reins, holding them firmly, talking gently to the horse until Maureen whinnied once or twice more then settled down, switching her tail nervously.

"Oh, thank you," Page said breathlessly.

He took off the hat that sat rakishly over one eye and made a sweeping bow. "Danny O'Shea at your service, pretty miss." He looked at the buggy. "This is the O'Leary contraption, but you ain't Catherine O'Leary, that's for certain."

So this was the terrible man Jeff spoke of so bitterly. Remembering all the terrible things she'd been told about Danny O'Shea she grew nervous.

"You do have a name?" Danny said when she didn't answer him.

"Carver. Page Carver," she managed, trying to keep her voice from shaking. She tried to maneuver Maureen away but Danny held her bridle firmly in his thick, long fingers.

At twenty-nine, Danny O'Shea looked older. He was a brute of a fellow with a wild head of red hair, coarse and uncombed, and a rough, stubbly chin that needed shaving. There was something cruel in the curve of his mouth as he stood leering up at her through his evil eyes. He had a thick neck and bullish shoulders that made Page think of half-man/half-beast, like some ogre out of one of those mythology books her father gave her on some forgotten birthday.

"I really must get home, Mr. O'Shea. Thank you again," Page said as she tried to back Maureen out of the man's grip.

"Having trouble with the old nag?" Danny said. "Here, let me help." Before Page could protest he leapt into the buggy, pushed her across the seat and took the reins out of her hands.

"Please, no!"

"No trouble, Miss Page."

Page noticed that the man was now between her and her only weapon of defense, the buggy whip. His forcefulness warned her of impending danger and when he turned the horse away from DeKoven

Street and put his hand on Page's knee, she panicked.

Shoving his hand away Page turned angrily toward him, her eyes on fire. "You get out of this buggy now or I'll scream my head off."

Danny laughed. "Scream all you like. You're in the Patch, little darlin', where a woman's scream is just a part of the scenery." He laughed again and pulled up in front of a saloon with a sign reading The Scarlet Lady.

Page thought of Jeff again. This was where he'd played poker, and as Danny pulled her out of the buggy and forced her toward the door, she prayed Jeff would be inside to save her.

As it wasn't yet eight o'clock, the saloon was practically empty. There were only two men at the bar and a few flashy women with an older, distinguished-looking man seated at a table near the back. The few people paid no attention as Danny forced Page through a doorway into a small room that was fitted under the stairs leading to the second level.

Danny kicked shut the door, pushed her onto a couch and stood over her, grinning, hands on hips, legs apart, the crotch of his torso in an even line with her eyes. She cowered back into a corner of the couch, unable to think or reason. This was the den of iniquity she'd heard so much about. Every place within several square miles was a house of the devil. What chance did she have if she screamed until her lungs burst? There was no help to be had in the midst of hell, she told herself as her eyes moved furtively about the room looking for some way to escape, some weapon of defense.

"Now," Danny said as he reached for her. "I

think you and I should get better acquainted, Page Carver."

"Please let me go," Page urged as she cringed away.

"But surely you want to repay me for having saved you from a possible accident." With that he reached for the neckline of her dress. Page kicked him soundly in the groin, doubling him over in pain. She saw her chance and made a dash for the door but Danny grabbed her, ripping the sleeve from the shoulder seam. Page screamed. She picked up an oil lamp from the marble-topped table and flung it at him, shattering glass in every direction. Danny only laughed and made a lunge for her. He caught her easily and backed her toward the couch.

With a hard shove he threw her down, reached out and ripped the front of her dress completely down to the waist. Again Page screamed and tried to cover herself, but Danny slapped her hands aside and tore the last remnants of her clothing from her, leaving her naked from neck to waistline, her lovely firm breasts, full and creamy soft, exposed to his lecherous view. He licked his lips as he looked at the nipples pouting at him defiantly.

He made a move to feast himself on the rest of her naked loveliness when suddenly the door broke open and three men burst into the room. Page screamed again, little realizing that her rescuers stood before her.

"Let her go, Danny."

The man who gave the order was the older gentleman Page had glimpsed sitting at the back table with the painted women. His age was difficult for her to calculate but she figured him to be about fifty or so, and though he stood leaning on a walking stick, strength was no hindrance because flanking him were two of the meanest, roughest men Page had ever seen.

The man with the walking stick said, "Now you wouldn't want my boys bloodying that Mick face of yours, would you, Danny?"

"She's just a dame, Karl," Danny said. "What do you care about just another dame?"

"I happen to disapprove of any man who mistreats ladies."

"What lady? She's a washerwoman who works for the O'Learys."

"A respectable young working woman, which is all the more reason she should be protected." Then, in a harsher, more threatening voice the man said, "Now back away, Danny. Brock and Ziggy here would be only too happy to have an excuse to see if Irish blood is red or green."

Danny stepped aside as the gentleman walked smiling toward Page, who sat trying to pull the torn pieces of her dress up over her exposed breasts.

"Permit me, my dear, to introduce myself. I am Karl Kane. If you would give me the honor, I'd very much like to escort you out of this disreputable establishment."

Danny sneered. "And take her across the street to that snake pit of yours, I suppose."

Page's eyes widened with a new fear. As honorable as the man appeared, if Danny O'Shea spoke the truth, this *gentleman* was nothing more than a dandified saloon keeper in the Patch, a man of the same ilk and character as the one from whose clutches she was being taken.

When Karl Kane extended his hand, Page quickly began sorting through the maze of doubts rushing through her head. She tried desperately to think what she should do.

She had no choice but to accept the man's offer of rescue and if a new precarious situation arose as a result then she would have to figure a way out of that, if possible.

Hesitantly she extended her hand to his, holding the other hand across her breasts.

"Ziggy!" Karl Kane barked, snapping his fingers. "Give the young lady your coat."

The man with the misshapen face grinned lewdly as he took off his jacket and draped it across Page's shoulders. As he did so he leaned close to her ear and said, "I'll take off everything else, honey, if you want." He let his hands linger on her shoulder.

"Ziggy!"

The goon gave her shoulder a suggestive squeeze and went back to his position inside the door.

"After you, my dear," Karl said. Page preceded him out of the room. Behind her she heard Karl say to Danny, "You must be mad to try this sort of thing with anyone connected with the O'Learys. They'll get you one day, Danny."

"No chance. I can buy Jeff O'Leary for a five-dollar bill anytime I want." He laughed. "Enjoy your booty, Karl. But I don't forget easily. Next time it'll be the other way around."

"If there ever is a next time for you, Danny. Just behave yourself and I'll see that you stay in business."

Page understood none of it. To her it was as if they were speaking in code, though she readily understood the remark about Jeff. For all he bad-mouthed Danny O'Shea, it was in O'Shea's saloon where he gambled and obviously spent his time. He might hate Danny O'Shea but there was something that held Jeff to him.

As they left The Scarlet Lady, Karl noticed the buggy. "I assume this is yours, Miss . . . You haven't told me your name."

She told him in a tight, nervous voice, clutching the jacket around herself. "The buggy belongs to the O'Learys. I was just returning there after making the laundry deliveries."

"You can hardly return in that condition. We'll have to do something about repairing the damage done to your gown. Come. I'll have your buggy delivered back to Mrs. O'Leary with my card, saying you're having dinner with me and for them not to concern themselves about your safety. Mrs. O'Leary knows me to be an honorable man. She won't object too strenuously." An impish gleam came into his eyes. "However, I fear I can't say the same about her two hotheaded sons."

Page frowned slightly, wondering how the man could consider Allan as being hotheaded; he was everything but.

"That's my establishment over there," Karl said. "I call it The Gilded Plume. My wife, God rest her soul, was very partial to yellow plumes." He reached for her arm and felt her pull back. "Now, now, my dear, I am not cut from the same bolt of cloth as Mr. O'Shea. You are perfectly safe with me and I have no intentions of taking you to my establishment. You're just about my dear departed wife's size and there are closets filled with lovely things of hers in my home, from which you can choose something to replace what you're wearing."

Reluctantly Page allowed herself to be led to the handsome landau with liveried footman and teamster. She felt she had no other alternative but to go with the man. If she turned and ran there were the two henchmen behind them blocking her escape to the buggy, and Danny O'Shea was standing in the doorway of The Scarlet Lady ready to pull her back inside.

Besides, considering herself somewhat of a fair judge of character, she felt this older gentleman a decent sort and aged as he was, she felt there was little harm he could do her.

They drove east along Division Street after Karl Kane wrote something on his business card and mumbled instructions to Ziggy and Brock.

"My house is on Lake Shore Drive," he told Page. "I built it for my wife as a wedding present. It holds many fond memories," he said sadly. "I suppose it does a man no good to live with the past, but I just never found a reason to move out."

It was the largest house Page had ever seen, set far back in a parklike setting of lawns and trees and sculptured topiaries. The house was of brick with white marble trim, three stories high, with wide bracketed eaves and a heavy, wide porch painted white.

As they entered the high, gilt-tipped wrought-iron gates Page stared in awe at the luxury of the place. Even the grand houses she remembered from St. Louis could not compare to this.

"There's dockage at the rear and, of course, a spectacular view of Lake Michigan," Karl explained proudly.

"It's lovely," Page breathed.

The interior surpassed the awesome beauty of the exterior. The rooms were mammoth. Karl told her there were twelve bedrooms alone and almost as many different rooms scattered about the first level. She'd almost forgotten that she was in the clutches of a stranger, until she was rudely reminded when he took her arm and started to lead her toward the grand staircase of white marble and red, plush carpeting that curved up to the next level.

Again Page pulled back. Karl laughed and reached for the bell cord at the bottom of the stairs. A moment later an older woman in black bombazine and a white cap and apron appeared from below stairs.

"Mrs. Chambers, Miss Carver had an unfortunate accident on my account, I'm afraid. See that one of the housemaids attends to her bath and dress. She may choose what she wishes from Mrs. Kane's closets. And while she's bathing and dressing, please set another place for dinner." He turned to Page. "You'll stay for dinner, of course."

Almost without realizing it Page nodded. "Thank you, yes. I am rather hungry."

"Good."

As she started up the stairs following along behind the housekeeper, Page wondered what she'd gotten herself into. The only way to find the answer to that, she decided, was to play the game to the end.

From out of nowhere she thought of Jeff O'Leary and how he'd taken advantage of her that day.

Karl Kane was far different from Jeff, but then perhaps he wasn't so different after all, she thought, as Mrs. Chambers led her into the elegant dressing room and threw open the closet doors. Page had never before seen so many beautiful things.

"You may choose anything you wish," the housekeeper said. "I'll lay them out for you while you bathe."

101

There'd be a price to pay, Page told herself. Then, with a sigh, she ran her hands over the expensive materials and decided she'd worry about the price when the time came.

Chapter Nine

To her complete astonishment, Karl proved to be a gentleman of his word. No repayment was even hinted at and by the time he drove her home Page was enthralled with him.

They were all up waiting for her when she came into the house. Page told her mother and the O'Learys she'd had a fall, ripping her dress, and how Karl Kane had come to her rescue.

"Karl Kane!" Jeff roared at Page, who looked like a princess in the ivory satin gown and ermine cape that hugged her chin and trailed on the floor, the clothes Karl had insisted she keep.

She glanced around the circle of disapproving faces. Jeff, Allan and her mother were scowling and shaking their heads. Lily wore a pitiful look and it was easy to see she'd been crying.

"How could you let this happen to you?" Lily groaned as she touched the ermine cape and fingered the satin flounces of the gown. "I thought I'd taught you right from wrong. Oh, Page, I am so ashamed." She broke down and began crying again.

Page put her arms lovingly around her mother. "There is nothing to be ashamed of, Mother. Nothing happened. I had dinner with Mr. Kane, that's the whole of it. On Father's grave I swear to you that I did nothing dishonorable."

Mrs. O'Leary bustled up to Lily. "I've been telling you, Lily, that Karl Kane's a right decent man. A widower these past few years and an admirer of beauty, but he has a good and generous heart and a clean soul from all I know of him." She glanced at Page. "These fancy duds he gave the girl are trifles to him. He has more money than he knows how to spend. He has vast cattle holdings in Kansas and he is a big investor in the stockyard as well as the grain market."

Lily shook her head. "Perhaps a good heart, Catherine, but no man gives expensive furs and dresses to a strange young girl without expecting something in return."

"Knowing the man, I'm sure he exacted no payment, nor expects any. Besides, the dress and cape are more than likely his dead wife's and were just gathering moths in the closets."

"He's a saloon keeper," Jeff reminded her.

His mother said, "And need I remind you that it's the one almost decent saloon in the Patch. At least he doesn't rent out rooms upstairs or water the booze or fix the gambling games. He's trustworthy and a fine, upstanding citizen."

Allan shook his head. "I'm not all that sure you're right, Mother. I'm afraid you're letting his kindness to you interfere with your judgment of him. Karl Kane is a rich and powerful man, true enough, but in these parts no man ever gets as powerful as he is by being honest."

Jeff eyed Page with disgust. "Get out of those ridiculous clothes. You look like one of those silly dalliers from Lake Shore."

She turned up her nose. "Karl Kane was every

bit a gentleman, which is far more than I can say for you, Jeff O'Leary."

He saw her knowing look and lowered his eyes as he shifted uncomfortably. "A gentleman to you, perhaps, but with the heart of a lecher."

"Do you say that because you compare every man's heart with your own?" Page snapped.

"Children," Lily said, coming between them. "I'll have no fighting." She turned to Page. "Jeff's right, dear. Take off the clothes and we'll pack them neatly and return them to Mr. Kane. Such finery is not for you. Though a man may present himself as wanting nothing in return for his favors, they all expect to be repaid in one way or another and I see no reason for you to remain in Mr. Kane's debt. You gave him delightful companionship in exchange for a lovely dinner and the loan of some clothing. That finishes the transaction between you. I see no need for you to ever see the man again."

"But he exacted the promise from me that I *would* see him again."

"I forbid it!" Jeff shouted.

She whirled on him, her eyes ablaze. "Who are you to forbid me? I'll do what I please and you'll have no say in it."

Lily patted her hand. "Again Jeff is right, darling. I too object to your seeing this Karl Kane again. It can serve no purpose. He's too far out of our class, Page. He wants nothing more from you except to satisfy his lechery."

"That isn't true. If he'd wanted anything of that nature he could easily have taken me against my will this evening. He had ample opportunity."

Lily said, "Some men enjoy playing with their victims, like cats sometimes do with mice, or little boys who take pleasure in slowly pulling the wings

105

off flies. They have a strange need to deny them-selves, making their conquest that much more pleasurable when it's achieved."

Mrs. O'Leary said, "Like fasting during Lent." She fluffed her apron. "But I'll not say a word against Karl Kane."

Allan explained, "It was Karl Kane who gave Mother the money needed to send Father to that desert ranch in California."

Jeff opened his mouth to add something but then shut it.

"He's a good man," Mrs. O'Leary insisted as a tear slipped down her cheek. She caught it with the edge of her apron. "If it hadn't been for Mr. Kane's generosity, Patrick would be dead and in his grave by now. There'll be no ill spoken of Karl Kane in my presence."

Despite the objections of her mother and the O'Leary brothers, Page kept her promise to see Karl Kane. She supposed her obstinacy was built on their jealous objections and in her young, innocent mind that's all it was. Allan and Jeff clearly resented the attention she paid Karl. Why her mother was so displeased with Karl, Page could not figure. Karl Kane was always kind and considerate and never once in all the times she had dinner with him or they went to the theater, had he ever so much as insinuated a desire for anything physical. He was an honest-to-goodness, twenty-four karat gentleman and Page found herself looking forward to their evenings together.

"Good evening, Miss Page," Mrs. Chambers said, opening the door just as the footman helped Page from the landau. As they went into the man-sion the older woman said, "Mr. Kane was called to his office on some important unexpected business. He said he wouldn't be long and asked if you wouldn't mind waiting."

"No, not at all," Page answered.

"Dinner will be a little later than usual, unfortunately."

"Is there anything I can do to help?"

Mrs. Chambers gave her a deprecating look. "Dear me, no." Uncomfortable, she stammered, "Thank you." She glanced toward the salon. "I've made a fire in the drawing room. I'm sure Mr. Kane will not be long. May I bring you a sherry?"

"Thank you, no, Mrs. Chambers. I'm sure I can amuse myself until Karl comes home."

The room was one she had seen only from a distance for Karl always preferred the small, more intimate sitting rooms whenever they dined at home. As she went into the drawing room she was overcome by its beauty. A massive chandelier of sparkling crystals flamed overhead, giving a delicate softness to the yellows and golds of the embroidered furniture. The fireplace was faced with marble and on its mantel sat twin crystal candelebra and an ornate gold clock with a china face and elaborate carvings. The floor was marble and a large, deep oriental rug of soft green dominated its center.

At one corner of the room Page noticed a pianoforte, its lid raised, lighted candles perched on either side of the music rack. The rosewood case and creamy ivory keys took her back into time when, as a small child of no more than seven or eight, she'd been made to practice at the keyboard at least one hour every day. She'd almost forgotten her music teacher, Mrs. Gerard, who'd stood over her with a yardstick in one hand and a pointer in the other,

107

smacking her between the shoulders if she slouched, jabbing the printed music score to call attention to an error in her playing.

Page smiled, wondering if she could remember anything of what she'd been taught. She slipped off her gloves as she went toward the square rosewood piano, flexed her fingers, then sat down on the velvet tufted seat. She tested the keys and found the instrument in excellent tune.

She played a few chords, then a scale and as she watched her fingers move over the keys more and more of what she'd known gradually came back to her, though she noticed she could manipulate both black and white keys only with effort, so decided she'd best play on all the white keys . . . the C Major scale, she recalled.

Amusing herself with little pieces she remembered, she suddenly began humming along with the melodies and without realizing it she slipped into an old song her father had always liked to hear her sing. She couldn't remember who wrote it but it was a favorite of his.

She closed her eyes and formed her fingers on the keys then began to sing in a sweet, mellow voice:

On wings of music roaming,
With thee, my sister, I glide.
Where the gay flowers are blooming
On the banks of the Ganges tide.

Surprised that it all came back so easily, she sang it through to the end, and when she finished, Karl Kane began to applaud enthusiastically.

Page jumped up and fumbled for her gloves, which she'd laid on the casing.

"Enchanting," Karl said. "I had no idea you sang so beautifully."

Her cheeks burned. "It's been so very long, I thought I'd forgotten how. I do hope you don't mind my taking the liberty of playing the pianoforte?"

"Mind? My dear, I'll have it delivered to your home so that you may enjoy it at your leisure every day."

"Oh, no," Page gasped, thinking of her mother's distrust of Karl Kane. "I'd never find time to practice and I must remind you that it isn't my house to furnish."

"Of course. But come. Sing me another song. Your voice is like a nightingale's."

Flattered but a bit nervous, Page sat down again before the keyboard as a jaunty little tune came into her head. Karl was content to sit and listen to her.

Later, as they were having their dinner at a table Mrs. Chambers had set up before the fire, Karl said, "Have you ever thought you'd like to sing professionally, my dear?"

Page buttered a crescent. "I suppose I did when I was a little girl. But then most girls want to be a singer or a dancer or an actress." She giggled. "Even though they are not looked upon as respectable professions."

"You have talent, you realize."

"Me?"

"Yes, you. Oh," he added as he cut into the fish with the back of his fork, "I don't mean Grand Opera or anything like that, but I'd bet a dollar to a doughnut you'd be able to become a first-class entertainer."

"Entertainer?" Page said, slightly wary.

"On the stage. There is a great demand for pretty young singers nowadays and the old principles against theater people are becoming quite relaxed. I have a friend, Ben Keith, who's talking of going on a tour with what he's going to call a Vaudeville Show. It's to be a form of entertainment made up of music, singing, dancing and every other type performers to be given in a series of short, independent acts."

"Vaudeville," Page repeated.

"It's supposed to come from the French, Benny tells me. He got it from a drinking song written by a man from Vaux de Vire. It's a valley in Normandy." Karl chuckled. "Benny's French is something terrible so he called it Vaux de Valley, clipping it down to Vaudeville."

Page thought for a moment, then shook her head. "No, I couldn't even dream of such a thing. I'd be scared to death to get up in front of a lot of people and sing to them."

"Nonsense. You sang to me, didn't you?" Karl leaned back and dabbed the corners of his mouth with his napkin. "Tell you what. How would you like to test your stage fright by singing at my place in the Tenderloin?"

"The Gilded Plume, in the Patch!"

Karl frowned. "I dislike that appellation, *the Patch*. I deal only with the more sophisticated clientele and we refer to The Gilded Plume as being in the Tenderloin."

"I couldn't," Page said, horrified.

Karl watched her for a moment. "I'll pay you ten times as much as you earn with Mrs. O'Leary, plus whatever additional expenses are incurred by wardrobe and such things."

Page gaped at him. He was offering her more

110

money than she'd ever thought possible to earn. "Just to sing?"

Karl laughed. "A singer, a good singer, brings in customers, dear girl. Customers spend money just to relax and be entertained. You'd be doing me a very great favor."

For the first time since meeting him, Page felt him take her hand in his.

"As a favor to me," Karl repeated, giving her hand a squeeze.

Tactfully Page withdrew her hand and fussed with her napkin. "Well, I don't know. I'll have to think about it."

"Contrary to what you may have heard, Page, The Gilded Plume is a highly respectable establishment, patronized by the very best of Chicago society. The mayor and his wife attended its opening and are frequent visitors, always in a party of equally distinguished ladies and gentlemen. Let me take you there and then you can decide. I know most people call it a saloon, but I think of it as a supper club."

It was one of the most beautiful night spots she'd ever seen—all red plush and gilt with tasteful paintings decorating the walls and tables draped in starched white linen with flowers and candle lamps on each. Along one wall was a stage and below it a roped area which Karl explained was reserved for musicians who accompanied the performers.

There was a goodly crowd of handsomely dressed customers, women in white plumes and flowing silks, men in evening dress with walking sticks and top hats. There was more elegance crowded in the one room than Page could ever remember seeing.

111

"Sing for them," Karl urged.

"I couldn't!"

But after her second glass of champagne she felt a little braver and hoped he'd ask her again. When he did, she accepted.

She sang a ballad she remembered about a girl abandoned by a soldier boy and then she followed that by a song her father had taught her, ending her short recital with the jaunty song she'd sung for Karl and this time she coaxed the audience to join in.

She was a tremendous success. The people clapped and stomped their feet and called for more. For the first time in her life, Page knew what it meant to be sublimely happy.

Chapter Ten

For weeks Page kept her new career a secret, working at the laundry during the day and going off to meet Karl Kane right after all her chores were finished. Lily was so angered by Page's stubborn refusal to not see Karl Kane that an open hostility grew between mother and daughter, a division that grieved Page deeply, yet she could not bring herself to give up the adulation of the audience that clamored for her every night. She had never known success and once having tasted it she was addicted.

It was only by pure happenstance that Jeff O'Leary came into The Gilded Plume that Friday night, in the company of a group of cattlemen.

When he barged into her dressing room after her last number, his face was hot with rage. "Good God!" he breathed. "So this is where you go every night?"

After the initial fright of seeing him, the disapproval in his expression only fired her obstinacy. "I see nothing wrong with it. You heard them. Listen. They're still calling for me."

"You must be insane! What will your mother say?"

"Nothing, if she isn't told," Page said coolly.

Jeff made a grab for her but she moved away, pressing herself against the wall. She picked up a heavy jar of face cream and threatened him with it. "You take one step closer, Jeff O'Leary, and I'll brain you with this."

Karl Kane appeared in the doorway flanked by his usual two goons, Ziggy and Brock. "I think you had better leave, young man," Karl said to Jeff.

"I'll leave," Jeff said defiantly. "But Miss Carver is coming with me."

"I believe that is up to Miss Carver," Karl told him. He looked at Page. "Do you want to leave with Mr. O'Leary?"

She stood there still menacing Jeff with the cold cream jar, her mind closed to everything but all the glamour, the happiness she'd found here. She gave her head a quick shake. "No. Leave, Jeff." Then in a softer voice she said, "Please."

Jeff let his shoulders slump and his fists relax. He gave Page a long, imploring look and saw the strength of her unbending will. He let out a sigh and moved his head slowly from side to side. "Very well, Page, if that's what you want." He turned abruptly and left the room.

The next morning Page knew what she had to do. The charade could continue no longer and painful as it would be, the truth would have to be told.

"I've been singing at The Gilded Plume," she told Lily when they were alone.

To her surprise Lily did not react as she'd expected. Her mother went on grating the yellow bar of soap into chips. "Singing, you call it?" She made a contemptible sound in her throat. "Well, that's as good a name as any for what you're doing."

"But it's the truth, Mama. I'm singing songs on a

114

stage. And the place isn't like those other places in the Patch. It's highly respectable. Why, even the mayor and his wife come there."

Lily lost patience and slapped down the cake of soap. "I have talked to you until I am blue in the face, Page. I know now that there is nothing I can say to bring you back on the road of righteousness. You're lost to me and to everything good and holy. That Karl Kane has corrupted your soul and I only pray the day will come when you'll realize it before it's too late. As far as I am concerned, Page, you are no longer my daughter. So if you want to do whatever it is you do in that den of sin, there is nothing stopping you. I wash my hands of you." She picked up the soap cake and began shredding it again.

"Oh, Mama," Page pleaded, the tears rushing freely down her cheeks. "It's not at all like you think. Listen to Mrs. O'Leary. She'll tell you. Karl is an honorable man. Never once has he asked anything of me but friendship. He pays me good money for singing in his supper club because it brings in a lot of customers. I've been saving all the money he's paid me. You don't ever have to work again. I'll get us a nice little place on the north side, just the two of us . . ."

"I'll never live on money made from liquor and vice," Lily vowed.

"Oh, Mama, there's no harm in making money by singing songs to people. It's fun and it makes me so happy to see other people enjoy themselves. And Karl is a very kind and generous man. If only you'd come with me one night and meet him, listen to me sing."

"I'll have nothing to do with that odious man, that . . . corruptor."

"I tell you he isn't what you think." Page gradually felt herself losing control. Her anger started to rise. "Why must you believe every man we meet is some kind of horrible monster? Why must you think evil of everyone? I am doing absolutely nothing wrong, Mother. No one has been corrupting me, I swear to you."

Lily whirled on her. "Then swear to me that you are still chaste and pure."

Page stared at her as she thought of Jeff O'Leary. She opened her mouth then closed it.

"Swear on your father's grave!"

Page felt the tears pour down her cheeks, streaming through the shame that burned her cheeks. She looked at her mother through her tears, then slowly lowered her face.

"I thought as much," Lily said as she turned back to the washing.

Page clenched her fists, fighting her frustration. She watched her mother crank the handle of the washing tub. A violent scream of rage began to take form deep down inside Page's chest. She held it back and in a swirl of skirts she turned and ran from the room, out through the kitchen, snatching her heavy cloak from the peg beside the door. Out she ran, into the cold morning. When she reached the gate she leaned on it, trying to quiet herself.

"You look terribly unhappy, Page," Allan said as he came up behind her. "What's wrong?"

She put her hand on his arm to support herself. She held fast to her resolve to carry the burden of her guilt on her own shoulders but its weight grew until she couldn't support it. "Oh, Allan," she said throwing herself in his arms. "I don't know what I can do."

Sobbing out her misery, she told him of her entertaining at Karl Kane's supper club. "I've tried to convince my mother of its respectability but she'll have none of it. I can't see how it will be possible to continue to live in the same room with her because I can't stop my singing. I can't," she wailed. "There is nothing wrong in what I'm doing and I do so enjoy it."

Allan took her hand and held it to his chest. "I know you are doing nothing wrong, Page, and I think in her heart your mother knows it as well. But for all its respectability, The Gilded Plume is only a clean façade for a very corrupt organization. Karl Kane may be kind and generous, but he is the lord of a very disreputable empire riddled with vice and gambling and political corruption. This is where he made the original fortune which he augmented with cattle ranches, railroads, and grain warehouses."

Page's eyes widened. "No, you're wrong, Allan. Perhaps that is how he got his start, but that's all behind him now. He told me he once led a rather adventurous life but he's changed all his old ways. Every dollar of his money is clean. I'd swear to it."

"You only see what you want to see, Page. Believe me, I know what I am talking about. Karl Kane is just as corrupt now as he ever was. He hasn't changed. He never will." He saw her anger and patted her cheek. "Don't believe me if it upsets you. The last thing I want to do is to cause you unhappiness." He took her hand. "Come, let's walk. The walk will help calm you."

The sun was bright and warm despite the coldness of the day. Page tried to sort through her troubled thoughts as they trod the wooden plank walkways.

"Why does everyone disapprove so of Karl?

117

Your mother is the only one who seems to take his part . . . besides me, of course."

"Oh, I suppose one can't really blame Karl Kane for what he is. Mudtown bred a lot of Karl Kanes."

"Mudtown?"

Allan chuckled. "One of Chicago's early nicknames, the Chicago that was here before the war with the South. It was practically all mud back then and plenty of jokes and stories about it. There's the one about a man sunk so deep in the middle of Lake Drive that you could only see his head and when someone asked him if he needed a hand out he said, 'Nope, I still got my horse under me.' "

Page laughed.

"Ah, that's better," Allan said, seeing her unhappiness fade a little. He tightened his hand in hers. "I suppose I shouldn't be so hard on Karl Kane. There's a lot worse than he. I think everyone who has money today made it dishonestly through graft, corruption, vice, gambling. Corruption was a way of life when the city started to grow and oddly enough it never seemed to go away like in other big cities. A lot of folks, even today, truly believe that Chicago is held in some kind of demonic possession, the Sodom and Gomorrah of the nineteenth century."

Page said, "Karl has been very good to me."

"I have no right to interfere in your life, Page. You know I am very fond of you and I would not like to see you involve yourself in the kind of life Karl Kane has to offer. He's not good enough for you." He felt himself flush slightly. "But then, I guess I don't believe any man is good enough for you."

She felt a swelling in her heart and hugged him tenderly. "I am very fond of you too, Allan, and

118

before I do anything more I will seriously consider all you've told me."

"Thank you for that, my dear."

She spent the whole of the day working at her usual chores of hanging clothes and ironing but she spoke little and pondered much. When the sun began to remind her that the day was finished and she should begin to get herself ready for her appearance at The Gilded Plume, she found she could not bring herself to go. What Allan had said made sense and though Karl Kane was a kind and generous man, there was no question that it would only be a matter of time before her exposure to the more unsavory elements of the Patch, which had so far been kept distant from her, would eventually take their toll. Reluctantly she had to admit that she closed her eyes to the heavy drinking of the customers, the bawdiness of some of the women, the great sums of money lost at the gambling tables. She was, of course, not directly involved in these things, but they were there.

With a forlorn sigh of loss, she walked to the window and watched the night fall, squarely facing her decision never to see Karl Kane again.

Later, when Page asked Mrs. O'Leary if there was any mending to be done, Mrs. O'Leary said, "Not going out tonight?"

"No, I think not."

The older woman saw Page's pained expression but thought it better not to pursue the subject. "Well, there is that cut on the brown cow's leg where she kicked into the roll of barbed wire. The dressing needs changing if you can manage that."

"I'll see to it now," Page said, anxious to have something to do. She took the lantern and went out into the barn.

Jeff was down on one knee rewrapping the cow's leg when Page came in. She gave a little gasp of surprise.

"Well, if it isn't Miss Nightingale." Jeff finished with the bandage and stood up, wiping his hands on a rag. "Did Kane give you the night off or are you playing the tease by not giving the customers what they want?"

Hearing his voice here in this place with its smell of hay brought back an uncomfortable memory. She could almost see his handsome face flushed with drink, his sensuous lips smiling with lust. A little shudder of pleasure and pain ran through her as she stood watching him walk toward her looking smug and malicious.

Page took a step back.

"Oh, you need have no fear of me," he said with a sneer. "As it turns out, I wasn't so far wrong about you after all."

The sensible thing for her to do would be to turn around and walk away, she told herself. Ignore anything he had to say, a little voice told her. Yet she found herself rooted to the spot. "What do you mean by that?"

"I took you for a doxy that first day I saw you. Stick with Kane and I'll wind up being right."

"Just because your mind runs like a sewer, doesn't mean mine does. Karl Kane is ten times the man you are."

"Ah," he said with a wink. "So you can compare us? I thought you two were still in the hand-holding stage."

"You're disgusting." She turned to go.

"That's right, Page, run away to that no-good, crooked bastard."

120

"I'd prefer to be in Karl Kane's company rather than yours any day."

"Then what's stopping you? Go to him."

"I will!"

Jeff rushed at her and grabbed her arm. "You won't!" he said hoarsely. "You'll never see that man again, do you hear me? If I have to lock you in the house and stand guard over you day and night, I'll do it. I forbid you to see him, Page," he said as he started to shake her. "I forbid it!"

Suddenly he wasn't shaking her. Her face was close to his, her body warm and soft, pressed tight against his own. He smelled the sweetness of her breath, gazed longingly at her beauty. The attraction he'd tried to deny rose in giant waves he couldn't fight against as he brought his mouth closer to hers.

With a violent kick to the shins, Page shoved him away and started out the door. "Don't you ever dare touch me again," she spat, shivering at the feel of his touch, trying to ignore the wet heat that was spreading out through the lower part of her. "I never want to see you again, Jeff O'Leary." She felt the threatening tears but held them back.

"Go to Karl Kane and you never will see me again."

Page stood staring at him, torn between truth and her selfish honor. A part of her wanted to throw herself into his arms and give herself to him here on the very spot where first he'd taken her, but pride forbade it, and as she fought back the tears she turned quickly and ran out of his life.

"Page!" Karl cried when he found her collapsed in tears before the dressing table in her little room at the back of the stage. "What is it, my dear?" He knelt beside her and peered anxiously into her tear-stained face.

Seeing his kind concern, feeling his love for her, Page could not restrain herself from throwing herself in his arms, the only refuge she could see where she might find some comfort and solace for her misery.

She told him everything, sobbing out her bitterness for their misunderstanding, hating Jeff, resenting her mother, even blaming Allan.

"I never want to go back there." But after she made her pronouncement she felt even more miserable than before, wondering how she would ever be able to stay away.

Karl tipped her face up and looked deep into her eyes. "Marry me, Page."

At first she wasn't sure she'd heard him correctly. She frowned. "What?"

"Marry me." He lowered his eyes. "Oh, I know you don't love me, but I love you enough for both of us. I'll make you happy, Page. You can have whatever you wish." When he looked at her again he saw her frightened look and felt her draw away from him. He clutched her hands.

He said, "I never thought I'd ever want to marry again until that day I saw you in Danny O'Shea's room. You are the most beautiful creature I have ever seen, Page. I'm no saint, God knows, far from it," he admitted. "Everything I have was through ill-gotten gain and I'm not proud of it, but I want you to know the truth about me before you give me an answer. I've never lied to you, Page, and I never will."

He let out a deep sigh. "I made my fortune during the war," Karl said evenly. "The people voted out all the prohibition laws and Chicago was a boom town where everyone came to kick up their heels and try to forget the Blues and the Grays slaughtering each other. I'd won some prairie land off some Indians." He lowered his eyes again. "No, that isn't true. I bought it from them for a case of whiskey." He looked up. "Cyrus McCormick was building all those automatic reaping machines, running them day and night over every inch of planted prairie land. The army and navy were paying top dollar for wheat and grain for bread and horse fodder. I made a small pile of money and started buying up land inside the city. There were a lot of sinful places here and the good people were only too anxious to see a brothel burn down or a gambling hall catch fire and I was there to buy the land and clean up the burned-out lot." He shrugged. "The good people of Chicago never questioned how the fires started. I told myself I was doing the right thing by torching those places and the city fathers just looked the other way."

Karl's shoulders were slumped. As he straightened he felt as though thirty years had been stripped away, leaving him young and fresh and clean again. "I've never told that to another living soul, Page, not even to my wife."

A deafening silence filled the little room. Finally Page looked at him.

"Thank you, Karl. I am deeply flattered both by your proposal and your honesty. I too will be honest with you. It's true when you say I don't love you, but I am more fond of you than of any man in all the world. Perhaps I will learn to love you. I must think on it. I can't give you my answer now because I feel pressured, finding myself with no place to go, no way to turn."

"I keep a very comfortable suite of rooms at the

Tremont House, which is at your disposal for as long as you want it," Karl told her. "Or if you prefer, I will have Mrs. Chambers arrange for an apartment of rooms at my mansion."

Page looked so horror-stricken that Karl was forced to smile. "I did not propose to shock your delicate scruples, my dear. Forgive me."

She smiled back, but weakly. "It isn't my reputation that I was thinking of, but my mother's shame." She toyed for a moment with the idea of blunt openness. She considered telling him that she was no virgin, but in the end could not bring herself to admit to the shame.

"Don't go on stage tonight, Page. You're upset. Settle yourself in at Tremont House. Tomorrow you'll feel better, I'm sure."

"No, I want to sing. They're expecting me and I shan't disappoint them. And it will help me as well."

And she didn't disappoint them. Night after night The Gilded Plume was crowded to capacity to see and hear the enchanting girl with the honey-blonde hair, the piercing blue eyes and the voice that gave pleasure to the coldest of hearts. Page Carver did become the most popular songbird in the Tenderloin, as she and Karl preferred to call the Patch.

They were seated in the lovely dining room of Karl's mansion having a late supper when Karl again broached the subject of marriage. Page, feeling a little giddy with champagne and flushed with the success of her evening's performance, touched her lips lightly to his.

"I want to say yes, Karl. Still . . ."

124

He cocked his head. "Is there someone else, Page? One of the O'Leary brothers, perhaps?"

"No!" She said it a little too quickly.

Karl smiled to himself and sipped his champagne. "Take your time, my dear. Whatever your reasons for delay, I will honor them."

Her spirits began to wane. For all her efforts to dispel any thought of Jeff O'Leary, to scrub away the feel of his hands on her naked breasts, his bare chest pressed against her own, his hairy legs forcing apart her thighs, the memory stayed in her mind. She hated and detested the man with all her strength. Still, she could think and dream of no other. Hard as she tried to replace Jeff's face with Allan's or even Karl's, it was useless.

As she sat sipping wine, chastising herself for her weakness, she suddenly wondered if perhaps the feel of another man in her arms might obliterate the haunting memory of Jeff O'Leary.

She glanced over at Karl from under her long, dark lashes and felt an odd sense of determination. It wasn't right that she continue to deny the one man who'd ever been so kind and generous to her. It wasn't as if she were parting with her virtue. That had been stolen from her weeks before so she would not be coming chaste into Karl's bed.

The more she dwelled on the matter, the more ungrateful she felt for having deprived Karl. He'd given her a world of glamour and excitement and luxury and she'd given him nothing in return. And again, perhaps his touch would ignite that last fragile piece of kindling that would set her love ablaze.

"Karl," she said in a soft sultry tone.

When he looked at her, no further words were needed. He saw in her eyes what she wanted to say,

125

though her desire was clouded by reservation, even fear. He reached out his hand.

Page hesitated. Then, she took his hand in hers and let him lead her silently out of the dining room and up the long, curving flight of stairs.

The bed had been turned down and a lamp was burning on each side of the high, mahogany headboard with its carved scrollwork.

Slowly, deliberately she turned to Karl and was surprised to see his nervousness.

He said, "Perhaps you'd rather not, my dear. It isn't all so very important, you know."

She didn't believe him. In consideration of her innocence, he was merely being overly solicitous of her. "It's all right, Karl. I want to," she lied. She smiled to give him reassurance.

On the far side of the room was a large side table with a tray with glasses and decanters of liquor. Karl went to it and poured two snifters of brandy and carried them back to Page. She sipped hers and put it aside. Karl finished his in one swallow and re-filled his glass.

Page couldn't understand why he was so nervous and thought that perhaps he felt awkward in the presence of a woman who wasn't his wife. But surely she was mistaken. Hadn't she first seen him in Danny O'Shea's with those painted women? He couldn't possibly have chosen celibacy after his wife died, it wasn't in his nature.

Perhaps he preferred the woman to take the initiative, she thought. She turned her back on him and began to undo the buttons of her bodice, determined to prove her appreciation for everything he'd done for her. She would prove to him that she was not the tease that Jeff O'Leary accused her of being.

The lamps were extinguished as she disrobed and Page supposed Karl thought it improper for a man and woman to see themselves naked. She heard him start to get out of his clothes and she was naked and in bed before he crawled in beside her.

For a long moment neither of them moved, then Karl turned on his side and reached for her. He began to caress her, hesitantly at first but then with more purpose, kissing her gently on the lips, the breasts, the nipples. Page lay waiting for something to happen inside her, the way it had happened that afternoon with Jeff. But nothing happened. There was no warmth spreading throughout her as Karl's fingers trailed across her stomach and began to caress the inside of her thighs.

When he rolled on top of her, the weight of him was oppressive. She struggled with her breathing as he raised himself up and tried to fit himself into her. She felt his fumbling but nothing was accomplished. His kisses grew more demanding, as though he were angry with himself. Finally, she felt him stiffen against her thigh. He aimed himself and penetrated her quickly. She heard him sigh as again he started to kiss her, this time more passionately.

For a moment she only wanted it to end, then at last she found a low, growing warmth being generated deep within her. As Karl made love to her, the warm feeling moved across her like tiny, flickering flames igniting dry grass and her sensual, natural woman's needs started to come alive.

Karl leaned over her, thrusting, panting, gasping. After a while a low growl escaped his lips. She felt him stiffen his spine and legs, as if in a sudden spasm of pain. He cried out something she didn't understand and grabbed his chest. His body collapsed on top of her then rolled off onto its side, then flat onto its back.

Instinct told her something was wrong . . . seriously wrong.

Quickly she lighted the lamp and turned the wick up high. "Karl," she said as she saw his wide-staring eyes and heard the harsh, gasps of breath. His face was scarlet, his lips ashen-blue and all puffed out. "What is it, Karl?"

Weakly he moved one hand from his chest and let it flop toward the drawer of the nightstand. "Pills," he managed to stammer. "Drawer."

Page threw back the coverlet, aware that she wore nothing at all and hastened around the massive bed. She pulled open the drawer of the stand and found a small box marked "Glycerin." Inside were several capsules. She stood there helplessly looking at the capsules, then offered them to Karl.

With trembling hands he took one of the capsules, spilling the others across the bed, broke it and put it under his tongue. Then, with a deep sigh he lay back against the pillows. After a few moments, with Page standing naked beside the bed, staring anxiously into his face, Karl's breathing began to relax.

A faint smile curled his lips. "You're beautiful, my dear, but you're apt to catch a chill."

Page realized that she was standing naked and hurriedly pulled a coverlet about her. "I'll call Mrs. Chambers," she said.

Karl shook his head weakly. "No. It's only a mild seizure. I experience them now and again when I drink too much brandy. The doctor warned me. That's why I keep the glycerin capsules on hand. Besides, Mrs. Chambers does not sleep in."

"I thought . . ."

"No, we're quite alone. Actually I prefer it this way." He gave her a wry smile. "Servants have always been something I've never managed to get accustomed to. They always seem to be eavesdropping or underfoot. Only my driver lives on the premises and his quarters are all the way down by the pier, over the boathouse."

"But suppose you had one of your seizures and could not reach the pills, as happened tonight."

"Now don't upset yourself unduly, my dear. You've made me a very happy man tonight. Don't spoil it for me by dwelling on unpleasantries."

It was impossible for her to sleep, though Karl dropped off immediately. Page found herself straining to listen to his breathing, holding her breath every time she thought it stopped.

He had no one, she told herself as she sat propped up against the pillows. For all he'd accomplished, for all he owned and all he could afford, he had no one to care for him. He had given her the world and as she turned and looked fondly into his sleeping face, she knew she would repay him for all his kindnesses by marrying him.

She would give him the one thing he needed most, someone to care for him. She felt the stinging behind her eyes when she thought of Jeff.

She let the tears slip from her lids and roll slowly down her cheeks and closed her eyes, conjuring up Jeff's handsome, young face.

Karl gave a little groan. Page's eyes shot open. She looked at Karl and watched until his breathing became even again.

"Jeff O'Leary will never need anyone," she said to the empty room as she turned her face into her pillow and began to cry.

Chapter Eleven

March was bitter cold with the freezing wind whipping the white peaks of Lake Michigan into a frenzy. As often as Page had dreamed of a June wedding, common sense dictated that the sooner they married the sooner she could move into the Kane mansion and assume her duties of wife and nurse. She had been deeply affected by his *mild seizure*, as Karl insisted upon calling it. She supposed it reminded her too vividly of the loss of her father. She didn't want to feel that oppressive loneliness and depression again. Watching over Karl would prevent anything happening to him, she assured herself, and so she agreed to be married on the fifteenth of March.

It was a small, quiet ceremony performed at the courthouse with only Lily, Mrs. O'Leary and Allan attending, and Lily was obviously there from a sense of duty.

Jeff's absence hurt Page deeply, but she wondered if his presence would not have hurt her more.

"Jeff isn't ill, is he?" she hesitantly asked Allan.

"No. He's at home. Had some pressing work, he claimed. I told him he was being rude to ignore your wedding but he said you'd most likely avoid his if the situation were turned around. I really don't know what he meant."

She did. The very thought of Jeff marrying someone unnerved her. Just then Karl slipped his hand in hers and Page forced Jeff from her mind.

Lily was cool but polite, declining, as did the O'Learys, Karl's invitation to come back to the house for the small reception. Seeing her mother's disappointment and Allan's pain, Page didn't insist and felt glad they all went off immediately after the ceremony. Her mother and the O'Learys represented a part of her life that was finished. They were more than welcome to become part of her new life. However, if they chose not to she would not pressure them. And especially her mother. Lily's resentment of Karl, Page thought, was unreasonable.

"She'll come around," Karl said when Page expressed her annoyance at her mother's coolness toward him. "We'll set her up in a nice little place all her own with a bank account of her own and a comfortable income. She'll refuse it all at first, naturally, but in time she will start missing you too much to make a total stranger of you."

As the weeks passed, Lily never changed her attitude and stayed with the O'Learys, refusing all help Page offered and after a month of begging and pleading, Page took Karl's advice and let her be for a while.

At first Page thought she'd be uncomfortable in her new position as Mrs. Karl Kane and for a short time she was. But before too long she found herself relaxing at the soirées Karl took her to, and even found enough courage to give formal dinner parties of her own.

Her days were taken up with entertainments of every kind, from high-fashion picnics at the racetrack to brunches and late suppers at any one of the new lavish marble mansions along Michigan Avenue. At the new theaters she laughed at the Christie Minstrels and saw the romantic sketches based on plantation life as it had been before the war. Clara Morris and May Anderson made her weep with their portrayals of luckless women.

By invitation from one of Karl's many friends, Page became involved with the newly formed Chicago Historical Society and with the Academy of Sciences, though she knew of nothing she could contribute.

"But you aren't expected to contribute," the mayor's wife said. "Karl does the contributing, dear, you just hold tea parties like this one and an occasional soirée. Next month you must come to a ground-breaking my husband's officiating at for a new park. What on earth we need with another park is beyond me but he claims it's a tax necessity, whatever that is."

Bertha Palmer said, "I do declare, Page Kane, I don't know how you keep looking so fresh what with your nightly concerts at The Gilded Plume and all the other duties you tend to for Karl. He's been under the weather, Potter tells me."

Page felt a little uncomfortable. "Nothing serious. He's working too hard and I've been insisting he rest more." She shifted in her chair and skillfully moved the conversation away from her husband, at the same time watching the door, praying Karl wouldn't stagger in. She heard him pacing the floor overhead and was sure the other ladies could hear him as well.

In Page's mind's eye she could picture Karl in his dressing gown, one hand pushed deep into the pocket, the other holding a glass of whiskey. Why

133

he drank so much of late she couldn't say but she supposed it was the pressures of remarrying and the fear of another of his seizures.

When at last she'd gotten rid of her guests and went up to her dressing room to change clothes, Karl came in looking exactly as she'd pictured him. Page asked him how he was feeling as she began sorting through her closet.

"Liquor seems to keep me relaxed," Karl said, more as an excuse for the drink he was holding.

"Do you feel up to The Gilded Plume tonight, darling?"

He swallowed the whiskey and looked at the empty glass. "No, I don't think so, my dear. I'm feeling a little tired."

She looked at him, trying to hide her concern. He was so haggard and drawn, his eyes were sunk deep in his head from lack of sleep and too much alcohol. She hesitated suggesting he see Dr. Evans again because it only upset him all the more whenever she mentioned it.

She patted his cheek. "Don't you worry about a thing at the Plume, darling. I'm managing very well, except when Danny O'Shea decides to be a perfect pest."

"O'Shea," Karl said angrily, his hand tightening on the glass.

Page saw rage build in his face. "There is nothing to be angry about. The boys at the Plume are very good at keeping everyone in line, including Danny O'Shea. Actually, he's very different than when I first met him. He's even apologized for that night when he troubled me." She smiled. "I haven't forgiven him, naturally, but I must admit I'm beholden to him in a way. If it hadn't been for Mr. O'Shea you and I may never have met."

"Has he been coming to the Plume regularly?" Karl refilled his glass and grew pensive for a moment. "Perhaps I shouldn't stay away so much."

"Now don't start worrying about anything to do with the supper club. You have enough on your mind with all those political things at the courthouse and your position on the Grain Exchange. We can manage very well, so just don't fuss about it and concentrate on your other more important affairs."

Secretly, Page knew it wasn't his business that was depressing Karl, turning him more and more to whiskey. In a way she knew it was her fault. Karl was having difficulty being a proper husband. Oh, he lavished her with expensive presents, exquisite clothes, jewelry and furs, and was as considerate and affectionate as a man could be. It was in bed that his frustrations grew out of hand, forcing him to fortify himself with alcohol. He tried too desperately to make love to her and always failed, no matter how much she tried to help, how much she encouraged him. But it seemed that the more encouragements she whispered, the more his inadequacies shamed him and he had to drink to bolster his shattered male vanity.

"How do I look?" she asked as she spun around in a swirl of pink taffeta.

"Much too good for the customers," Karl said, taking her in his arms. His face grew serious. "I love you very much, Page. Please be patient with me. It's just . . ."

She kissed him lovingly on the mouth. "I love you too, Karl." She knew what he meant to say but it embarrassed her to speak of it. "You rest yourself. I'll be back as early as I can."

"By the way, darling, I may have to go to Abilene in a few days on business," he said.

"Abilene?" A cold hand gripped her as she remembered all too vividly the squalid shack by the railroad tracks, the horror of Bull Ramsey's attack.

"I have a large interest in Texas longhorns in Abilene and there has been a bit of a squabble brewing between the cattlemen and the farmers. It happens every spring when the new herds start coming in from down south." He grinned. "I thought perhaps you'd like to see if your old town has changed in the last several months."

She never wanted to see Abilene again and was tempted to use The Gilded Plume as an excuse to stay behind. With a chilling thought she wondered how she'd ever forgive herself if anything happened to Karl and she wasn't there to take care of him.

She forced a bright smile. "Yes, that may be fun. After all, we never really did have a proper honeymoon." She saw the instant hurt and bit down on her lower lip as she turned away and started out of the room. From the corner of her eye she saw Karl go toward the whiskey decanter.

When the quiet of the room dropped over him after Page shut the door, Karl looked at his reflection in the mirror. "What in hell's the matter with me?" he asked himself. He refused to admit it was his age that was causing his impotence. He knew older men than himself who were frequent customers at Carrie Watson's brothel on South Clark Street. Maybe that's what was wrong. Perhaps he needed to return to his old habits.

With a disgruntled shrug Karl turned away from the glass. No, a visit to a bordello, even one he owned, wasn't the answer. He had all he ever

136

wanted in Page. "Why then," he demanded, slamming his fist down on the bureau, "Why?"

An itching suspicion gave him his answer. He'd married an innocent, chaste girl, pure in thought and intention, who never suspected that her husband was one of the most corrupt men in the middle west. He'd deceived her and his conscience was making him suffer for it.

Pacing back and forth, sipping his whiskey, Karl tried to convince himself he should make a completely clean breast of his so-called business success, not that half-assed little sob story he'd told her when he first proposed. It was true enough as to how he'd gotten the land that started him off, and it was true enough about his cattle holdings in Abilene, even though it was illegal longhorns he brought in from Texas. But how could he explain that most of the brothels and gambling houses in the city were owned by him and other men like him, men who ran the city of Chicago? Could he reveal to Page that he was just another crooked millionaire on the take? Everything about him was rotten and sordid and every time he lay naked beside Page, his unworthiness took hold of him and the only comfort found was in a glass of whiskey.

Now Karl poured himself more whiskey and lay down upon the bed. He'd drink himself to sleep, he decided as he moved the decanter within reach. That way he'd be asleep when Page returned and he wouldn't have to suffer the repeated humiliation of his impotency, his inadequacies as a husband and a man.

As he closed his eyes he pictured his beautiful wife in her pink taffeta gown standing behind the new limelights he'd had installed, her voice rising sweetly, her smile dazzling her admirers.

Page's smile flickered and started to fade when she saw Jeff O'Leary help the lady off with her wrap and hold the chair for her. The words of her song faltered as she watched him order drinks and reach for the lady's hand. Quickly she pulled herself together and pretended not to have noticed them.

This was the first time she'd seen Jeff since marrying Karl and the slight of his not attending her wedding still stung her. Oh, what did she care about Jeff O'Leary? she asked herself as she left the stage to a roar of applause and shouts. He meant nothing to her and thinking of the flashy woman he was with tonight, she obviously meant nothing to him any more.

Still, she knew the instant she heard the tap on the door that it was Jeff.

"Yes?"

His smile was as devilish as ever and his eyes danced with amusement, as though reminding her that he well knew what she looked like naked. "I just thought I'd come back and apologize for not having attended your wedding." He made a little bow. "I apologize."

"Allan explained," Page said. "You needn't have bothered."

He frowned. "Allan," he slurred. "I just bet he explained." He fidgeted. "You're happy then, I take it."

She turned and looked up at him with angry defiance. "Extremely happy."

She saw him wince with pain, then smile quickly to hide it. "I'm glad." He continued to gaze at her. "I must say, marriage agrees with you. You are beautiful."

138

Page felt herself beginning to weaken under the desire that gleamed so clearly in his eyes. "I'm sorry, Jeff," she said as she turned back to her mirror. "I must change."

"Yes, of course. I must be getting back too. I left my friend alone at the table." He laughed. "Anyplace else in the Patch she'd be abducted by the time I got back." He paused. "I give you credit, Page. You've made the Plume downright respectable."

She felt the need to hurt him, drive him away so he'd never want to come to see her again. "It was always respectable. My husband saw to that. It's one of the many things I love and admire about Karl, that and the honor and esteem he holds for women, even doxies," she said with deliberate malice.

Jeff's eyes narrowed. He took a step toward her, wanting to feel her body against his. Something held him back. "I'm sorry," he said, fighting down the need he felt for her. "I . . ." He clamped his mouth shut and turned quickly and left the room.

The moment she was alone she felt the tears.

"Two minutes, Mrs. Kane."

"Ready," Page called back as she pushed back the tears, and with them she pushed Jeff O'Leary out of her life once and for all and reached for her change of gown.

Chapter Twelve

The train ride to Abilene was a far cry from the one she and her mother had taken only months before. Page looked around at the luxury of the private railway car, admiring the mahogany-paneled walls, the etched mirrors, the crystal chandeliers, the velvet-upholstered couches and chairs. In a sudden moment of girlish abandon, she slipped off her shoes and curled her toes into the deep, soft pile of the maroon carpet, as thick as moss.

Outside the landscape again intrigued her, and she marveled at the openness, the massive emptiness of the rolling plains, the seemingly unending stretches to the horizon. She'd seen pictures of buffalo herds, but seeing them in the flesh just outside the window, there was something terribly sad about them. She leaned back into the deep comfort of the armchair and watched the grazing buffalo herds that seemed to cover the entire terrain.

"There must be millions of them," she said as Karl laid aside the newspaper he was reading. When he looked quizzical she said, "The buffalo, there must be millions. I don't remember seeing them when Mother and I came to Chicago on this route."

"They were south. It was the middle of winter then, remember." He looked at the herd. "According to the government, they estimate there's almost twenty million of those beasts. That's why they've authorized the shoots. The buffalo are a growing menace and are becoming a bigger menace every year. The cows bear their calves about this time—May and June—that's why the government organizes these shoots before the young are born."

"It seems a shame to thin them out by having to kill them."

"Killing them serves several purposes," Karl explained. "The Indians live on the buffalo. They eat their meat and oil, wear their hides and build their tepees from buffalo skins. Even the animals' bones are used for tools and jewelry. Unlike the white man, the Indians waste none of whatever they kill."

Page frowned. "But if the buffalo are so necessary to the Indians, why not let the Indians kill them?"

Karl chuckled at her innocence and took her hand. "You sweet little girl. Your hard life in Abilene taught you little about the realities of this world." He leaned back in his chair and reached for the decanter of whiskey. "Washington is having a lot of trouble with the Indian tribes, as you may have read about in the newspapers. The government feels that if the buffalo are gotten rid of then the Indian problem will disappear too."

Page's eyes widened in horror. "You mean the government intends to kill off *all* of the buffalo?"

Before Karl had a chance to answer there was a knock on the door and a uniformed soldier said, "Excuse me, sir, but we will be pulling up to a stop in a couple of minutes. Did you want to join the

142

party in the adjoining coach or do you intend doing your shooting from here?"

Karl saw the color leave his wife's face. "I think I'll join the others." To Page he said, "You'll excuse me, my dear." He left the private railway car with Page sitting there staring after him.

She felt she should make some kind of protest, but a protest against what?

Still, as the train began to slow and she looked at the poor unsuspecting herds, she could not but think the whole scheme downright barbaric. And what of the Indians? They'd starve and die of exposure. It was all terribly cruel and horrible to think upon. But surely, she told herself as the train jolted to a halt, Washington had plans to see to the Indians' welfare once the buffalo were exterminated.

She was totally unprepared for what happened next. It seemed as though the entire world exploded in a deafening roar as the dozens of guns began blazing from the windows and doorways of the carriages. Within seconds hundreds of beasts fell before her eyes as the herds stampeded, trampling the dead and dying buffalo under their hooves. Groups of men on horseback came charging down the ramp from the cattle car at the end of the train, galloping in fast pursuit of the herds, corralling the stampede in a straight line, forcing the beasts to run parallel with the railroad tracks.

The locomotive belched a huge puff of steam as its wheels screeched and the train lunged forward. In a matter of minutes the train kept an even pace with the galloping buffalo. Guns blazed, and Page screamed in terror as the beasts dropped. Hundreds upon hundreds of the animals were slaughtered as Page buried her face in the cushions of the chair and held her hands tight over her ears, not so much to shut out the sound of gunfire as to shut out the bellowing agony of the wounded and dying animals.

A sudden wave of nausea gripped her as she pushed herself away from the window and groped her way toward the private lavatory at the end of the car. She happened to glance toward the front of the train and saw an even more horrible fate awaiting the blind, galloping beasts. Immediately ahead was a trestle that spanned a deep chasm. The cowboys were herding the beasts directly toward the precipice. They had nowhere to go but forward to their death.

There was the unmistakable hollow sound of the wheels racing over the high trestle and within seconds the gunfire stopped and Page found herself standing in the midst of the most deadly silence imaginable. Every part of her was trembling as she closeted herself in the lavatory alcove and splashed cold water on her face, wrists and the back of her neck. The mirror over the basin reflected a face she didn't immediately recognize. The eyes were wide and staring, as if reflecting the horrors of hell. Her skin was white and stretched taut across her cheekbones. Her lips were chalky gray and pulled so thin they almost weren't visible.

Karl found her collapsed on the Victorian rosewood rest-bed at the far end of the private car. "My dear," he exclaimed as he hurried to her. He took her hand. "You're burning up," he said, laying his other hand on her forehead. "What happened?"

"The shoot," she managed as she tried to sit up. "It was so horrible."

"There, there, my dear. Relax. I'll fetch you a brandy. It'll put you right in no time." He brought her the glass. "I should have drawn the curtains. I had no idea you were unfamiliar with buffalo shoots. They've been going on for some time."

"Please, Karl. I'd rather not think about it," she said as she sipped the brandy. "Those poor, helpless beasts," she groaned as she lay back and put her arm across her eyes.

"Two men were killed," Karl said. "Which is far worse than killing a lot of dumb animals."

"Two men?" She sat up, gaping at him.

Karl shrugged. "It happens. Damned fools. It's no one's fault but their own for coming on a shoot with men who have a grudge against them. It's a easy way to get rid of an enemy. I doubt if anyone will question that it was just accidental."

"Two men were shot?" Page said unbelieving.

"Gabe Spencer and Tom Fisher. They were two windows away from me in the next car."

"But how? Who shot them?"

"It just happened," he said with a shrug. "One of their enemies hires a gunman who rides herd on the buffalo, usually a crack shot with a rifle. Instead of firing at the buffalo heads he gets paid to take a couple of shots at Gabe's and Tom's heads. Hickok's back there now asking questions. Wild Bill's just doing what he's hired to do, going through the formalities. Nothing will come of it. It happens all the time." To Page's utter amazement Karl laughed. "You know, Hickok beat his own record. He claims he got off 165 shots and never missed one bull. He never shoots cows," Karl said, smiling. "Says it ain't gentlemanly to aim a gun at a female." He laughed again. "Says he would have got more but the barrel of his Sharps was starting to melt." Laughing, he shook his head. "Wild Bill's trying to catch up to Bill Cody. You know, Page,

145

Buffalo Bill Cody killed over 4,000 bison in eighteen months. Now there's a crack rifleman."

Page waved her hand weakly. "Please, Karl," she moaned and turned her face into the pillows. She closed her eyes but immediately opened them again against the image of the stampeding herd which stayed in her mind. For the rest of her life she knew the memory of that brutal carnage would haunt her.

"I'll let you rest," Karl said as he took a crocheted throw and tucked it gently around her. "A few hours' sleep will put the whole thing out of your mind." He looked down at her, then turned and started out of the car.

From under her lowered lids Page saw him pick up the whiskey decanter and go into the adjoining car where he'd talk cattle and politics and drink too much. She didn't care. All she wanted to do was try and forget what she'd experienced. She was certain she'd never be able to sleep but before she knew it Karl was shaking her shoulder, telling her dinner would be served shortly.

She wasn't hungry but managed to eat some cracked crab and a bit of the caviar. After two glasses of champagne she found herself beginning to feel closer to normal.

Karl saw the color gradually come back into her face and laid his hand lovingly on her arm. "I'm glad you're looking better. I hope you're feeling better as well."

"Yes, a little, thank you, dear."

"Good."

A strange glint came into his eyes and it was not the usual glow from whiskey. He looked oddly excited, almost exhilarated and said as much.

"I suppose all that action today brought back the

spirit in me, Page. I suddenly feel like a boy again."
He toasted her with his champagne glass. "To the
most beautiful woman in the entire state of Illinois."

The wine was making her light-headed. "But if I
am not mistaken, Karl, we are out of Illinois by
now and well into the Missouri territory."

"Then you are the most beautiful woman in Missouri as well," he exclaimed raising his glass again.

Gradually she began to recognize the strange
light in his eyes. She'd seen it before all too often
but it had never before shone as brightly as tonight.
He wanted her. She suddenly hoped with all her
heart that he would not fail to fulfill his desire.

Cautioning herself to resist the urge to encourage
him, Page let Karl move at his own pace, and the
champagne helped them both make the game of
seduction even more enjoyable.

When the clock chimed the hour they were
wrapped in each other's arms. Usually Page was the
first to move toward the bed but tonight she made
Karl take the initiative. She let him undress her
in the full glow of the gas lamps, refusing to show
any embarrassment or shame. Then she lay back,
completely naked as Karl undressed. She watched
him devour her with his eyes. She felt like a harlot
but she didn't care. She would be whatever he
wanted her to be, and do whatever he asked, even
demanded.

He began to caress her, his touch gentle and soft
as feathery wings. His lips touched hers, then
moved down to kiss her breasts, suckle her nipples.
Page felt them respond, grow taut and hard as Karl
nibbled them gently with his teeth. His hands
roamed over every part of her and she began to feel
a stirring deep inside, a stirring she'd almost forgotten was there within the depths of her core.

As Karl's mouth again covered hers, her lips parted to his and their breaths became one warm desire. The feel of his nakedness began to arouse in her a feeling of wanton need. She never believed she could respond to him the way she was responding, but there was nothing she could do to control the way she was beginning to feel. Wherever he touched her, her flesh tingled with a burning sensation as her heart pounded in her breast and her blood rushed madly through her veins, sending wave after sensual wave of passion throughout her body.

A new emotion suddenly took her firmly in its grip. It started in the lower part of her body and began to grow hotter and hotter, shooting tiny sparks up and down her neck.

"Oh, Karl," she heard herself moan as she pressed herself tighter against him. For a second she felt him stiffen and she feared her words had brought on failure.

The throbbing, hard shaft pressed against her thigh reassured her. His tender caresses continued, then began to increase in their intensity, their daring. His fingers grew bolder as he dug into her, testing the depth, the heat of her desire. At last he moved over her, probing gently, then more anxiously. Gradually he entered her and her life began anew as a pleasure she'd almost forgotten swept her up into its gossamer web and held her suspended in a delicious agony of passion.

He moved slowly with her, leading her toward a sublime feeling of fulfillment. Page was aware of nothing but the sensations of touch and heat as an unrestrained desire began to lift her higher and higher.

As Karl started to move faster, more urgently,

she clasped him tightly. He called out her name with a shuddering gasp as he plunged deep into her very existence. Page felt a warm surge of pleasure flow into every part of her as she held him in her arms, clinging to him until the spasms ended and she felt his body begin to relax.

They lay a long time locked in a loving embrace. Finally Karl heaved a sigh and rolled onto his side. A sly smug smile of self-satisfaction crept across his mouth and a moment later he was fast asleep.

Page hugged herself as she turned and looked at her sleeping husband. She felt happy and satisfied. Still, as she looked at Karl's face she felt something was missing.

She shrugged and smiled to herself as she turned on her side and went to sleep.

Chapter Thirteen

During the months she'd been away, Abilene had greatly changed. The early spring months always brought cattlemen and cowboys, but their number this year seemed to have increased tenfold as she walked with Karl from the depot to the Drover's Cottage Hotel. Fewer weedy lots bordered it and more pitched-roofed houses and stables and stores cluttered the wide dirt street which, despite the earliness of the season, was already dried and cracked and gritty.

Men lounged about, basking in the unusual warmth of the day, and ladies strolled the boardwalks delaying their town shopping as long as possible, as it was their only respite from the work that was always waiting for them at the farms and ranches.

Contrary to Abilene's growing reputation as the leading cattle town in the midwest, the people who lived here year round were mostly farmers, not cattlemen. The bulk of the cattle in Abilene were driven up from the south by Texas drovers, and the cattle brokers came from cities in the north and east, such as Chicago and New York, where beef was in demand.

151

On their stroll from the station, Page noticed the tavern owners were beginning to sweep out the winter dirt from their saloons, getting ready for the cowboys and their bosses.

There was a sudden rumbling sound behind them that shook the earth and made Page and Karl turn around in time to see a small herd of about two thousand longhorns move toward the fences of Joe McCoy's stockyards. The herd was led by a Texan in a broad-brimmed hat and chaps. The herd of cattle was boxed in by a complement of eight cowboys, all looking very young, Page thought, but she supposed that was why they were called cow boys.

"Those two men in the front of the herd are called the two points," Karl explained. "A right and a left point. They keep the herd moving in the right direction. Those two about a third of the way back are the *swing* men who, together with the two boys farther back, the *flankers,* keep the herd in a rough form of box. Those men have the tough job of keeping the cattle from bunching up and becoming overheated."

"Overheated?"

"Sure. That many steers moving side by side at a steady pace generates a great amount of heat. Heat melts off fat so the heads have to be kept apart for ventilation of the herd."

Page saw the two men at the very rear. "I don't think I'd much like their job."

"They're called the two *drags.* They get all the dust, depending upon the direction of the wind and the direction in which the herd is moving. Those two are more than likely the newest or youngest hands."

When the billowing clouds of dust started to move toward them, Page and Karl walked more quickly toward the hotel as the drovers hooted and urged the cattle into the pens.

The hotel where she and Lily had worked as washerwomen was as different as the town itself, but she had to remind herself that this time she was being ushered in through the front door and not the service entrance in the alley that led down to the basement. It was as if she were seeing the place for the first time. A luxurious three-storied hotel with forty-five spacious, well-appointed chambers looked vastly different in the eyes of a guest than in the eyes of a washerwoman. Now, on Karl's arm, she could look at it critically. The exterior was somewhat Italianate, rather devoid of ornamentation except for a shallow gable at one end and green runged shutters at the sides of each window. The wooden sidings were painted tan, like the dust of the street in front; a lengthy veranda ran across the front and two sides.

As they were shown to their suite of rooms Page said, "I know I shouldn't involve myself with your cattle business, Karl, but I can't help wondering why you felt it necessary to make the trip here. Couldn't one of your agents handle the buying and shipping?"

"Buying cattle for the Chicago market is only a small part of the reason for our being here. The Cattlemen's Association has heard rumors of trouble brewing between the cattlemen and the Kansas farmers."

"What kind of trouble?"

"To be perfectly frank, bringing longhorn steers this far into Kansas is against the law and the farmers want to keep them out."

"But why? Surely the influx of cattle business only adds to Abilene's prosperity."

"Texas longhorns," Karl explained as they settled into their rooms, "carry what is called splenic fever. The steers bred in the southern states don't contract the fever, they just carry it. The northern cattle are very susceptible to splenic fever and so the Kansans don't want their few heads infected by the fever brought in by the longhorns. The government established what they call a 'quarantine line' which we're supposed to stay behind. But the railroads don't have tracks that far south yet and the Kansas politicians want the business so the quarantine line is ignored by everyone except the farmers. They're the ones who are complaining to the governor and threatening to drive out the longhorns with gunfire if the governor doesn't intercede, which he doesn't want to do because he has too many supporters in the cattle business and in railroad, like me."

"Gunfire?"

Karl reassured her. "I would never have consented to bring you here if I thought for a moment that there would be any possibility of danger."

"How do you propose to pacify the Kansans?"

"There's a meeting at the dance house tonight. My partners and I have a proposition which I think will satisfy everyone." He went toward the windows and looked out toward the railroad tracks and the sprawling stockyards of Joe McCoy. "The foolish farmers," he said almost to himself. "They should realize that Abilene's days as the leading cattle town in Kansas are very few. The railroads will eventually bring cattle trains southward, closer to Texas and westward, closer to Oregon. The drovers won't have to herd their heads this far. Abilene will die as a cattle town." He laughed softly. "They hate it when you call it a *cow* town, you know, but that's exactly what it will become. I own too big an inter-

154

est in the Abilene cattle market to let that happen, at least not until I've recouped a reasonable profit on my investments."

Page walked to the windows and leaned her head on her husband's shoulder. "I have a feeling Abilene will be a very important city one day," she said as she looked at the stores and people and horse traffic. "The railroad will always be here and if they don't ship cattle, they'll ship farm produce."

Karl kissed her forehead. He chuckled. "Very astute, my dear. I thought the very same thing, that's why I own a rather large parcel of land here. Perhaps one day you and I will retire here and I can become a gentleman farmer. Would you like that?"

Page smiled but a nagging urge told her she didn't ever want to leave Chicago. The city was too alive, too comfortable, and . . .

A gasp caught in her throat and her eyes widened when she recognized Bull Ramsey as he came out of the saloon directly across the street. She knew she wasn't mistaken. There could be no doubt that that massive frame, like an ox, that hideous face belonged to anyone but the fiend who'd tried to rape her. It was the same man, the same thick, powerful shoulders and short, squat legs. She saw the eyes narrow beneath bushy dark brows, just as they'd narrowed that day he'd ripped her clothes from her body and had flung her on the brass bed. Even now those eyes were still filled with an animal cunning and the mouth was as cruel and thin as she remembered.

Quickly she buried her face in Karl's chest.

"Page? What is it?" he asked, looking anxiously down at her, then studying the street to try and recognize whatever it was that had frightened and upset her.

155

"That man," she gasped, pointing but not looking where she pointed.

Karl saw several men whom she could have meant. "What about him?"

How could she tell him about Bull Ramsey, the man who saw her mother split a man's skull with a stone and leave him to die in an alley not a hundred yards from where they now stood. That horrible New Year's Day came back with sordid, horrifying clarity as she stood, pressed against Karl. If he knew his mother-in-law was a murderess everything would be lost. She couldn't tell him. He must never find out, Page told herself as she fought to compose herself.

"What is it, Page?" Karl asked again, his face lined with concern.

Forcing herself to hide her fears, she looked up at him, then carefully glanced toward the street. "I'm sorry, darling," she managed to say. "I thought I saw someone who . . . who I used to know." She forced a little laugh. "It couldn't possibly have been the same man. The man I knew is dead." When she thought she had her fear well masked, she looked up into his face. "It was as if I'd seen a ghost. It startled me, that's all."

He put his arms around her. "Ghosts have no place in your life now, my dearest. I'll not permit them," he said, laughing. "As far as we are concerned, Page, neither of us has anything unpleasant in our pasts. We only have a dazzlingly happy future to look forward to."

But all day long Page found herself reluctant to look out of the window, let alone go out into the street. It was as if a harbinger of doom, the vulture of death was perched just outside the hotel waiting to snatch her up and carry her off into hell.

After dinner Karl said, "I do wish you'd come with me to the meeting tonight, my dear. There's entertainment planned. I know you'll enjoy yourself and it would please me so much to show you off to all my friends and business associates. They've been flocking into town all day long. Already the hotel is crowded. Please say you'll come with me."

She didn't want to, but she couldn't bring herself to add to the hurt look he was wearing. Besides, if Bull Ramsey were at the dance house meeting, surely he wouldn't recognize her as being the scrawny, pale little washerwoman he'd tried to rape.

By the time she finished her coffee and the brandy Karl had insisted she have, her nerves were more settled and her courage stronger. "Yes, I think I'd very much like to go to the meeting."

Page had heard the gossip about the dance house but had never been inside it before. It was a long frame building with a good-sized hall and a bar up in front with sleeping rooms in the rear. The hall was used for dancing with the girls who belonged to the house, who charged the men a price for dancing and another larger price for visits to the sleeping rooms, which Page heard were kept busy before, during and after the dancing hours, both day and night.

When they went inside, with Page nervously clutching her husband's arm, Texas cattle herders wearing brimmed sombreros and with giant spurs on their high-heeled boots were dancing side by side with farmers in overalls and well-dressed city dudes, all of whom were partnered with painted, bejeweled ladies of obvious easy virtue.

Karl noticed Page draw back and smiled reassuringly at her. "The ladies should have been sent away before this. We must be a little early. I'll see to it."

"No," she said, holding tight to him, keeping her eyes lowered. "It's all right, Karl, just please don't leave me."

"I wouldn't think of it."

A man in a tailored suit and silk ascot called Karl's name and came toward them. "You're early," he said. He bowed to Page. "We weren't expecting you'd bring Mrs. Kane." He glanced at the painted ladies, then quickly added, "But I'm honored you came, Mrs. Kane."

Karl introduced Page to Joe McCoy and the latter turned to the little orchestra in the alcove and waved to them. The music stopped and Page felt the color rise in her cheeks when everyone turned toward them. After an uncomfortable moment or two, the doxies began to slip quietly back toward their rooms in the rear. In another moment chairs were pulled onto the dance floor and the men began to quiet down. Their expressions and postures changed as they forgot what they'd just been doing and started thinking about the real reason for being here tonight.

The meeting was quick to get down to business when one farmer, obviously a spokesman for his fellow Kansans, protested loudly against the impending invasion of the Texas longhorns.

"Just remember the Bible," the farmer stormed. "Cain was the keeper of the land and Abel the keeper of the animals. Like Cain, the farmer needs fences and is tied to the land. The land is all he has and he'll kill to protect and preserve it."

"Now, now, Zeke," Joe McCoy protested, "There'll be no talk of fighting or killing." His voice was like oil. "There isn't any reason the farmer and the rancher can't get along and live peaceably with one another. Cain and Abel lived a long time back; surely we've had a lot of time since then to learn how to be civilized."

As he talked Page noticed the cattlemen drifting through the farmers, talking in whispers. She looked at Karl and frowned.

"It's the cattlemen's intention to buy up the farmer's produce at handsome prices. That way they know they'll always have a ready market for all they grow as soon as the cattlemen arrive with their herds," Karl said in a whisper.

Joe McCoy announced, "And as far as splenic fever is concerned, Karl Kane and the rest of the Cattlemen's Association are willing to pay any farmer for any of his cows that die from the infection. Now I call that about as fair an offer as can be made."

At the end of the meeting the farmers seemed content with the promises, especially when Karl told them the generous price he would pay for any infected cattle.

"At least," Karl said to Page, "I believe we've averted the crisis for the time being." He shook his head. "But the Kansas farmers will never completely accept ranchers trampling over their acres and cattle drinking their water. The long cattle drives will soon be a thing of the past, Page, so take a good look around. This may be one of the last friendly meetings of ranchers and farmers that will be held."

Page glanced around and again she gasped and clutched at her throat when she saw Bull Ramsey lumber into the hall from one of the back rooms.

Karl was talking to one of his partners and didn't see her fear. She stared at Bull, feeling much the same as the mouse hypnotized by the snake's eyes. He was looking at her, wearing a quizzical expression, as though he was trying to remember where he'd seen her before.

When he smiled, showing his crooked yellow teeth and started toward her, Page clutched Karl's arm and got to her feet. "Can we leave, Karl?"

The anxiousness of her tone made him look at her with concern. "Of course." To Joe McCoy he said, "We're not needed here any more, are we, Joe?"

"No, go along. Pleased to have met you, Mrs. Kane.

Page lost little time getting out of the dance house and as they started toward the hotel Karl said, "Is anything the matter?"

"No, Karl. I suddenly became quite weary. The train ride has tired me more than I suspected."

Back inside the dance house Bull ambled up to Joe McCoy. "That good-looking little lady with Kane, who is she?"

"The new wife," McCoy told him. "A real looker, ain't she?"

"Yeah," Bull said rubbing the stubble on his chin. "That she is."

McCoy said, "I thought you were going back to Chicago, Bull. Don't you still work for Danny O'Shea?"

"Danny says for me to stay quiet for a while longer." He kept looking toward the door through which Page left. "Does Kane still have the place across from Danny's?"

"Yes. Maybe that's where you've seen the wife. She sings there."

"No, I haven't been back to the Patch for quite a

160

spell." He screwed down his brows. "But I've seen her, that's for sure. It's just that I can't figure where."

Hard as Bull tried to remember, he couldn't. But then, Bull thought with an ugly laugh, there'd been an awful lot of pretty ladies in his life and how could he expect to remember any particular one of them?

However, the following afternoon Bull did remember. He was across the street when Page and Karl came out of the Drover's Cottage Hotel and started along the boardwalk. Bull leaned back into a shadow and watched their progress, moving parallel with them.

Page stood stalk still and gaped when she saw the brass bed in the store window. There couldn't be two such fine beds, she told herself as she saw the enamel finials, the elaborate brass scrollwork that formed the letter "C" in the center of the headboard.

"Something you fancy?" Karl asked as they looked in the store window.

She told him about the last thing she and her mother had managed to salvage from their once luxurious life. "It was my parents' bed," she said. Then with a jubilant cry she said, "Oh, Karl, let's go in and look at it. My father had a small brass plate mounted on the main cross-stay with his and mother's name on it and the date of their marriage. It was one of his honeymoon presents."

It was indeed the same bed.

"Please, Karl, could we buy it?"

Karl smiled and reached for his billfold. "You can have the entire store shipped to Chicago if you wish."

"Just the bed," Page urged, overjoyed at her

good fortune. Her mother would be so pleased, she thought. Perhaps the bed would help narrow the rift that was getting wider between them.

She had no possible way of knowing that the shiny brass bed was her undoing. Through the window Bull Ramsey watched the purchase and as he looked from Page to the bed and back at Page, it suddenly all came back to him with crystal clarity.

His memory started with the shack by the railroad, next to McCoy's stockyard. It had been cold. Sure, that was it, he told himself with delight. It had been New Year's Day. He remembered how he'd watched the drunk try to rape Kane's wife in the alley and how her old lady had conked him with a rock.

Bull chuckled when he recalled their terror when he told the old lady he'd seen her kill that drunk. She hadn't killed him but they didn't know that.

He remembered trying to get into the young bitch on that same big shiny bed, but she'd drugged him or something because he'd passed out and the two of them had hightailed it away by the time he'd come to.

"Hightailed it to Chicago, obviously," he said as he moved back into the shadows as Page and Karl came out of the store. "Ran off thinking they'd killed a man."

"Well, well," Bull said, rubbing his chin. Danny O'Shea was always trying to get some dirt on Karl Kane and he'd always wanted Kane's fancy club across the street. Maybe Danny would be grateful to hear Bull's story. Karl Kane's mother-in-law a killer. At least she believed herself to be one, which was just as good, and Kane's wife an accomplice to murder.

Bull chuckled again. Danny would pay plenty for

the information and Bull was positive his boss wouldn't be too upset if he returned to Chicago earlier than he was supposed to.

"Yes, pretty lady," Bull said as he eyed Page. "I have a feeling you and me are going to get reacquainted very soon, and next time you won't get the chance to cold-cock me with no drug."

The day was pleasant and bright as Page and Karl meandered down the street, stopping to look in the store windows, chatting with people Karl introduced to her.

Sheriff Hickok doffed his hat as he recognized Page from the train. "How are you enjoying our little town of Abilene, Mrs. Kane?"

"It isn't so little any more," Page said.

"You're right there. Things are growing so fast around here I'm finding it hard to keep up. Too many strangers moving in," Wild Bill said. "I'm even thinking of giving up my badge soon's my term of office is over."

"You!" Karl said. "You'll never be happy without those two guns strapped to your hips, Sheriff."

"Oh, I wouldn't give up my firearms, Mr. Kane. I got an offer to travel with one of those new Wild West Shows that are getting to be so popular all over. Bill Cody asked me . . ."

Suddenly Karl grabbed at the searing pain in his chest. He groped for something to support him but his hands clawed the empty air. Page gave a tight little scream as Sheriff Hickok reached for Karl, but too late. Karl fell to the boardwalk, his lips blue and swollen, his eyes wide, his breathing labored.

"Get Doc Wooster," the sheriff yelled to one of his deputies. To another man he said, "Here, give me a hand getting him into the jailhouse and onto a cot."

Page's heart was in her throat as she watched the stream of spittle flow out of the corner of Karl's mouth as he gasped for breath.

As the men carried Karl into the Sheriff's office Page tried to hold back the tears.

"Oh, please, dear God," she prayed. "Don't let him die."

Chapter Fourteen

It was not a fatal seizure but the doctor was adamant that Karl stay in bed at least several weeks.

"Nonsense," Karl said after the doctor left. "I'm feeling fine."

"You'll pardon me for saying it, darling, but you do not look it. You've lost all your color," Page said.

"Being cooped up in this blasted hotel room for three days would take the color out of any man." He threw back the coverlet and swung his feet over the side of the bed. "I'm getting up."

"No, you aren't!"

He stood but a second later he was back on the bed, his head spinning. "It's just that I've been off my feet," he said as an excuse. "I've got to be up and around, Page. I can't afford to languish like a pet dog."

"Would you prefer to languish in bed or in a pine box?" she asked sternly as she coaxed him back against the pillows and tucked the coverlet around him.

Karl laughed. "A pine box? Really, my dear, surely you'll at least lay me out in mahogany. After all, you'll be able to afford it with the amount of money I'm leaving you."

"Don't even jest about such things, Karl. It disturbs me."

"Come here, my pet," he said pulling her down and cradling her against his chest. "I am as strong as a horse and intend staying that way. You heard the doctor and I'll listen to at least a little of what he said. I'll not overwork and I'll ration my whiskey."

"He said *give it up completely.*"

Karl cocked an eye. "I said I'd listen to a little of what the old codger said, not all of it. And . . ." he continued, ". . . I'll rest in bed. That is," he added with a chuckle and a hug, "if you'll rest with me." He caressed her breasts.

Playfully she slapped his hands. "Get away with you, Karl Kane. I do believe it'll take more than a heart flutter to cool your ardor." She got up and fluffed his pillows.

"Seriously, Page, we must get back to Chicago. I can't afford to stay here. The drovers are coming in like invading ants. I'll never get any rest with the noise and hootin'-it-up they'll do night and day."

Page had to agree there was something in what he said and said as much to Dr. Wooster.

Several days later Karl was tucked comfortably in bed in their private railway car and before the end of the week they were back in the mansion on Lake Shore Drive.

Gradually Page found herself a prisoner in her own home. It wasn't that she was forced into the position; she felt it her responsibility as a dutiful wife to stay beside him at all times. When first they arrived home it was fun to prepare little teas and parties to entertain the many people who came to visit Karl. But as time passed Page came to the realization that healthy people hated visiting people who weren't well, and the personal visits were replaced with flowers and notes and an occasional brief "stop in," which was always sandwiched in between some other important engagement that had taken the caller into the neighborhood.

Karl was much improved, but he tired easily and so they seldom went anywhere. Invitations had to be declined and after several weeks the invitations ceased to come. Like a dutiful wife, Page gave every waking moment to her husband's comfort, agreeing to engage only a night nurse, insisting she wanted to care for her husband herself.

And there among all the beauty of the mansion and the affluence of her position, her glamorous life began to pale. She tried desperately to convince herself that she was happy and content and that it would be only a matter of time before she'd be back singing at The Gilded Plume, attending fabulous dinner parties, hostessing elegant soirées.

Staring at herself in her mirror one evening, she came to the realization that that really wasn't what she missed. With all the glitter that surrounded her, with all the roaring cheers that followed her songs, she discovered she had no close friends. There was not a single person with whom she could kick off her shoes and put up her feet and relax completely. She thought about her mother and of the O'Learys and dearly missed those evenings around the kitchen table drinking tea or coffee, her bones aching from the day's backbreaking work, and still able to laugh in spite of it, or because of it.

Tomorrow, she decided, she'd do as Karl had been insisting, she'd get out of the house. She'd go to visit her mother and the O'Learys.

"A wonderful idea," Karl said when she told him. "Remember that brass bed you installed in the big guest room. Try to convince your mother to come and sleep in it again. We'll give her the whole north wing, an apartment all her own right here in the house."

Page saw her mother's eyes light up when she told her about finding the brass bed, but Lily did not warm to the idea of moving into Karl Kane's house.

"I'm perfectly content where I am," Lily said. "The O'Learys have been good to me and the least I can do is repay them."

"Don't you see, Mother, we can repay them a thousand times over. I am a very wealthy woman. Karl and I can give you and the O'Learys everything."

"Is that why you're here, Page, because you have everything?" Lily asked giving her daughter a meaningful look. "You are unhappy. I can see it in your eyes." She thought suddenly of her daughter just having returned from Abilene. Her eyes widened. "Nothing happened in Abilene . . . I mean, you didn't see . . . you didn't have any trouble."

Page averted her eyes in case her mother could see her lie. "No, I saw no one in Abilene. Everything went very well." After a moment she turned back. "I'm unhappy because we've grown apart."

"And we will grow farther apart if you insist upon living with that man."

A stormy look came into Page's eyes. "He's my husband. And Karl is a good, decent man."

"To you, perhaps, but it is dirty money that buys him his decency. I'll have none of it. And I'll have none of you so long as you live on that money."

168

Page's anger flamed as she snatched up her bag and gloves. She got up from the table. "You're being very stubborn, Mother. I only want to help."

"I don't need your kind of help."

For a long moment Page stood looking down at the frail, aging woman. She saw the determined tilt of the gray head, the unyielding line of the mouth, the obstinate set of the jaw. There was no way she could break down her mother's resolve, that she knew. Feeling frustrated and piqued, she turned sharply and started toward the door.

Just as she reached for the knob, the door opened and Page found herself staring up into the surprised face of Jeff O'Leary.

"Jeff!"

"Hello, Page," he said after he recovered himself. He glanced toward the table and saw Lily sitting there as though etched in stone. He'd heard Lily's mutterings over the past months and knew how much she disapproved of her daughter's marriage. Looking at the old woman now, he could easily tell that this evening's confrontation hadn't ended on a happy note.

"I was just leaving," Page said.

"I'll walk you to your carriage."

Page turned to her mother. "If you change your mind . . ."

"I will have no change of mind, Page. Good night."

Outside the night air was cool but not cold. Page pulled her coat collar up around her chin more in an effort to fend off her mother's chilling words than the drafty night air.

"Your mother is a very principled woman," Jeff said.

"Yes." Page sighed. "I just can't understand why she dislikes Karl so much."

Jeff stopped and turned her to him. "She doesn't see him with your eyes."

He studied her face to see if their separation had erased any of her beauty. It hadn't. She was still the most ravishing creature he'd ever seen.

Page looked up at him and for a moment her heart stopped as she felt a disquieting stirring deep inside her. It was the same face that had looked down at her that day in the barn, a face alive with lust and wanton desire, yet so sensual and manly she fought to keep herself from touching it to make certain he was real and not another of her dreams.

He wanted her. She saw it in his eyes. Even standing in the innocent light of the moon, talking of ordinary things, the undercurrent of lust pulsed like a pounding surf.

Bit by bit Jeff watched her defenses fall away under the weight of the desire that showed clear and bright in her eyes. "Page," he murmured. He reached for her.

She saved herself in time by reminding herself of who she was, what he was, how much she despised him for what he'd done. She turned abruptly and started for the carriage where her driver was waiting to take her back to her husband.

"You aren't happy," Jeff said. The tone of his voice was suddenly different. Earlier it had been casual, even, polite; now he'd honed a sharp edge to it, giving it a low, guttural sound. Even the expression on his face had changed from sensual to angry.

"I'm perfectly happy," Page said as she felt Jeff take her arm and force her into the shadow of the barn.

"Let me go!"

"A man like Karl Kane could never make you happy, Page. He's too old for a woman like you."

"And I suppose you think a man like you is what I need."

"Absolutely," Jeff said, an easy smile again curving the corners of his mouth. "At least I'd give it a damned good try."

"Like that day inside there," she said, motioning with her head toward the barn door.

Jeff laughed deep in his throat. "It must have been a good try on my part because you never seem to forget it."

"You're contemptible. I'll remember it until my dying day with disgust. You took the only thing a woman prizes above everything else. I'll never forgive you for that."

He stood undaunted, legs apart, arms crossed over his chest as he looked down at her with undisguised desire. He'd purposely stepped aside to let her go. She didn't move. "Who would you have rather given your virtue to, me or that old man? At least I made you enjoy it."

She raised her hand to slap his face. He grabbed her wrist and pulled her against him. He kissed her passionately on the mouth.

An instant later he pushed her roughly away. "Is that the way Kane kisses you, Page?"

Her entire body was trembling. She told herself it was rage that she felt, yet the feel of his lips against hers, the taste of his breath, the hardness of him made her head swim.

When she found her voice she snarled, "You're nothing but a filthy beast."

"Perhaps. But I know when I want a woman more than life and I want you, Page. I get sick to

171

my stomach every time I think of you and that bastard in bed together. The thought of his touching you makes me want to put my hands around his throat and squeeze the life out of him." He glowered down at her. "But perhaps it's your neck I should squeeze. You're a perfect little fool!"

She clutched her throat and backed against the side of the barn. "You're insane," she gasped.

"About you," he said as he reached for her again and before she could scream he covered her mouth with his own. When he looked into her lovely face he said, "You don't know what you do to me, Page. For the first time in my life I want to do what's right."

"Don't do me any favors. Besides, I doubt if you know what *right* is. You take whatever you want and throw it aside when you're bored with it. You can never change what you are."

"You're dead wrong. You know nothing about me."

Her eyes glazed with defiance. "I know enough to know I want no part of you, Jeff O'Leary." An inner torment was ripping her heart to shreds. There was a stabbing pain shooting through her as she said words she knew would send him out of her life forever. She felt a terrible need to be cruel, to hurt him for the way he had taken advantage of her.

His eyes went dark and a demonic smile settled on his mouth. "Well, if you think me so base, then I might just as well behave as you expect me to behave." He grabbed her and began kissing her passionately. He fondled her breasts and pressed his leg between hers, proving the firmness of his purpose. Page struggled but in vain as Jeff began forcing her toward the barn.

172

"The carriage," she managed as one part of her shook with anticipation, the other trembled with fear.

Suddenly Allan's hand came down heavily on his brother's shoulder. He pulled Jeff away from Page and spun him around. A second later Allan's fist connected with Jeff's jaw and Jeff went sprawling on the ground. He started to get up but Allan shook his fist at him.

"You stay right where you are, Jeff," he snarled, "unless you want your teeth knocked down your throat."

Jeff rubbed his jaw and gingerly moved it back and forth to make sure it was still in one piece. He said nothing, just stayed where he was.

"Come, Page," Allan said, extending his hand to her. "I'll tie my horse to your carriage and ride home with you."

Page took a hesitant step toward him, trying to quiet the urgent little voice that was telling her to rush to Jeff and make certain he wasn't seriously hurt.

Then with an angry toss of her head she remembered her weakness and took Allan's hand as he led her to the carriage.

As they drove away she looked back. Jeff had gotten to his feet and stood looking after them. Her heart pained to see the closed look on his face.

"Jeff isn't really a bad sort, Page. Try not to judge him too harshly. Unfortunately he never had the chances I had. When he was growing up our parents were set on one of us getting proper schooling. I took to lessons and Jeff seemed quite willing to work." Allan glanced back to make sure his mare was still hitched to the carriage and following on behind.

173

"Father fell sick when I was in school and there was no one to provide. Jeff volunteered to quit school and insisted I complete my studies and pass the State Law Examinations. I owe Jeff an awful lot. We all do. Too bad he fell into bad company right from the beginning." He shrugged. "Of course even now a teenage kid can't get any kind of decent work except at slave wages. Only the shadier jobs, the ones you get in the Patch, pay decent money." He was silent for a moment. "Jeff has always been in some kind of trouble, but I'll say one thing for him, he never shares his troubles. I know of a dozen tough scrapes he got himself involved in but he said he'd beat the tar out of me if I ever got even remotely involved in any of his business." Allan chuckled. "And despite my lucky punch back there, Jeff could easily have knocked me silly."

Page suddenly remembered Danny O'Shea's remark to Karl that night in Danny's saloon. "Just what does Jeff do?"

"When he isn't helping Mom with the deliveries, it's anybody's guess. Jeff never talks about where his money comes from. Mom and I have stopped asking long ago."

The carriage pulled up under the north portico of the Kane mansion. Allan helped her out and unhitched his mare. "I'll repay my brother one day. I owe him everything, that's why it is so important that I amount to something one day. I'm not ambitious only for myself, I want it for my family."

Page put a gentle hand on his arm. "You'll be a great man one day, Allan. I know you will."

"Well, let's hope it's soon."

She extended her hand. "Thank you, Allan. I'd ask you in but Karl may be asleep."

174

"Good night, Page. It is so wonderful seeing you again. Please don't stay away so long next time."

"I promise."

Karl wasn't asleep. He was sitting propped up on pillows with an open periodical in his lap and a glass of whiskey in his hand.

"Oh, Karl," she said as she took the glass out of his hand. "You know you're not supposed to be drinking."

"I got bored. Nurse Fleming fell asleep in the sitting room so I decided I'd have one small drink as long as my watchdog wasn't at her post."

She touched her lips to his and noticed that he'd obviously had more than one small drink.

Later, as she lay beside him, she started to think about Jeff again, letting all that Allan had told her run through her mind.

Her thoughts scattered when she felt Karl's hand touch her thigh. She turned and smiled at the slightly tipsy look he was giving her. She kissed him, but not with any seriousness. "You had better think about sleep, dearest."

"I want you," he whispered. Then showing a lecherous grin he said, "The doctor said exercise wouldn't do me any harm."

Page laughed softly and fitted herself into his arms. The remembrance of Jeff's body against her own, the taste of his mouth made her bold as she reached for Karl and found him hard and throbbing.

When he moved over her Page closed her eyes and gave herself gladly, willingly. A faint image of Jeff O'Leary flitted across her mind and she could almost feel the roughness of the hay bale against her naked flesh as she thought of the way he'd bound her, the way he'd deflowered her. Against her will, the more she thought of that afternoon the more she urged Karl on.

He kissed her eyes, her hair, her throat. "You're so very beautiful," Karl murmured, his breath short and anxious.

His hand went between her legs, stroking the soft inner flesh of her creamy thighs. Page gave an involuntary cry of desire as she felt him enter her, quickly, urgently. She wanted it to go slower, to last forever so she could linger over the forbidden dream that was floating around inside her head. Her hands caressed Karl as he moved against her nakedness. Page felt the tensing and untensing of his back muscles as the cadence of his breathing and thrusting increased. His breath grew more labored, his face strangely contorted as he pushed and drove deep into her.

Suddenly his eyes widened and with a gasp his whole body went rigid. Page threw herself up to him, though she was far from wanting it to be over. Her fantasy had only begun.

Karl let a long, low moan escape his lips as he fell heavily on top of her. She lay feeling unfulfilled, oppressed by the weight of his body.

"Karl," she said softly as she tried to move from under him. When she got no response she again called his name. "Karl!"

He didn't move. He didn't answer. Suddenly with a scream building up in her throat Page realized that his breathing had stopped.

Karl was dead.

Chapter Fifteen

Page grieved deeply and her tears were genuine; still a sense of freedom seemed to hang about her which made her feel ashamed. She'd hardly learned to be a wife before she was a widow.

As was the custom, the wake was held at the home. It lasted three days and three nights and was more of a party than a period of mourning. Everyone of importance came to pay their respects, women veiled in black sat with the corpse in the large salon, drapes drawn, black bunting hung throughout the room, the flower-draped casket sitting on a raised dais.

The men retired to the library and back parlor where they smoked and drank and ate. Servants were loaned from the prominent families and for the three days of mourning the comings and goings at the Lake Shore mansion went on endlessly.

It was Page's duty as widow to preside over the mourners, sitting straight and stiff at the head of the coffin, accepting the murmured expressions of condolence and trying to ignore the boisterous talk and laughter coming from the men in the other parts of the house.

Blocks of ice had to be fitted into the galvanized containers secreted under the bier to keep the corpse fresh. The emptying and refilling of the containers was done only in the middle of the night when just the appointed vigils were present in the mourning room. It was an honor to be asked to serve in the all-night vigil, an honor given only to the men.

The wake finally ended in a procession of black-draped carriages with black-plumed horses carrying the mass of mourners to the cemetery at the northern outskirts of the city, where Karl Kane was put to rest in the ground and a mound of flowers laid over him. Everyone then returned to the Lake Shore mansion for one final feast in his honor. It lasted well into dawn of the following day and by the time the house was at last quiet, Page dragged herself wearily up the long, curved staircase and dropped, fully clothed, onto the bed.

When at last she awoke she lay quietly trying to figure out the day, the time. Even the room seemed strangely different. Gradually everything began to sort itself out inside her head as she pushed herself up and sat on the edge of the bed. Her mourning clothes were rumpled, her hair in terrible disarray and her face no better, she noticed as she picked up her hand mirror from the night table. In the three long days of mourning she felt as if she'd aged ten years.

"Ah, you're awake," the housekeeper said as she came in carrying a tray of coffee and toast.

"Good morning, Mrs. Chambers."

"Good evening would be more like it, madame. It's nine o'clock."

178

"Heavens. Have I slept all day?"

"Almost two days to be precise, Mrs. Kane. I didn't feel it would be right to disturb you so I kept the house quiet and let you rest yourself. You've been through an awful ordeal these past days," the kindly old woman said.

"We all have, Mrs. Chambers, especially you. I know how fond you were of Mr. Kane." She touched the woman's hand. "Thank you for standing beside me all during the wake."

"Oh, I got my chances to rest, Mrs. Kane. Unfortunately a man's widow can't do that. People seem to enjoy seeing how much a woman mourns." She put down the tray and began helping Page off with her widow's weeds. "How do you feel?"

"Rested."

"Your mother's here. She didn't ask to see you actually. She just stopped by for a cup of tea in the kitchen and inquired as to how you were bearing up."

"She's here now?" Page asked anxiously.

Mrs. Chambers nodded. "She was having her tea when I came up. But as I said, she never asked to see you, just inquired as to how you're bearing up."

Lily had made one formal appearance at the wake, kissing Page's cheek and reciting an expression of sympathy. As was expected, she sat for three hours, then left after a second expression of sympathy. It was as though she were a distant relative or an acquaintance doing a duty.

Mrs. O'Leary, on the other hand, had been in attendance throughout most of the wake, always nearby in case Page needed anything at all. And of all the mourners, Catherine O'Leary was the only one who had looked truly grieved.

Lily was just finishing her tea when Page hurried into the kitchen. Lily let herself be embraced.

"I've just come to make sure you're getting rest," Lily said. "No sense in burying two corpses in a week's time. I didn't like the look of you when I paid my respects and I can't say I much like the look of you now."

"Mother, please come into the front rooms. I want so much to talk with you."

"Your husband's death changes nothing between us, Page. You have nothing to say that would interest me. You're my daughter and I am concerned for your health, nothing more."

"I'm alone here now, Mother. Won't you please move in and share my house? Your bed's upstairs in the north wing. You'd be such a comfort and I know I could make you happy."

"It isn't your house, Page. It will always be Karl Kane's house and I'll never be in that man's debt even if he is dead." She pulled on her shawl. "Get rest and some food into you. You know where to find me if you need me for anything serious."

"I need you now," Page insisted.

"Being alone in a house too big for you is not what I consider a serious need. Good-bye, Page." She turned and walked out the back door.

Page stood looking at the closed door, her pride holding her back from rushing after her mother.

"Pardon, Mrs. Kane," the housekeeper said, "there is a gentleman to see you. I put him in the parlor."

"Oh?"

"A Mr. O'Shea."

Page's breath caught. "Danny O'Shea?"

Mrs. Chambers nodded.

"What does he want?"

"I'm afraid he didn't tell me that, Mrs. Kane."

As Page went toward the parlor she pushed her difficulties with her mother out of her mind to make room for this new problem, because that's surely what Danny O'Shea was bringing her.

Fortunately, as it turned out, Danny did not cause a problem. He made her a proposition.

"The Gilded Plume is obviously yours now, Mrs. Kane. I thought perhaps you'd like to sell it to me, or better still, let me buy myself in as your partner."

For the first time since Karl's death it occurred to Page that as his widow she was also his beneficiary. "I—I never thought," she stammered as the idea of inheriting so vast a fortune began to make its impact on her.

"Haven't Karl's lawyers been to see you?"

"I suppose they were here to pay their respects, but no one spoke to me of business matters."

Danny chuckled. "Knowing Karl's lawyers they're most likely trying to see how much they can grab off the top before turning over Karl's estate."

"But how do you know Karl left me The Gilded Plume? He may not have had time to sign a will in my favor. After all, we haven't been married all that long a time."

"Karl was always a businessman first, Mrs. Kane. You can bet your last penny he drew up a new will."

Page was flustered as she began to pace. "I don't know, Mr. O'Shea. It's much to early for me to think about business matters."

"I know I'm rushing things a bit, but I wanted to be the first to make the offer. I would suggest you speak to your husband's attorneys and then we can talk some more." He narrowed his eyes on her. "I believe you and I can come to some mutual agreement. I want The Gilded Plume very badly."

She sensed something ominous in his voice and studied his threatening expression. "I'll speak with the lawyers and will be in contact with you. Good day, Mr. O'Shea."

"Good day, Mrs. Kane. And take my advice and contact the lawyers as soon as possible. As you know, I am not a very patient man."

She didn't like the way he was looking at her. It was as if he knew something she did not, something that gave him a hold over her. As she walked with him to the door she came to the decision that if it turned out that she did own The Gilded Plume, Danny O'Shea would be the last man on earth she'd sell it to and she would certainly never share it with him.

"I'll be waiting," Danny said.

Page closed the door and leaned back against it, thinking. She'd heard Karl speak of lawyers, of course, but she never paid any attention to names. "Allan," she said brightly as she pushed herself away from the door and started up to her room, deciding that Allan O'Leary would surely be able to help.

Page had just stepped out of the door and was starting toward the waiting victoria with its liveried driver when a white carriage with four pearl-gray, well-curried horses pulled into the drive. In the carriage sat a bejeweled, overdressed woman with three younger women, all of whose occupations obviously were not respectable ones.

The older woman, ablaze with diamonds, adjusted the girls' sunshades so as not to blemish their cream-and-pink complexions as the carriage pulled to a stop beside Page.

"Mrs. Kane?" the woman said in a soft, sensual voice. "I'm Carrie Watson. Perhaps you've heard of me?" Then she laughed and nudged the girl beside her. "But then you'd only know who I am if you spoke to the wrong people."

Trying to hide her embarrassment Page said, "I'm afraid I haven't heard of you, Miss Watson, but what is it you want of me?"

"Well, that all depends on what you want from me, honey."

"I don't understand."

Carrie glanced at her girls. "I have a place on South Clark Street. That is, I have *half* a place on South Clark. Your husband, that is your late husband, had the other half. I assume you own that now and me and the girls here were wondering what you intend doing with your share."

The color rose in Page's face until it burned the roots of her hair. Carrie slapped her thigh and laughed. "Talk to Clyde Evans, honey." She noticed Page frown. "He's Karl's mouthpiece. He'll advice you. I'm willing to buy you out, of course, at what I think is a fair price."

"I'm sure, Miss Watson, whatever you think right will meet with my satisfaction."

Carrie laughed again. "Karl would turn over in his grave if'n he heard you say that, but good enough." She tapped the tall-hatted Negro coachman with her parasol. "Let's go, Joshua." To Page she called, "My lawyers will be in touch, honey. And drop by for a visit sometime." She and her girls giggled happily as the carriage swung on down the drive.

It shocked her to think that Karl would have a fifty percent interest in the type of place Carrie Watson obviously ran.

More surprising facts were disclosed to her when Page, in company with Allan O'Leary, visited the law offices of Clyde Evans, a distinguished-looking gentleman well up in years who reminded her of a charming country gentleman with an amiable disposition and a heart as pure as spring rain.

"Your husband did indeed make a new will after your marriage, Mrs. Kane," Evans told her. "I've taken the liberty of making a list of his holdings, all of which pass to you."

It took several readings before Page realized she was now one of the richest women in Chicago.

"Good Lord," Allan breathed. "I had no idea Karl owned so much." He began pointing to the numerous entries. "Railroads, cattle ranches, farmlands, industrial buildings, and look at the list of real estate." Page noticed he quickly skipped over the address of Carrie Watson's place on South Clark Street.

"You are indeed a very wealthy young lady," Evans said as he leaned back in his chair. "I am sure that you will want to dispose of some of these holdings, so if I can be of any assistance please do not hesitate to call upon me or my partners."

Once outside Page found her blood racing and her head reeling. "I'm rich," she breathed.

"Richer than Clyde Evans wants you to believe. The man has a reputation for holding back inherited assets. Knowing Evans, this is only about half of what Karl Kane left you."

"How much do you think it is all worth? I mean, how rich am I, Allan?"

"Very rich. Even with what Evans and his cronies succeed in stealing from you, I'd say you're well worth upwards to about thirty or forty million dollars."

Page gasped and put out her hand, groping for his support. "I don't believe it," she breathed.

"That's only an estimate. I'd suggest you convert it into solid securities and live the rest of your life in luxury without a care in the world."

But Page wasn't ready to retire into a life of idleness. She knew, of course, she had no head for cattle selling or grain manipulations, nor did she know anything about banking or the stock market, or real estate investments; but deep down she had an urge to go on with managing The Gilded Plume. She missed singing for the captivated audiences.

As they rode back toward Lake Shore Drive, Page idly mentioned the conversation she'd had with Carrie Watson. "Did Karl own any other places like that, Allan?"

He hesitated for a moment. Then, with a forced sigh he said, "Your husband was not a very reputable man, Page. Everything he owned he acquired through some kind of shady dealing. I know how fond of him you were and I don't mean to destroy your memory of him, but you should face the truth. Karl was a very dishonorable person, rich and powerful and totally corrupt."

"I don't believe that," she snapped. "You can tell me as often as you like but I'll never believe it."

Allan started to drive his point home but changed his mind and closed his mouth. He put his hand over hers. "You'll find out for yourself, I'm afraid. Just be prepared, Page. He was not well liked."

"But his funeral was one of the biggest ever held in Chicago. Everyone was there, including the mayor."

"Karl owned all those people. He still does, even in death. And you," Allan added ominously, "inherited them."

Page pulled far within herself and sat quite still as a chill ran through her. She squared her shoulders and pulled her shawl tighter about herself. "I never thought of Karl as anything but a good man, a man of principle. I can't see your version of him any more than you can see mine, Allan, so let's not discuss him further."

"As you wish, Page. But if you don't believe me, then ask Jeff." He paused. "Jeff worked for Karl for a while."

Though stunned, she held up her hand. She didn't want to hear another word.

Later however, in Karl's study, she began sorting through the papers in his desk, finding evidence of truth in what Allan had told her. There was a curt note from an alderman mentioning:

"Here's the last of the money. I hope you'll not demand any more."

In a strongbox at the bottom of a deep drawer she found thousands of dollars in cash, letters from politicans thanking Karl for his support and promising every type of favor. There was even a letter from Carrie Watson thanking him for sending over two girls.

With a shudder of disgust Page slammed the drawer. She gathered up her skirts and ran from the room.

As she sat at the windows of her upstairs sitting room, Page came to a decision. If Karl had done wrong she would right the wrongs. If his gain had been ill-gotten, then she would repay it, even if it took every cent of her inheritance. The major question in her mind was where should she start. Then Allan's parting words came back to her.

"Ask Jeff," he'd said.

Chapter Sixteen

She had refused to acknowledge that she'd been looking for an excuse to see Jeff and even as she started out alone for the O'Leary cottage she told herself that it was merely his counsel she needed. If Jeff had indeed worked for Karl, then Jeff would know the people connected with him and how they should be approached.

"He's down in the Patch as usual," Mrs. O'Leary said as she lugged a load of wet wash out of the soaking tub and began twisting it, piece by piece, around the wooden wringing pegs. She used a broom handle for added leverage when the twists got too tight.

"And my mother? I didn't see her in the yard."

"Lily went out to pick up Mrs. Mahoney's work." She strained at the wringing. "Ask your boys at The Gilded Plume, Page. They'll more than likely know where you can find Jeff."

She got back into the buggy and started toward Wells Street. Seeing the Patch again in broad daylight she'd forgotten how tawdry and delapidated it was. The plank streets were rotting from the marshes they rested on, the buildings were flimsy and unsafe. It surprised her that the gusty winds from the lake hadn't long since blown the whole place down. Yet, with all its dereliction, its flashy gambling men and gaudy women, she still longed to stand on that little stage inside The Gilded Plume and listen to the applause of the crowds. Night and gaiety hid all the seediness, the debauchery for which the Patch was so notorious. Besides, she told herself, The Gilded Plume was not in the same class as the other places. It was a respectable night spot and it was free of corruption and crime.

Hitching the buggy to the post in front of the Plume, Page started to get down and immediately felt a man's assistance.

"Mrs. Kane," Danny O'Shea said as he tipped his hat. "Have you come to see me or are you just checking up on a parcel of your inheritance?"

"Hello, Mr. O'Shea. As a matter of fact I've come seeking Jeff O'Leary. Have you seen him, by any chance?"

"Actually I have. He's over at my place."

"Your place!" Knowing what the O'Learys thought of Danny O'Shea it stunned her to think that Jeff would so much as step foot inside.

Reading her thoughts Danny said, "Men like Jeff change their minds pretty easily when given the right provocation."

Page started across the street with Danny at her side. "I don't imagine you've reached a decision on that matter we discussed?" he said.

"I've seen my husband's attorney. I've made no definite decisions on anything, Mr. O'Shea."

"You know then that you're a pretty wealthy lady. And as such you and I could really put this old town on its ear."

"I wouldn't put too much stock on you and I being in any way associated."

He merely gave her a lopsided grin. "I wouldn't be too sure about that, Mrs. Kane."

As he held the door open for her, Page hesitated. All the horror of that first time here with Danny O'Shea came back in shuddering, ghastly detail.

"I'll wait out here. Would you kindly ask Jeff to come out, please?"

Again Danny gave a snide laugh. "Remember what happened the last time you were caught in front of my place. No, Mrs. Kane, I think for your own safety you'd better step inside. There's a lot of ugly articles loitering about nowadays." He saw her reluctance. "You'll be perfectly safe, Mrs. Kane. I give you my word as a gentleman."

Knowing he was far from a gentleman she continued to hold back, but when she saw a trio of roughs staggering along the boardwalk she hurried inside.

The place was deserted, very much like it was that day Danny dragged her into that little room under the stairs.

"O'Leary should be back there," Danny said, indicating a curtained archway at the end of the long, oak bar. "First room on your right."

There was a leaden feeling in her feet as she left Danny and started toward the rear of the saloon. It hadn't occurred to her that Danny might be lying, that Jeff wasn't here at all and that she'd been trapped once again. Yet Danny had turned away and had left her alone so obviously he'd told her the truth.

Beyond the heavy velvet curtains she found herself standing in a short corridor with several doors leading into rooms. She paused before the first door on her right. Her knuckles remained poised in front of the panel. Then, taking a deep breath to fortify her sagging courage, she knocked.

"It's not locked," she heard Jeff call out.

Page turned the knob and pushed open the frame door. It swung easily on its hinges and as she stepped into the room she froze.

"Page!" Jeff gasped as he hurriedly threw the bed covers over the naked girl lying beside him. Quickly he tucked a sheet up around his own naked body.

"Page!" he cried again but she fled in a flutter of skirts, trying desperately to hold back the tears that were stinging the backs of her eyes.

The girl on the bed propped herself up on her elbows and looked at the empty doorway. "So that was the popular Page Kane. If she sings as great as she looks, no wonder everybody's clamoring to get into The Gilded Plume."

"She does," Jeff said. There was a terrible ache in his chest. It hurt so badly he found it hard to speak. He lay back against the pillows still seeing the shock on her face and feeling a terrible painful longing for her.

"I see why you talk about her so much," the girl said.

"I don't talk about her," Jeff grunted as he rolled over on his side, turning his back to Melody Sharp.

Melody cuddled up against him, pressing her firm, round breasts into his shoulder blades. She started to toy with the disheveled hair that curled over his ears. "I suppose now that she barged in on us, you won't want to make love to me."

"What are you talking about?" He rolled back and took her in his arms. "Page Kane means nothing to me. Nothing at all," he repeated as he forced her onto her back and began kissing her eyes, her throat, her breasts.

It took a woman to know when a man was making love and when he was performing. At the moment, Melody knew Jeff was performing. They'd met only a month ago and had become lovers that very first night. That is, Melody had fallen in love. Jeff was all she'd ever wanted in a man, but she was smart enough to know that he didn't love her. She was also smart enough not to ever let him know how desperately she loved him. Her love was futile, but she didn't much care about that. She wanted Jeff on whatever terms he laid down and when he stopped wanting her, well she'd think about that when it needed thinking about.

She just made sure she never made any demands on him, other than to let him know how much she wanted him sexually, which seemed to please him. Melody never let herself forget that Jeff loved Page Kane. Oh, he'd never admit it to himself, in fact he went to extremes to deny it and prove his denial just as he was doing now as he thrust into her cruelly, violently. ·

She saw his closed eyes, his clenched teeth and knew he was fantasizing. To him, Page Kane was the woman he was assaulting, hurting, making suffer for the pain she caused him.

Jeff worked more feverishly as his orgasm began to build. He knew he would spend too soon but he couldn't help himself. Page's face was clearly etched before him and he wanted her to be unsatisfied, he wanted her to feel the emptiness that gnawed at his insides.

He heard Melody speak his name as she moved under him, pushing herself up to meet his onslaught, but to him the woman was Page Kane.

With a powerful lunge forward he buried himself deeply into Melody's willing body and let her softness enfold him, soothe him, milk him of his last vestiges of strength as he fell heavily to his side. He put his arm across his eyes and tried to black out everything but the pleasurable release from his frustrations.

"Jeff," Melody said softly as she pressed close to him. "Sleep now."

Danny O'Shea's voice from the doorway shot open Jeff's eyes. "Hey, you two, don't you have any decency or do you get an extra kick out of doing it with the door open?"

"Get out of here, Danny," Melody yelled as she threw a pillow at him, then drew the sheet over themselves.

Danny laughed and came into the room. He boldly pulled up a straight wooden chair, sat down beside the bed, lit a cigar, then leaned back, propping his feet up on the edge of the mattress.

"Jesus," Melody moaned as she burrowed deeper into the covers.

Jeff eyed him suspiciously. "What in hell was the idea of sending Page Kane back here? You're the only one I know who'd pull a lousy stunt like that."

Danny puffed in his cigar.

"What was Page doing here in the first place?" asked Jeff.

"She said she was looking for you, so I told her where she could find you."

"What did she want?"

Danny shrugged. "All she said was that she wanted to see you. She did mention that she'd been to Kane's lawyers and knows she's a very rich lady." Danny blew smoke at the ceiling. "If Kane left her everything, she's just about one of the most vulnerable women in Chicago."

"Vulnerable?" Jeff thought for a moment and suddenly sat up and began pulling on his clothes.

Danny continued to puff on his cigar as he watched him.

Melody said, "Where are you going, Jeff?"

Danny answered for him. "To protect a damsel in great distress, of course."

Jeff put on his shirt and quickly buttoned it up. "Page is practically a member of my family. I owe it to her and her mother to point out the dangers she may be in. With Kane dead there are a lot of incriminating papers many important people would like to get their hands on and they wouldn't raise an eyebrow if it meant killing off a widow."

"Sir Galahad to the rescue." Danny chuckled. He let his eyelids droop until he was watching Jeff through tiny slits. "I want The Gilded Plume, if you are going to start helping the little lady dispose of Kane's shadier assets."

"I'm sure she'll be only too happy to sell it along with everything else that has Kane's dirty fingerprints on it. I'm familiar with most of Kane's dealings, more than he ever thought I knew. I'll see that Page comes out clean . . . and rich."

"And yourself as well, I'm sure," Danny said.

"I don't want anything out of this." He went over and kissed Melody lightly on the cheek. "I'll try and get back tonight to catch your act."

It took Jeff most of the afternoon to find Page and when he did she was sitting at the table in the O'Leary's kitchen talking to Allan and his mother. Lily sat quietly beside the stove expertly darning a hole in a linen tablecloth that belonged to one of their wealthy customers.

Allan had a collection of papers and ledgers in front of him which he was explaining to Page. When Jeff came in Page eyed him coldly, nodded, then bent back to what Allan was saying.

"Now these are mineral rights that Karl bought on various pieces of real estate from here to Missouri. They're honest enough holdings but I'd suggest you get rid of them. There's little likelihood of any profits being made out of anything here, and the cost of drilling wouldn't pay for the profit you'd eventually realize."

She nodded. Allan made a note on a large yellow pad, then picked up the next stack of documents. "These are deeds to cattle lands, some in Kansas, some in Oklahoma, some in Texas. My advice is to sell them, unless you want to go into the cattle business."

"No, I have no interest in ranching."

"I'll find buyers without much trouble and I know I can get you good prices."

Jeff stood listening, then pulled up a chair beside his mother after pouring himself a cup of coffee. "I was told you were looking for me earlier," he said to Page.

"Yes," she admitted, glancing at his mother. She forced herself to try and forget the scene that was still playing before her eyes. Remembering the sight of Jeff's naked torso made her heart pound, but remembering the blonde girl's naked breasts made her blood boil. Without looking at him she said, "I was told you were familiar with some of my husband's business affairs. I thought you might advise me."

"Do as Allan's telling you. Sell everything, Page.

Everything," he said emphatically. "Don't hang on to anything connected with that man. Get rid of his house, his papers, his real estate." He looked at his mother and stopped. In a softer tone he said to Page, "I know you believe your husband was a nice man, and I don't want to say anything against him because you won't believe me. But he had a lot of enemies and there are a lot of damaging papers in his safe that must be destroyed and the people concerned with them must know they were destroyed or returned. I'll take care of it if you'll permit me."

Page gave him a hateful look and started to refuse him but Allan anticipated her. "I think you should let Jeff help, Page. He knows what should be done and how to go about doing it."

There was a gentle quiet over the kitchen with no sound but the crackling of the wood fire in the stove. "Very well," Page said with a sigh. "But I intend keeping one thing. I want The Gilded Plume."

"No!" Lily said as she dropped her sewing and got to her feet. "It's unthinkable."

"Lily is right," Catherine O'Leary said. "It's one thing your singing in the place, but owning and running it just wouldn't be right, not to mention that running a saloon in the Patch is a dangerous business, child."

"Mother's right," Allan urged. "Sell it with the rest."

"Danny O'Shea wants to buy it," Jeff told her.

Page turned slowly toward him, arching her brows and tilting her head at a haughty, defiant angle. "That friend of yours, the blonde girl, Mr. O'Shea told me she's a singer in his saloon."

"Yes," Jeff admitted, not knowing what she was getting at.

"Danny O'Shea also told me he wants to buy

The Gilded Plume, that he'll even go partners with me if I do not want to sell out completely. Well, I don't want to sell at all and if anyone sings in The Gilded Plume it will be me."

"Page!" Lily said harshly. "I'll not have it!"

Her daughter turned angrily toward her mother. She could see in all their faces that they were against her.

"I'm sorry, Mother, but ever since we came to Chicago you have disapproved of everything I've done. I am now an extremely rich woman and if you will all permit me, I can see to it that none of us will ever want for anything again."

"We'll not be charity cases," Mrs. O'Leary said gathering her dignity about her.

"Once you were very kind to me, Mrs. O'Leary. Just let me return the kindness."

"There is nothing I want that I don't already have, Page, my darlin', including your love and your concern for my well-being. Enjoy your money if it pleases you but, saints preserve us, child, don't run a saloon in the Patch. It was the likes of Danny O'Shea that almost killed my Patrick and sent him so far away from us. You can't let yourself be lured into the devil's playground."

"The Gilded Plume, as everyone knows, is an honest, decent place for entertainment. I'll see that it's run clean and proper. It'll set an example." She saw their stern looks of disapproval. "I was going to ask you to help me make it a place the entire city could be proud of, but I see I'd only be talking to the air."

Lily lowered herself back into her chair and resumed her mending. "You want to make a spectacle of yourself with your singing, so don't try to disguise your selfish purposes with talk of lofty ideals.

Go sing to the riffraff in the Patch. I have nothing more to say to you."

"I just do not understand you, Mother. I can give you the world. I can bring back all the luxury you once had. Why do you deny me?"

"Because I will have nothing that was bought with unclean money."

"But it's my inheritance."

"Give it to the poor. Burn it. Don't touch a dollar of it. Look what it's done to you. You've become a conceited, spoiled little fluff with a temper to match."

Page sat, then slowly her whole body began to sag. She thought about the horrible shack near the railroad tracks in Abilene, the smelly stockyards in the summer, the horrible men like Bull Ramsey who represented an ever-existing threat. She remembered the backbreaking hours over the washtubs, the freezing cold of her hands as she hung out line after line of wet laundry. She could never go back to that.

It was all well and good for her mother to sit in judgment. She'd had all the advantages of money when she was young. She'd married a wealthy man and all her pretty years had been spent in solid comfort and ease. But she was old now and she could afford to be self-righteous and sanctimonious.

I still have my whole life ahead of me, Page reminded herself. And as she glanced from one to the other she realized that they all were living the kinds of lives they wanted to live. Well, she was entitled to do the same.

She straightened in her chair and began collecting her things. "Sell everything but The Gilded Plum, Allan," she announced as she got up. She turned to Jeff. "If you wish to go through Karl's papers, I would consider it a favor."

"We can do it now, if that is convenient, Page. Besides, there is something I would like to explain."

She gave him a withering look. "I neither want nor need explanations." To Allan she said, "Please let me know when you have everything ready for my signature."

"Don't keep the Plume, Page," Allan implored. "Or at least sleep on it and we'll discuss it again tomorrow."

"There's nothing to discuss. I'm keeping The Gilded Plume." She started toward the door. "If you are coming with me, Jeff, please come along." Keeping herself tall and straight she walked out the back door.

Jeff went over to Lily. "Don't worry now," he said to her. "I'll talk to Page. I think I can talk her out of it."

"Please," Lily said fighting back her tears. "Please try, my boy."

He patted her cheek and hurried after Page.

Chapter Seventeen

To her complete surprise, Jeff never mentioned The Gilded Plume. They rode back to the Kane mansion and Page asked Mrs. Chambers to fix dinner, which she asked be served in front of the fire in the study where she and Jeff began sifting through the stacks of notes and letters and documents.

As they worked together, she looked at him from time to time and wondered why the image of the naked blonde girl grew more faint as the minutes passed.

Jeff reached for some papers, read through them then folded them quickly and put them inside his pocket.

"What's that you're taking?"

Jeff patted the hidden papers. "Only another part of Karl Kane you don't need to know about."

She remembered Carrie Watson and her parasol-toting doxies and the letter thanking Karl for the girls. "The house on South Clark or some other?"

Jeff stared at her, then a gleeful laugh burst from him. "How in the deuces did you know about the house on South Clark?"

"Carrie Watson spoke to me about it."

201

"She didn't!" Jeff said, aghast.

"She did, indeed. This very morning, in fact."

Mrs. Chambers came in followed by a maid. Jeff and Page sipped the wine Jeff had opened earlier and waited until they were again alone.

"Did Karl have an interest in many such places, Jeff?"

"A few."

The wine was making her bolder and more kittenish. "I've always had an idle curiosity about what those places were like, I mean the really elegant ones. Are they as fancy as I've heard them gossiped about?"

Jeff laughed. "Complete with solid silver seats in the water closets." He saw her turn crimson. "I've never been in such places myself, of course," he added quickly.

"Of course," Page said and giggled.

"But take Lou Harper's mansion on Monroe Street, for example."

"That huge house with the oversized numbers?"

Jeff nodded, feeling silly and extremely devilish. "Red lights are only for the lower classes." He leaned closer and confided, "Miss Harper even has her own engraved calling cards, as do her young ladies. The mansion is said to be the most opulent in Chicago with great solid golden oak doors and polished brass plate everywhere. Ostentatious and swank is the only way to describe the place. The ladies are never introduced on a first-name basis and they always are dressed in the latest of fashions, including silver scent bottles suspended from their bosoms in case they faint if a gentleman utters a vulgarity. It's very posh, I tell you."

Page doubled up in peals of laughter. "No

202

more," she gasped, falling onto the couch, trying to contain her laughter.

He walked over and smiled down at her. The smile faded as he reached out his hand. Page's laughter gradually subsided as she saw his earnest expression, the hunger in his eyes.

She let him help her up but expertly avoided his attempt to embrace her. "The dinner is getting cold," she said as she quickly seated herself at the table.

"That girl," Jeff started as he took the chair opposite her and spread the napkin across his lap. "Her name is Melody Sharp."

"I know her name, Jeff. Danny O'Shea was only too anxious to tell me all about her. Your relationship is none of my concern so I see no need to discuss it."

"I don't love her."

Page went on spreading butter on a roll. "I am not in the least interested in your feelings toward her, Jeff. I've asked you here strictly for business reasons and I believe we should stick to that."

"And forget the fact that we've both been enjoying ourselves immensely?"

"That was a mistake."

"Page."

"Please, Jeff," she said, slamming her knife down on the edge of the plate. "If you persist in bringing your personal life into this evening, perhaps you had better leave."

He leapt to his feet, threw down his napkin and glowered at her. "I'll go, if that's really what you want, Page, but I honestly don't think it is."

With a flustered move of her hand she pushed aside her plate and got up from the table. "I asked for your help with Karl's papers."

"Look at me, Page, and tell me that's the real reason you came searching me out this afternoon."

She whirled around but when she looked at him her voice betrayed her and she could not speak. She made a helpless gesture, then turned away. Not seeing him gave her courage. "Yes," she said firmly. "That's the only reason I came looking for you."

He went toward her and put his hands on her waist, turning her roughly. "That's a lie and we both know it."

"Let me go," she said, starting to struggle.

"No." His mouth covered hers. She beat weakly against his chest and tried desperately to squirm out of his arms, trying to deny the glowing warm feeling that spread through the lower part of her body as she felt his desire throb against her thigh.

"No," she murmured softly as her strength began to fail.

"Yes," he said firmly. He moved her toward the couch and forced her down, holding her tight against the cushions with the weight of his body.

Page continued to struggle but it was a different struggle, a feeble struggle to rid herself of the underthings that he was so recklessly tearing aside.

"I hate you," she groaned as he entered her quickly, smoothly, anxiously.

"I love you," he answered as he covered her mouth again.

She gasped as he plunged deep into her, then began moving with the practiced rhythm of an athlete. He drove into her until he felt her begin to respond, then suddenly removed himself and left her panting on the couch while he quickly went across the study and locked the door.

A moment later his mouth burned a trail down over her throat, her breasts, igniting tiny flames as he knelt and kissed the insides of her thighs. She yawned wide for his caresses, tightening herself about his shoulders as he lavished his wanton desire on the very center of her existence.

Page writhed and cried, squirming, fighting to be free of the sensations he was creating. She kept telling herself she wanted him to stop, to leave her, but she feared his leaving, and she clung to him.

Again he was upon her, in her and she felt incapable of not responding to his expert manipulations. With aching joy she felt him touch the innermost recesses of her, going deeper, deeper, deeper until she knew their souls were lost, bound as one.

Her flesh yielded to his every move, his every need as she enveloped him, clinging wetly to the hardness of his desire. Page found herself sobbing helplessly as hot, searing waves of delirious pleasure swept over her. Her body thrashed and writhed as she urged him on faster, harder, deeper. Nothing existed except the hot, blinding sensations that he was producing inside her. Then, in a blasting phantasm of light and fire, she found herself collapsing in his arms as his powerful, manly body consumed her with its strength.

They lay in each other's arms listening to the crackling fire, oblivious of everything but the pounding of their hearts and the comfort of each other's arms.

Finally Jeff stirred and Page became aware of where they were. She started putting herself back together as best she could. Again she had the sense of having been used and an odd mixture of contentment and resentment confused her mind.

She said, "You always take whatever you want, I see."

He was adjusting himself back into his trousers. "You wanted it to happen as much as I did," he said as he slicked back his hair.

Page walked to the table by the fireside and picked up her wineglass. He was right, of course; she had wanted him to take her, but his accursed male superiority infuriated her. He could read her as easily as a book and it annoyed her that she was so transparent. She thought of the love for her which he'd murmured and wanted to believe it to be sincere but she knew it had only been said in the heat of passion. That was the way of men, she'd heard her mother say all too often. Yet Page was tempted to ask him to repeat his protestations of love.

When she turned to him he was back at work going through the rest of Karl's private papers and somehow Karl's presence was suddenly back in the room and the moment was lost.

"I've gotten to like this big house," Page said, for want of something to say. She went over and casually unlocked the door.

He didn't look up. "It's too grand."

"What do you mean? I have plenty of money. I can afford it."

Jeff put aside the documents he was reading and shook his head at her. "Big houses, Page, are for old people. Haven't you ever noticed that people who don't really need space always have it?"

"Regardless," Page said, just to be ornery, "this house has some fond memories for me."

"What fond memories?" Jeff smirked. "Having some old lecher pawing you? Is that what you call a fond memory?" He picked up another document and began scanning it. "This is Kane's mausoleum.

206

Get rid of it and everything else connected with that man."

"And where, may I ask, am I supposed to live?"

"I haven't thought about that yet." He let a sly smile tease his lips. "I might decide we'll live in a one-room flat over some gambling hall."

"*You* might decide!" His arrogance was annoying but the thought of living with him made her tingle with happiness.

"I'll look around." He threw the last of the papers back into the metal box and clanked it shut. "I'll take care of disposing of this stuff. Allan will handle the rest of it. All you need do is pack whatever you want to take with you and we'll start out tomorrow looking for a place." He tucked the box under his arm and looked around the room. "All this should bring quite a few dollars. The land alone is worth a fortune. Oh, by the way, I think I can get you a nice price for The Gilded Plume. When Danny O'Shea wants something badly enough he gets a little reckless with his money."

"I am *not* selling The Gilded Plume. I thought I made that adequately clear."

"You *are* selling the Plume and that's final." He saw her square her shoulders. "Who in the blazes do you think you are, Page? You're not some seasoned doxy who was born and dragged up in the Patch. You haven't the slightest idea of what it takes to operate a saloon down there."

"The Gilded Plume is not a saloon."

"There! That's exactly what I mean. You think you can refine the place, bring a little dignity to that hellhole. Forget it, Page. You're too naive. You're selling the Plume and I'll hear no more about it."

Page slammed down her glass so hard the stem
207

snapped in two and the wine splashed across the damask cloth. "I am *not* selling the Plume. Just because I'm a woman doesn't mean I'm stupid or naive. I ran The Gilded Plume when Karl was sick so I know what it entails."

"How about the payoffs?"

She gave him a blank look.

"I thought so. Do you think the dives in the Patch operate so openly because nobody in the courthouse building cares? Every owner down there pays off any number of politicans and blue-coats to keep their places open. Every time you turn around there'll be some big shot with his hand out and if you don't know which hand to grease you'll be shut down in a week."

"Then I'll learn."

"And who's going to teach you? Not me," he fumed. "I'll be damned if I'll let you run some gin mill just so you can stand up on a stage and have guys ogle you. You want the Plume because you need a showcase for your ego, Page. Well, I'll not lift a finger to help you. So sell the dump, burn it to the ground—anything, just to be rid of it!"

"No!"

Jeff slammed his fist down on the desk. "I demand it!"

"You what?" Her eyes blazed. "How dare you? Who do you think you are to demand anything?" Her temper flew beyond her control and the words tumbled out against her will. "You're nothing but a two-bit reprobate who never did a lick of honest work in his life. You're even pals with your father's enemy. Where do you get off running down places like The Gilded Plume? You wouldn't know anything about decency if you stepped in it. I'll run The Gilded Plume and I'll sing and dance and do whatever I please without any help or advice from you."

She watched him walk toward the door with the tin box still tucked under his arm. Still she could not stop her tirade.

"Don't you ever tell me what to do, Jeff O'Leary. Ever!"

At the door he turned and looked at her, his hand resting lightly on the knob. "I never will, Page," he said, fighting to keep himself in check. "Never again. If you want to become just another piece from the Patch then I suppose there's nothing I can do about that."

He turned and started to leave, then stopped. He gazed at her for a long, loving moment, then shook his head. "You're a stupid little idiot."

A second later she found herself alone. She stood with fists clenched, nerves taut. Suddenly she picked up the broken glass and hurled it into the fire, then threw herself on the couch and started to cry.

Chapter Eighteen

Allan, like his brother, was opposed to Page's keeping The Gilded Plume, but his disapproval was far less adamant than Jeff's, especially when he saw how determined she was to operate the place.

"I suppose you know what it takes," Allan said. "I'll help all I can, of course, and most of Kane's boys are as trustworthy as any other of that lot. At least they'll be loyal if you pay them enough."

She mentioned the payoffs that would be expected. He saw she was resolute, that nothing would dissuade her. In his mind, it would be wiser to help than oppose her. Left on her own, heaven knows what would happen to her, he told himself. "I'll check around," he said. "Every respectable lawyer must have contacts in all sorts of places if he's to remain respectable," he added with a wink.

He loved her. Every time he saw her his love grew until he felt his whole insides begin to ache. He knew she didn't love him but somehow that didn't matter. She needed him, which was just as good if not better than loving him. In time, after she'd rid herself of her widow's weeds, she'd start to look around and he would be right there beside her, reminding her how much she depended on him and what a good, upstanding citizen he was. True, the police and the courts were controlled by the courthouse crooks and the state politicians, but gradually things were changing for the better. Decent men like Marshall Field, Cyrus McCormick, and Potter Palmer were having stronger influences on the way things should be run.

All knew for certain that there were one or two members on the city council who were comparatively honest, decent men, interested in seeing an honest, clean future for Chicago. The mayoral election would be held this fall and Allan had put his name up as a candidate.

"I'm going to run for mayor, you know," he told Page as they rode away from the mansion on Lake Shore Drive.

"Allan, how wonderful! Your mother must be very proud."

"I was hoping you'd be proud."

"But I am. I didn't mean . . ."

He saw her embarrassment and came to her rescue. "Chicago needs a good housecleaning and I, with the help of a few friends in the city council, think I might be the best man to wield the broom."

"You'll make a wonderful mayor, Allan. You're exactly what the city needs." She looked about as they came toward the central business part of the city. "I wonder why Chicago has such a bad reputation? There's vice and crime in every city, I know, but why is it so pronounced here? Where did it all start?"

"Chicago started out bad before it was a city," Allan said. "It took tough men and women to try and survive in a place where the Indians' favorite pastime was scalping whites. Then the two Beaulieu brothers came along and kind of integrated the place." He grinned. "Squawman Beaulieu fathered twenty little half-breeds and brother Jolly Mark sired twenty-three. They brought a kind of understanding between whites and redskins and the massacring eased up, especially when their kids started mixing with both races. After a few years it didn't seem to matter much who was what."

He turned the buggy onto State Street. "So as things got quieter more people moved into the area. A canal connecting the Mississippi with Lake Michigan was proposed and Jefferson Davis, he was in Congress then, won a political fight with Stephen Douglas to make a harbor at Chicago." He laughed. "There's a funny story some people like to tell that the city got its name from the Indian *Chickagaw* which means 'big stink.' If you hold your nose and say *Chickagaw* it comes out 'Chicago.' "

Page laughed.

"But as I told you when we first met, there's a lot of stories about how Chicago got its name; however, they all have to do with bad smells. Anyway," he continued, "Douglas wanted the harbor at the mouth of the Calumet River below Chicago but he lost out, and when the harbor was officially opened here, naturally, it brought in more trade and more settlers. Land was going fast and the politicians were quick to start taxing everything from pleasure buggies to clocks. A fast-writing lawyer back then could make a fortune just writing and selling titles to land parcels, which changed hands almost daily, at increased prices, of course.

"As the harbor grew the politicians got richer and if they stumbled upon a good money-producing enterprise like a gambling house, a saloon, or a brothel, they found it more lucrative to tax it rather

213

than shut it down. Today it's called graft; back then it was considered good, sound business, all for the welfare of the people and their new city.

"They say nobody will ever clean up Chicago, that its roots are too deep into corruption, so deep that to pull them up would kill the city completely, it would never blossom again. The clean air would poison it."

Page frowned. "Then why are you going to run for mayor?"

"Perhaps it is a mistake on my part, but I'd like to have a chance to put the city to the test. I truly believe Chicago can be as decent a place as any other, that we can clip off the rotten parts of the roots and splice clean healthy roots onto the main stalk. Just because a 'corrupt' label is sewn into a lining doesn't mean the garment's bad."

With an encouraging smile Page said, "If anyone can do it, you can, Allan."

"Thank you." He switched the horse as they got closer to his meager office at the end of State Street. "Of course the Civil War didn't help matters here. I don't know whether you know or not, but Chicago's sentiments lay mostly with the South and the southern gambling influences were very quick to establish themselves here. Chicago was a wide-open city during the war years. Men back from battle had lots of money to spend and gambling doesn't tax a man's strength the way whiskey and doxies do, so gambling houses were awfully popular, especially when a soldier knew he was going back into action, deciding he'd just as well be broke as rich."

He fell silent, thinking. " 'The strong preying on the weak,' that's what Chicago's ethics are. And do you know why the criminal element is so hard to get rid of, Page?" He didn't wait for her answer. "Because the big boys who have the real power aren't just some thugs who made their dollars running sporting palaces; they are men from so-called fine, respectable families, well-educated, well-heeled . . . fine society people. Unfortunately, that fine façade coupled with hearts of thugs makes a very difficult combination to beat. They all operate under the same old motto: Let's make money now and apologize later."

Page said, "Which is one thing you won't have to do, Allan . . . apologize later. You'll make a very fine mayor and I will do everything I can to help you get elected in November." She cocked her head and smiled softly. "I'm a very rich woman, remember."

"All I want from you is your moral support."

Before Page could insist she saw a familiar figure standing in front of Allan's modest office.

"Danny O'Shea," Allan grumbled. "What in the devil do you think he wants?"

"I have a pretty good idea. News has obviously gotten around that you're handling my affairs. Mr. O'Shea has the ridiculous notion that if I won't sell him The Gilded Plume he will insist upon bringing himself in as a partner."

"Mr. O'Shea can be a very ugly enemy, Page. The worst, in fact."

"I'll neither sell him the Plume nor have him own any interest in it. I'd burn it to the ground first," she vowed, then suddenly remembered Jeff having said something similar.

"As for selling the Plume, Page, I think you're making a mistake by keeping it, but as I told you, if you have your heart set on running the place I'll

215

help all I can, including keeping Danny O'Shea out of your hair."

"Thank you, Allan."

Danny O'Shea hadn't come to see Allan about The Gilded Plume, though it was mentioned.

"Too bad you don't want to sell it, Mrs. Kane. It's bigger than my place and a lot fancier. But," he said with a shrug, "Let's let that piece of business be for the moment. I really came to see you, Allan, on an entirely different matter."

"Oh?"

"The election in November. I hear you're going to run for mayor."

"That's right."

"So am I," Danny said flatly.

Allan stiffened slightly, then let himself relax. "That, naturally, is your privilege. It's a free country."

Danny glanced at Page then back at Allan. "I see you've been working on your campaign backing. It'll take a lot to beat me, Mrs. Kane."

Her eyes narrowed. "I just happen to have a lot, Mr. O'Shea, and I am willing to spend every cent of it if it means defeating you."

Danny clucked his tongue. "Too bad you don't appreciate me more, Mrs. Kane, especially since there's a distinct possibility I might be your only salvation one day."

"What is that supposed to mean?" Page asked icily.

Danny merely smiled. "Let's just say 'Abilene' and let it go at that for the time being."

Page flinched but still did not completely understand. What could he possibly mean or know? It never occurred to her to make a connection between Bull Ramsey and Danny O'Shea. "I don't know what you're implying nor do I care to know." She put out her hand to Allan. "I have some shopping to do, Allan. Thank you for all you're doing."

"I'll see you this evening?" he asked hopefully. "Dinner, perhaps?"

"Yes, I'd like that. Until this evening, then."

As she drove away leaving Allan and Danny O'Shea looking after her, she couldn't for the life of her figure what Danny meant by his reference to Abilene. Karl's cattle investments, most likely. Like everything else that was being uncovered, there had to be as much illegalities there as in everything else Karl had left her.

It was strange, however, that with all the proof she'd been shown of Karl's badness, she found it impossible to think ill of him. He'd lifted her up out of a life of drudgery and want into a life overflowing with comfort, beauty, happiness.

Happiness? She thought of Jeff and unconsciously tightened her hands on the reins. She gave a little toss of her head and refused to let him occupy her mind.

Purposely she forced herself to think of Allan and his ideals. With his talk of the city, Chicago was suddenly all she could think of. It was really the first time she was aware of the scope and size of the place. He had made it come alive for her and had given it depth and dimension. It wasn't just a city where she lived in a house and rode over its streets. This was Chicago, where more than three hundred thousand people lived and thrived on a spot six miles long and three miles wide, sitting on the shore of a lake. It was a city divided in three parts by a river in the form of a rough "T" with its base in Lake Michigan and with twelve new wooden bridges spaced about two blocks apart, holding the three parts of the "T" together.

The only trouble with these new modern bridges, Page thought as she pulled up behind a long line of wagons, horsecars and shays waiting to cross, was the fact that they pivoted on a fixed pier in the center of the river so that the ships could pass up or down. There were two tunnels, but she was already in the middle of the congestion so with a sigh she contented herself to sit and wait.

It had to be the most promising city in the world, she thought as she steadied the horse. Allan would make it clean and decent and she was here to see the beginning of that marvelous change and here she'd stay, she told herself. And like the booming city itself, she'd make her own success.

Despite everybody's opposition to her running The Gilded Plume, she felt it her duty to try to improve the Patch, just the way Allan wanted to improve city hall. One hundred passenger trains came into Chicago every day bringing new people, new ideas, new ways of life. The crime and vice that flourished in the Patch could be stamped out if only she could rally all the good citizens together. She would do that by offering a place in the Patch where people could come for wholesome, clean entertainment. In time the good would overpower the bad; it always did, she'd been taught.

The line of traffic began to move, slowly at first but then with faster regularity as she bumped her way over the pine blocks that paved the downtown streets. Fences of pine and hemlock neatly separated the various lots, giving each individual plot a character all its own.

An idle thought passed through Page's head as she wondered where the wood would come from for building expansion when all the surrounding forests were depleted. Of course there was evidence already of wrought iron and stone and brick but only where the marshy land beneath could support the weight.

As she drove into the more fashionable area of State Street she saw the phaetons, the victorias. Mr. McCormick's splendid pair of roans were tethered in front of the Palmer House beside Bertha Palmer's French charabanc with its leopard skin upholstered seats.

Page told herself she could now afford to be as sophisticated as they. She'd buy matched bays and a custom-built carriage with the high-stepping trotters in silver-mounted harnesses. And no one of any real culture employed any but an English coachman. Bertha Palmer once told her that a darkie in livery was just too, too common.

She had to remind herself, however, as she stepped into Fair and Carrs that prices were going up, it seemed, every single day. She picked up a chic straw hat and glanced at the price. Only last month it had been $2.00, now it was marked $2.75. The shoes she'd come in to buy were an extravagance. For a moment she thought she'd best go over across the street to Palmer's Dry Goods Store, where they had that new policy of allowing customers to take home merchandise and inspect it at their leisure; they even made exchanges and gave refunds.

But she felt like indulging herself. Fair and Carrs' prices were always much higher but she didn't care; after all she could well afford to spend such an outrageous price as $5.00 on a pair of shoes if she felt like it.

Later, as she picked up the menu in the fashionable ladies' lounge of the Palmer House, she noticed at least the food prices weren't inflated. Steaks were still 50¢ and their delicious lamb chops 35¢.

"Why Page Kane," Bertha Palmer breathed as she came over to Page's table. "Why didn't you let me know you were coming in today?"

Mrs. Potter Palmer was from southern aristocracy and spoke with a delightful cultured drawl. She was a lovely young woman who wore her clothes with style and flair and had a penchant for wearing pink tea roses in her hair and a glittering assortment of diamonds and pearls. Today she was dressed in a gray-flared gown trimmed in Chinese red braid. She looked the epitome of elegance.

Though not a close friend, Page liked Bertha Palmer. She was an independent sort, much like herself, and was an advocate of women's rights and liked to say, "One hears so much about the new woman, that one is in danger of being bored by her unless she arrives quickly." Page enjoyed Bertha's company because she wanted to be just like her.

"I really didn't know I was coming in myself, Bertie. I had a sudden impulse to buy a new pair of shoes and decided I was suddenly ravenous."

Bertha Palmer studied her for a moment, then sat down beside her. In a conspiratorial whisper she said, "I know it's expected, my dear, but black just does not suit you. Surely you don't intend wearing weeds for twelve months?"

"Gracious no, Bertie, only until I feel comfortable out of them. I miss Karl. I really do."

"Of course you do," Mrs. Palmer said, but she didn't believe Page for a minute. Page Kane would be remarried in a month's time; everyone was saying so.

"So," Bertha said, resting her arms delicately on

220

the table covering. "Have you decided on what you want to do?"

"Allan O'Leary's helping to arrange for the disposal of everything of Karl's. That is . . ."

"Splendid," Mrs. Palmer broke in. "Convert everything into cash or jewelry, my dear. Let men have their bonds and their investments. Men so like to deal in everything complicated." She looked around at the Palmer House dining room. "Perhaps you should own something like a hotel."

Page admired the room. "This is beautiful. You must be very proud of the hotel."

"I was, up until Potter showed me the plans he has for a new one." She began to bubble with enthusiasm. "You should see it, Page; it makes this place look like a cheese crate. He's planning to start building next year."

"I'm seriously interested in keeping The Gilded Plume in operation," Page told her.

Bertha's eyes widened in surprise. "That adorable little supper place where Potter took me—where I first heard you sing?"

"Yes."

"Too bad it isn't in a better location." She shrugged her lovely shoulders. "Oh, well, perhaps between us we'll bring some class to the Patch."

Page looked at her with surprise. "I mentioned it, Bertie, but I never dared hope . . ."

Again she didn't get a chance to finish. "You mentioned it because you need all our help and, of course, I'll do what I can. I'm all for the independent woman, remember. Just let me know when you're opening and we'll make it a class party. I'll see that everybody who is anybody will be there." She happened to glance up and her voice fell. "Oh, no," she groaned. "If only we had a law keeping that type out. You know who he is, don't you?"

For the second time within two hours Page spoke his name. "Danny O'Shea," she said with a sinking feeling. They both ignored his bow and grin as he passed the table. "He's running for mayor in November," Page told her.

"Against Allan O'Leary, I hear," said Bertha, giving Page a knowing look and closely watching for her reaction. She saw the color rise in Page's cheeks. "Well, if gossip holds any truth, I'm pleased it's Allan and not the younger one."

"Jeff." She felt her heart give a little tug.

"Potter and I will get behind your Mr. O'Leary, even if he is a *Mick*," she said, laughing. She glanced at Danny O'Shea and saw he was staring in their direction. "Come on, Page. Let's go into the private dining room. I have a few guests but you know them all and we won't have to feel that man's eyes boring into us."

Without looking in Danny O'Shea's direction the two women gracefully left the dining room, ignoring the feel of Danny's eyes on their fashionable backs.

At his table by the windows Danny watched until the ladies were gone, then looked about the room. He hated Potter Palmer's hotel with its tall palms and fat rubber plants, its pink damask and the heavy smell of feminine perfume. He only came here to antagonize all that snooty crowd from the north side whom he held in such contempt. They were all a bunch of hypocritical snobs, phony toffs who liked to be seen at Potter Palmer's luxurious hotel. Danny smiled arrogantly at two men who were seated not far from him. They quickly looked away, pretending they hadn't noticed O'Shea.

They were just two more of the many two-faced bastards who were only too quick to smile at him when they came to The Scarlet Lady looking for a little amusement, Danny told himself. And their pompous ladies were no different. Too many of their closed carriages tied up to the alley entrance so they could slip unseen into the upper rooms where the young studs were only too happy to take their money and their favors. It was one of the reasons Danny O'Shea needed more space. His business was booming because he offered something no other place in the Patch had to offer—discreet accommodations for ladies.

The idea of a male service for women had occurred to him years before when a well-heeled matron slipped him a dollar after he'd delivered her parcels from Drayton's. He had always had a calculating mind and knew it wasn't meant as a tip, especially when she tickled his palm with her finger. He was just as randy and eager to help her out as she was to help him, even if she was old enough to be his mother.

When he could finally afford his own place in the Patch, thanks to the money his father left him—money that rightfully belonged to Patrick O'Leary—male studs were one of the first things Danny made available, and tactfully and discreetly let the northside ladies who could afford the luxury know they were available.

As he studied the menu he just happened to glance out the window at something that caught his eye and started out of his chair. Bull Ramsey was coming across the street. Page Kane mustn't see them together at any cost, Danny told himself as he threw aside the menu and hurried out to intercept Bull. The time wasn't ripe yet to have Page know that he knew all about the Abilene murder. Bull had told him the truth about who killed the drunk in the alley. It made Danny laugh to think that Bull was too dumb even to let the lie stay a lie.

Bull Ramsey never did have very many smarts but he was fast and deadly with his hands and moved like a cat in the dark. When he told Danny about killing the guy and later making the two women think they'd done the killing, Danny made a mental note that Bull was getting smarter; he'd have to watch him a little more closely.

Outside, Danny grabbed Bull's arm and pulled him into an alleyway. "What in the devil are you doing here?"

"Looking for you. The boys told me you come here for lunch sometimes."

"Damn you, how many times must I tell you I don't want you in this part of town. Kane's widow is inside. She might have seen you and recognized you. And if she saw us together she'd hightail it out of here and then where would we be?"

"I guess I didn't think."

"You never think, unless it's to get yourself a piece of tail."

"Yeah," Bull admitted with a lopsided grin.

"Now you listen to me, Bull. I don't want to scare Mrs. Kane off so don't plaster your mug all over town. I told you to stay put in Abilene and I have a good notion to send you back."

"Aw, boss, that cow town's dead as old meat."

"Okay, but if you want to stay here do as I tell you. After I get what I want out of Page Kane you can do whatever you like."

"I want Kane's widow."

"Be my guest, just don't make a move on her until I tell you to. She's not too anxious to give up

224

The Gilded Plume; we may have to persuade her." He gave Bull a shove toward the back exit of the alley. "Now get back to the Patch and try to stay out of sight until I tell you it's time."

Bull Ramsey lumbered away, thinking of all the pleasure that lay in store for him. His boss had promised him that Abilene bitch and he'd have her till she wouldn't be able to ever have any other man. His flesh crawled with anticipation as he thought of what he was going to do to Page Kane, especially toward the end. He's made her pay for having made a fool of him. She's never get the chance to do it again to anyone else.

Where some men found extreme pleasure in a woman's flesh, it was torturing her that Bull found most exciting. Just thinking about how he'd go about it made him sexually aroused as he scurried along the back streets that dead-ended at the river. There were so many fantastic ways to abuse female flesh, ways which he knew a woman liked. So many times he'd paddled a doxy's backside until it was raw and bleeding and he'd find her nipples hard and pouting, her body panting for more.

As for Page Kane, he knew what he'd do to her this time. This time he'd rip every shred of clothes off her body, then tie ropes around her wrists and attach the ropes to an overhead beam. Then he'd spread her legs apart and tie her ankles so she couldn't close her thighs.

He adjusted himself in his pants as his blood pulsed and throbbed, thinking of her vulnerability. He'd ravage her brutally; he'd make her do every filthy, obscene thing he could think about. She'd be his slave, always there to service him in whatever despicable way he ordered her to.

"Hey, watch where in hell you're walking," a

225

wagon driver yelled as Bull stepped in front of the team, making them rear.

In an instant Bull's fantasy was gone but as he walked slowly along the river he knew that it would only be a matter of time for it all to become real.

Chapter Nineteen

Bertha Palmer was, as usual, as good as her word. She mustered all her friends from the elegant section called Chicagotown to launch the grand opening of Page's new Gilded Plume. The Swifts and the Armours—who were scarcely friends—the Marshall Fields, the McCormicks, the Stantons, Mayor Mason and his wife, even the governor, John Palmer, came to lend their endorsements of dignity to the establishment. The early summer vacationers were streaming in from the plains states and the warmer regions to the south.

Page hugged Allan's arm as they surveyed the elegant crowd at the tables and on the dance floor. "It's lovely, Allan, and I could never have accomplished it without your help."

"It's the least I can do for all the support you're giving my campaign."

Page giggled. "I noticed that even Mayor Mason went out of his way to shake your hand when he arrived. He obviously wants to stay on the right side of his rival."

"There's talk that he is going to withdraw from the race. The competition is getting too stiff, especially with Danny O'Shea's crooks blackmailing votes. O'Shea's going to be my major rival."

"Then you have nothing to worry about," she said.

"Don't be too sure. Danny knows how to twist arms and he is very well acquainted with all that courthouse corruption."

"You'll handle them," Page assured him, "Just like you managed to get this place opened for me."

She didn't realize how much her remark stung him. What he'd been forced to do to accomplish Page's dream for a decent Gilded Plume appalled him, but he swore that she'd never know the depths of degradation that he'd had to stoop to. The vice and graft of the city was far more widespread than he'd ever imagined. It didn't stop at city hall; there were the aldermen who controlled the individual districts, the men who put the councilmen into office, the politicians in Springfield, the representatives in Washington. But one consolation was that he was learning just how much filth he had to clean up.

Chicago was strategically situated right in the middle of the nation's roads of trade. Every railroad led into and out of Chicago. Twenty-one major lines of track crossed through the city and there were powerfully rich men behind those railroad tracks, each with an avaricious eye out for profit. The same went for the men who owned and controlled the massive grain elevators through which sixteen million bushels of wheat passed every twelve months. Among the owners of twenty-one packing houses in Chicago, few had ungreased hands. The ships, the barges, the boats on the lake and the river all had prices they asked for all types and kinds of services and products. People poured into the city through which passed all of the new riches of the growing nation and everyone had to be satisfied. Those who displeased any of the men in control of the city just weren't permitted to exist. Business space was at a premium so in order to survive you met the price of those who tolerated your enterprise or you were sent packing.

Thanks to Allan, Page had no way of knowing the extent of what it had cost in graft alone to open The Gilded Plume. In time, if business fell off, there would be no way for her to survive; the sharks would eat up every inch of her and her fortune. So Allan steeled himself to the fact that it was up to him to make the place a success as he knew Page would be lost to him forever if he didn't.

In his mind he was convinced that the only way he could gain her love was by making himself indispensable to her life-style. His sacrifice had already alienated him from his family, but Allan had all he wanted—or almost all. And in due time, perhaps later tonight, he told himself, he'd have the rest of it.

Just the feel of her hand in his made it all worthwhile. What he was doing was wrong, he knew, but it was only a temporary wrong. All his life he'd dreamt of becoming a great, highly respected man with a woman like Page at his side. When he became an important, influential man she'd come to love him, and if not love him be content to be his wife. Yet, oh, how he wanted her to look at him the way she looked at Jeff, the way she was looking at Jeff right now as he came through the doorway to the cabaret.

Page's expression changed when she saw Melody Sharp on Jeff's arm. "Hello, Jeff," she said pleasantly enough. "I'm surprised to see you here."

229

"Curiosity," he said, looking around. He motioned to Melody. "You remember Miss Sharp?"

"We've seen one another," Page said coolly.

Melody giggled and hid the lower part of her face behind her fan. "Unfortunately, Mrs. Kane, you had the opportunity of seeing more of me than I of you."

Page felt the color rise in her cheeks. Flustered, she awkwardly introduced Allan.

Melody put out her hand to him. "You do resemble your brother, Mr. O'Leary." With a mischievous wink at Jeff she added, "But you didn't tell me he was so much better-looking."

Jeff laughed. "He's unattached, from what I understand."

Page slipped her arm protectively into Allan's and gave Melody and Jeff a stony look. "I'll have the maitre d' show you to a table."

"Maitre d'," Jeff mimicked arching his eyebrows. "Real high class."

Page glowered. "I'm surprised you know what a maitre d' is."

"Contrary to what you may have heard about me, Mrs. Kane, I do get out of the Patch on occasion. Tonight, unfortunately, is not one of those occasions."

She was tempted to order him out, but instead of motioning to one of the bouncers standing cross-armed on either side of the archway, she smiled up at Allan and said, "Darling, ask Phillippe to take especially good care of your brother and his friend."

She saw the look that passed between Allan and Jeff; one of anger, the other of smug defiance. Her heart ached when she realized that her childish jealousy had caused the rift between the brothers to widen. The last thing she wanted was to bring pain to the O'Learys and yet everything she did lately caused friction. Why did they insist upon refusing her help, resenting everything she tried to do?

If only Lily would accept the fact that she could live in comfort now, that there was no need for her to stir the soap vats and churn the washtubs. Too many times she'd begged and pleaded only to have their visits end in argument.

"In time," Allan had advised. "Perhaps if you would marry me."

His proposal had shocked her, coming so suddenly and so quickly in the wake of Karl's funeral. Page had wanted to talk to her mother about Allan's proposal but knew it would only upset her, knowing as she did the growing bitterness that was developing between the brothers.

And so she had confided in Bertha Palmer, the only woman she could call a friend here in Chicago.

"Good," Bertha advised. "Accept."

"I couldn't," Page said, shocked. "It's too soon."

"I told you a month ago, Page, that widow's weeds do not suit you."

"I don't love him."

"What does that have to do with anything? Few women love their husbands, you know. Some day a woman will be allowed to marry the man she wants to marry and not one her family decides is suitable." She sipped her tea. "You didn't love Karl, did you?"

"Surprising as it may be, Bertha, yes, I think I did."

"Bosh! You were thankful and appreciative." She put down her cup. "Look, Page, one day Allan O'Leary will occupy a very high position in this city, if not in this state, maybe even in the country. We women are made in such a way that we find important positions most attractive. We respect position; and, therefore, we do it good service, especially when it's in the family, like a husband's or a father's. Now an exceptionally beautiful wife—a woman like yourself—is always a tremendous asset to a man in everything social. Furthermore, if she is ambitious—again like you and me—her ambition will only serve to help her husband." She let her eyes slide away and said, "Unless she seeks to destroy him, which is highly unlikely because she'd only wind up destroying herself."

Page was unconvinced. "I'd have to be in love with Allan to marry him."

Bertha gasped in horror. "But that's the worst possible situation for a wife." She leaned forward. "Let's suppose you were passionately in love with Allan O'Leary and married him. It would be a terrible misfortune for Allan because a wife passionately in love would indubitably create unending scenes of jealousy, mistrust, always insisting on having all her husband's time and attention. No, an overly loving wife is often too possessive and therefore a tragic liability to any man."

Page laughed. "You're a cynic, Bertha Palmer."

Cynic or not, Page thought as Allan came back and took her hand, perhaps it wouldn't be so wrong to marry Allan O'Leary. As she glanced toward Jeff and Melody with their heads together laughing at some private joke, she decided she'd give Allan's proposal more serious thought.

"Oh no," Allan whispered. "My adversary just came in." He nodded toward Danny O'Shea, who looked almost respectable in his evening clothes. In spite of his elegant attire, however, there was no way he could hide the aura of coarseness that clung to him.

Danny was in a foul mood but covered it with a smile as he greeted Page and Allan and complimented Page on the obvious success of The Gilded Plume. "You haven't forgotten how much I'd like to buy in, or buy you out."

"I haven't forgotten."

Danny grinned and glanced at Allan. "I must admit, I'm surprised you two carried it all off. There's more to making a success of a place than just a lovely lady with a beautiful voice."

Allan said, "The business end is more or less my responsibility. It wasn't too difficult to learn the tricks of the trade, if you know what I mean." It galled him to have to show himself on O'Shea's level but he wanted Danny to know that he now could fight dirty too if he had to.

"You learn fast, counselor, but then I'm sure Mrs. Kane's money made things easy for you."

Page was quick to see the threat of a fight. "Let's not spoil my opening by talking business, gentlemen. If you will excuse me, I must get changed for my first number. Have a pleasant evening, Mr. O'Shea."

"Thank you, Mrs. Kane, I'm sure I will." As Page started away he said, "When can we have that little talk about this place?"

"Never," she said with finality.

He continued to grin. "As I told you once before, I always get what I want."

"Not this time." She gave him a slight bow of her head and started away again.

"Give my regards to your mother," Danny called, putting a sinister sneer into the tone of his voice.

233

Page didn't answer but as she made her way to the backstage area she found his parting comment disconcerting. Why did he speak of her mother? How did he even know she had a mother living in Chicago?

She suddenly put the remark together with an earlier reference Danny had made to Abilene. Was there some way Danny O'Shea had found out about what had happened last New Year's Day . . . about the man Lily had killed with the stone?

Her blood suddenly ran cold. If anyone was capable of learning a person's darkest secrets she felt sure it would be a man like Danny O'Shea.

"They're waiting for you," Allan said as he came into her little dressing room after tapping on the door.

Her troubled thoughts scattered. "I'm almost ready," she told him.

Later, with the applause still ringing in her ears, Page sat before her mirror and again began worrying about Danny's seemingly idle remark. It was possible, of course, that Bull Ramsey and Danny O'Shea were known to one another; men of that ilk often are. And she had seen Bull Ramsey in Abilene when she was there with Karl. It wouldn't have been difficult for the thug to have recognized her as well and found out who she was.

"You're frowning again," Allan said as he came up behind her and touched his lips to her hair. "You can't have anything to frown at, Page. The place is a roaring success. Thanks to you, decency has finally gotten a toehold in the Patch." He thought of the graft that had been paid out and reminded himself of what a hypocrite he was.

"I was thinking of my mother."

"I have a perfect solution to bringing her around."

"Oh?"

"I offered it before, remember? Marry me, Page."

She looked up into his wide, handsome face, his eyes so deep green that one could get lost in them, his sandy-colored hair so thick and wavy. He was a stunning-looking man, if a man could be called stunning. What Bertha Palmer had said flashed through her mind.

Page stood and kissed him lightly on the mouth. "Let me think about it for a few more days."

"I'm a very patient man, darling."

She saw the desire in his look. "Take me home, Allan. We can go out the back way and avoid everyone. I'm really quite tired."

"Of course."

All during the carriage ride home and the coffee and brandies before the fire in the sitting room, Page knew she had to find out how she truly felt about Allan O'Leary. He was an extremely handsome man, intelligent, capable, ambitious. He had all the qualities any woman could want in a husband and yet, wrong as she knew it was, there was the physical part of marriage which she'd learned was an essential part of two people's married life. It was brazen of her, of course, to even entertain such notions but she could not help herself.

When Allan fell silent and came toward her she knew she wanted him to kiss her, but not as they had kissed before.

Her lips parted as he took her in his arms. The kiss was demanding and urgent, like the hunger only deprivation can create. She felt his tongue and tasted the warm wetness of his mouth as his initial

235

gentleness became more ardent, more demanding. Page tried to keep herself aware that these were Allan's arms, Allan's lips, that it was Allan's body that pressed so hard and commanding against her own.

Cautiously she sensed his hands moving upward toward her breasts. A moment later he was caressing them, cupping them lovingly, running the flat of his thumbs against the fast-hardening nipples.

"I must have you," Allan said.

Her consent was a soft moan as she kissed him more passionately, wrapping her arms tighter about his strong young body.

"Come," she said gently easing herself out of his arms.

A moment later they were in her bedroom and again wrapped in a passionate embrace.

"Undress for me," he said huskily. "I want to see you naked so I can ravage you first with my eyes."

She frowned slightly, suddenly seeing Allan in a different light. She'd never expected the staid and proper Allan O'Leary to propose such a thing. Still, there something exciting in the way he was devouring her, like an impatient little boy waiting for a longed-for reward.

As she reached for the cameo at her throat and unpinned it, she noticed that Allan seemed taller, more powerful as he stood watching her. She let down her hair and began undoing the buttons that ran down the front of her gown. There was something harsh, almost brutal, in the way he was watching her. Slowly she let her dress fall in folds around her feet. She stepped out of it, keeping her eyes firmly fixed on his. Every so often she noticed the delicate movement of his tongue across his lips, wetting the corners. His hands were clenched as if fighting back an inner force that was taunting him.

It was as if it were all a fantasy. Page let herself undo the laces and hooks of her underpinnings and boldly let them drop away until she stood before him in all her lovely nakedness. She knew she should feel ashamed, should cover herself, but the way Allan was gazing at her erased all feelings of shame or humiliation. She felt strangely proud seeing the admiration and lust in his eyes.

"You're ravishing," he breathed almost inaudibly. He opened his arms and she came into them. They kissed long and passionately as Allan caressed her naked flesh. Then suddenly he swept her up into his massive arms and moved toward the bed. Gently he laid her down, propping her against the satin pillows, then stood back.

She found herself incapable of looking away as he stood over her and began to remove his clothes. Slowly he slipped out of his jacket and undid the buttons of his close-fitting vest. With agile fingers he removed the pearl studs from his boiled front shirt after taking off the black bow tie and celluloid collar.

Page lay naked and hypnotized as she stared at the broad, hairy nakedness of his chest, glistening like silver in the light of the lamps. Then, stooping to remove his ankle-high shoes, he quickly stripped off his black silk stockings and stood over her, feet planted well apart. Button by button, he began to undo the front of his trousers.

She squirmed in anticipation as he dropped his trousers over his hips, every moment slow and tantalizing and seductive. An almost maliciously evil grin curled the corners of his mouth as he stepped out of his trousers and saw the way Page's eyes were riveted to the powerful erection that jutted out from his loins.

Almost casually Allan let his hand drop and his fingers curl around his long, heavy shaft. He stood taunting her with the naked perfection of his body, the evidence of his need for her, the throbbing evidence of his passion.

A gasp escaped her lips as she found herself tormented with a desperate desire to be possessed by him. She pulled her body tight against his as Allan crawled onto the bed and took her in his muscular arms. The stiff curling hair on his chest tickled her breasts as she shivered with wanton desire.

"Page," he murmured as he covered her mouth with his own.

"Yes, Allan, yes," she heard herself whisper, not fully recognizing her own voice. "I want you," she murmured as he began kissing every part of her. She found herself becoming bolder as he made love to her body. She wanted to fondle and touch him the way he was touching her. A craving urge to explore every part of his masculine strength and power obsessed her as involuntarily her hands moved impatiently, pulling, feeling, caressing the hairy flatness of his chest, the rippling hardness of his stomach, the hard, steel-like power that showed how much he wanted her.

"Oh Page," Allan moaned as he felt her hands on him, guiding him, urging him on.

She felt strangely in control as she manipulated his passions from one peak to another. Easing herself onto her back, she moved so that he could fit himself between her aching thighs.

It was all going too fast, too quickly, and Page never wanted it to end but as she molded her body against his she knew they had reached that point of no return as the hard impatience of him suddenly drove slowly, deliberately, into her very core.

After gaining his advantage he held himself motionless, allowing her to adjust to the length and thickness of his desires, letting her become a part of him. In another moment he began to move, slowly at first, then more urgently, more forcefully as he held her pinned down under the force of his assault.

"I adore you," he breathed as he began to pound her unmercifully, feeling her rise up to meet his violent thrusts.

"Yes, oh, yes," she moaned as her body rose higher and higher into some vast beautiful void alive with color and sensation. She moved with him, matching pace for pace, rhythm for rhythm, desperately trying to hold back the flood that was building up inside her. She was lost in a world of lust and knew there was no salvation for either of them.

His movements became faster, sharper, more urgent and then suddenly, like the snapping of a branch, she found herself falling into the soft, velvety arms of a down-filled abyss that slowly enveloped her, smothering her into oblivion.

"I love you," she heard him whisper as his lips touched her. It was the last thing she remembered until morning came and she found herself alone in her bed.

Chapter Twenty

It was a glorious summer for Page. The Gilded
Plume was a raging success and she was certain
that the affection she felt for Allan would blossom
into love. Everything about him was so pleasing, so
completely comfortable. Why she kept putting off
naming their wedding date she couldn't understand.
She blamed it on her excitement over making the
club a success and the other campaigns she'd
launched into with Bertha Palmer to clean up the
Patch. None of their campaigns got very far off the
ground but they kept her busy with meetings and
teas and social affairs. There were too many important appointments on her calendar to fit in anything
as time-consuming as the planning of a wedding.

It was all an excuse, of course, Page told herself
when she wanted to be truthful about it all. Deep
down she knew Allan was resentful of the fact that
she was extremely rich and he was more or less de-
pendent upon her for his own success. This was a
minor irritation to him now, Page reminded herself,
but minor problems had a habit of magnifying
themselves when things were legally tied together.
In her mind it was far the best to let things ride

along as they were and not succumb to Allan's anxious requests that she set their wedding date.

"I don't much like the idea of marrying in a cold month again," Page told him. "How about a June wedding, darling?"

Allan looked crestfallen. "But it so far away. I know this is only the first of September but its still quite warm; hot, in fact."

Page gave him one of her irresistible smiles. "Please, let's wait until next June. That way we'll have so much more time and fun to plan for a really big affair." She became serious. "Besides, it isn't all that long since we buried Karl. It might have a damaging affect on your mayoral campaign. There are any number of straitlaced people in Chicago who put a lot of stock in a widow's mourning period."

Allan nodded. "Perhaps you're right. I'm having enough trouble with my supporters as it is."

"Oh? Who's giving you trouble?"

"Just about everyone who disapproves of my connection with The Gilded Plume."

Page looked surprised. "But most of those who support you come here to enjoy themselves."

"There are thousands of voters who wouldn't be found dead coming to a place like this."

She heard the derision in his voice and turned on him. "Really, Allan, you make it sound like another den of iniquity. You know how hard we've both worked to make this a decent, honest place."

He hesitated. Perhaps it was just as well she learned the truth about what he'd had to do to keep The Gilded Plume's doors open, the palms he'd had to grease, the graft and bribes that were secretly paid out and which never appeared on any ledgers except the private record he kept himself, the one

242

hidden in his old room at his mother's house. It was the only safe place he could think of after he moved into the comfortable apartment on the second floor of The Gilded Plume. His present quarters would be the obvious place to hide such incriminating evidence, so it seemed wise to put the book in the most unlikely place, yet a place he could have easy access to.

To Page he said, "There's more to running a club like this than you think."

"What do you mean?"

"Let's take the liquor we buy," he started, deciding to test the water before plunging in completely.

"What about it? We pay good prices for good quality merchandise."

"Selling liquor requires a license. Licenses aren't just handed out to anyone who asks for one."

It took only a moment for her to see what he was driving at. "There are one or two greedy politicians in every city and state. I expected there would be a few men with their hands out."

"Not a few," Allan said, feeling the floodgates suddenly collapse. "A lot. An awful lot."

Page's brow crinkled. She put her hand on Allan's arm. "How many?"

"Too many," he said. He suddenly felt disgusted with himself for having failed in his resolve. "It's been necessary to pay off a great many people and payoffs like that always are found out. Those who get paid boast to their friends who then want to be cut in. Word gets around." He ran his hand through his hair. "Word's gotten around about me. The Plume is killing my chances in the mayor's race, Page." He turned back to her and looked into her lovely face. "We really should close the doors."

She didn't hesitate. "No."

"After I'm mayor we can reopen. I'll let you have a dozen clubs, anything you want," he pleaded.

"No. The Gilded Plume stays open. If it is your connection with it that is hurting your reputation with some of the voters, then sever your connection. I can run the club. You can tell me who needs to be paid and when. I'm not really Little Nell from the farm any more, Allan. I know bribes are being paid. Even some churches pay bribes to keep from being taxed by the political bosses in Springfield. But if it is your relationship with me that is the real cause of people turning against you, then that's another matter completely."

"It isn't that." He reached for her hand and squeezed it. "You're the biggest asset I have."

She kissed him on the cheek. "Thank you for that. Well then," she said, "disassociate yourself from the club. It's as simple as that."

He shook his head stubbornly. "If you care anything about me, you'll close down the place."

"That isn't fair."

"If you and I are a couple, The Gilded Plume will always be a thorn in my side as long as it's open, whether I'm helping to manage it or not."

Page studied his face. "There's something else behind this, isn't there? Has Danny O'Shea been getting to you?"

"Of course not. It isn't anything like that. It's exactly what I told you."

Her pride in the success of The Gilded Plume wouldn't permit her to believe him. Besides, Danny O'Shea was becoming much too persistent lately about wanting the place, almost to the point of making physical threats. She could understand;

being just across the street, her club was making his place look like the rat hole it was.

All Danny O'Shea could think about was the money he was losing. His second-floor-room customers weren't coming any more because they were afraid they'd run into people they knew who frequented Page Kane's place. And, oh, the money he could make if he had The Gilded Plume. The fact that it was now established with a face of first-class respectability made it all the more perfect for his purposes. He could so easily and discreetly add his special kind of amusements upstairs.

"I've got to have the Plume," Danny told Bull Ramsey, who sat with his feet propped up on the edge of Danny's desk. "And the time's come to take it."

"She really hates your guts, boss," Bull reminded him.

"I haven't much love for hers either, even if I wouldn't mind sticking it to her. But I'm not interested in sharing ownership. I want her place all to myself and I suppose the only way I'm going to get it is by forcing her to hand it over."

He gave Bull a nod. "It's time we got moving, Bull. Find out where the old lady is. Page didn't leave Abilene without her mother, so the old doll's got to be around here someplace."

"I'll tail Kane's widow. What do I do when I get my hands on the mother?"

"Bring her here. We'll hold her as a kind of ransom. All I need do is tell Page Kane I have her mother, the woman who killed a man in an Abilene alley by bashing in his skull with a rock. Unless they both cooperate by giving me exactly what I want, I'll turn the old doll and Page over to the police, one for murder and the other for complicity."

He uttered an ugly laugh. "I'll get what I want and send them both packing in the bargain."

Bull swung his massive feet to the floor and lumbered out of his chair. "Me and the boys will start shadowing her today. She should lead us to the old lady soon enough."

But after several days had passed Bull was getting frustrated. He and his cohorts watched Page day and night, but not once in almost a week did she make contact with her mother . . . and Danny was getting angry.

"She's got to be in Chicago," Danny yelled as his impatience grew. "Find her, damn it, if you have to put every good man we have on following her."

It was Danny's raised voice that caused Melody Sharp to pause outside his office door and listen. It was easy to learn he was furious with that odious Bull Ramsey for something or other but exactly what Melody had no idea.

"I want that old lady found!" Melody heard him yell, then she had to scurry into her room when she heard Bull's footsteps start for the door.

What old lady? Melody had no idea, but she decided she'd keep an eye on Bull and see just what he and Danny were up to.

On the first night of Bull's second week of tailing Page his feet started to hurt and his mouth watered for a shot of whiskey. Unfortunately he was stuck in his secret spot behind The Gilded Plume, where he had an unobstructed view into Page's room backstage. She always stepped behind the screen to dress and undress but the glimpses he got every now and then of her bare flesh made him blind to everything but his raging lust for her body.

Usually she left The Gilded Plume in company with the older O'Leary brother and he usually saw her home, then left her there to return to his rooms over the club. Several times a week, Bull noted, the two of them would go up to O'Leary's rooms after the place closed down. Bull's imagination of what went on in that upstairs bedroom made his blood race; his sexual desire for her caused him to lose control, forcing him to do things to himself that angered him afterward . . . but what could he do? He was stuck on watch. All this he filed away inside his head. The day would come soon when he'd have the bitch all alone, all to himself and then he'd do what he liked with her.

He pulled back into the shadows when he saw the back door of the club open and Page Kane step up into her buggy. Bull saw his chance. She was going home alone; O'Leary wasn't with her.

Bull knew the route to her house only too well and quickly ran through the building he used as a cover and was hiding in an alley a few blocks away when Page's buggy clattered toward him. As it turned away from the glass-enclosed gas lamp on the corner of the street, Bull took the advantage and stepped in front of the buggy. The horse reared but Bull easily grabbed the reins and quieted it.

Before Page could fumble for the derringer lying in the folds of her skirt, Bull was next to her on the seat. He grabbed the buggy whip out of her hand and palmed the derringer when she managed to finger it.

It took a moment or two for Page to recognize him. At first she thought he was just another drunk looking to rape and steal, but when she saw Bull Ramsey's face she knew it meant much more trouble than she'd bargained for. An ordinary rough could be threatened and paid off once learning who she was; Bull Ramsey was another matter entirely.

She opened her mouth but the scream never came. Bull fisted her neatly alongside the jaw, knocking her unconscious.

When she came to she felt the jostling of the buggy and heard the rinky-tink sound of a piano playing as they trotted slowly down a narrow alley between clapboard buildings. There was a damp, musty feel and smell over everything and before opening her eyes Page knew she was somewhere along the docks, in that southern part of the city's shoreline where the dregs of society liked to congregate and where the police rarely came, except to collect payment for leaving the inhabitants alone. The Patch was almost honorable in comparison to this section, which they called the Levee. Allan had told her it got its name from long before the Civil War when gamblers from the southern states got off the big packets to play games of chance and to gorge themselves with every conceivable type of sexual depravity.

When she glanced at Bull she found him leering at her. "Scream all you want, pretty lady; it'll just mean somebody's enjoying himself."

Page knew he spoke the truth. She decided she'd be better off reserving all her strength for the chance to escape. "What do you want with me?"

"Surely you remember old Bull, missy? From Abilene way? Had ourselves a cozy little time cooking and all till you slipped some knockout drops to me. Now that wasn't very nice of you, missy, nor your ma neither."

He pulled the buggy into the open doorway of a dilapidated warehouse that reeked of dead oysters and rotten fish. Page quickly calculated that they were in the back of one of those lakeshore dives that ran an all-night oyster bar, shucked right there at the bar and served with hot sauce and half a lemon. The food was bad enough up front; back here was where they stashed all the debris and dead stuff before dumping it all back into the lake come morning.

As Bull grabbed her and carried her easily out of the buggy he said, "How's your old ma, missy? Haven't been visiting her too often, I see."

"What do you know of my mother?"

He backed her toward a small tack room after closing the doors leading to the alley. "Now don't you go forgetting that I was the one who offered help after your ma bashed in that fella's head and left him dead."

"It was only to protect me," Page blurted out.

"Well, that may be what it was, but it weren't too nice of you to treat me like you did for trying to help you and your ma." He grinned, showing yellow, crooked teeth. "I just wanted you to be nice to me. Was that too much to ask, missy?"

"Please," Page pleaded when he moved closer and she felt the rough, splintered boards of the wall pressing against her back. "Don't hurt me. I have money. I can pay you," she said, desperately snatching up her bag and pulling open the drawstring that had been looped around her wrist. She fisted a wad of bills and held them out to him.

Bull slapped the money away and grabbed her in his powerful arms. Page screamed and kicked and clawed but she knew there was no way for her to escape him.

"I don't want no money. I got plenty of that from Danny and I'll get plenty more for snatching you."

Page's eyes widened as she stopped struggling and stared into his ugly face. She smelled his fetid breath and felt the clammy sweat of his body as he continued to paw her.

"Danny O'Shea? What does he have to do with this?"

"He wants your old lady," Bull stupidly admitted.

It was as if Bull suddenly realized he'd made a mistake and had to rectify it. She'd tricked him into saying something he shouldn't have said. His anger flared.

"Damn you," he snarled, punching her alongside the head and knocking her backward down onto the grimy floor. Then he fell on her and began tearing her clothes from her body, his mouth watering with lust.

Chapter Twenty-One

Melody Sharp got up from her chair in Page's sitting room and began pacing the floor. She checked the time on her lapel watch with that over the mantel. Surely Page Kane should be home by this time. The housekeeper said she was usually always home by midnight and it was already half past. Melody started to get the feeling that something was wrong. But then it was common knowledge that Page sometimes spent time with Allan after her last show, although she always sent word to the housekeeper that she'd be a little late.

The whole evening was going wrong. If she hadn't had that silly argument with Jeff, Melody reminded herself, she wouldn't have gotten up the nerve to have it out with Page Kane. She heaved a sigh, glanced at the clock again and continued to pace. She had to know exactly where she stood in her relationship with Jeff. He was obviously in love with Page but was too blind and stubborn to admit it. If his love for Page was all one-sided, as she prayed it was, then there was a chance that Jeff would marry her one day. If Page was in love with Jeff then there was no sense in beating a dead horse and she might just as well accept that job offer in New York and try to forget all about Jeff O'Leary.

A confrontation with Page Kane, Melody had decided, was the only thing that would clear the air. Men called it "laying the cards on the table" and that's exactly what Melody intended doing, laying bare her soul, determined to sacrifice her own happiness if Page's cards turned out to be higher in value than her own.

Mrs. Chambers came into the sitting room. "I really can't explain it," she said tugging her heavy night robe around herself and looking very concerned. "Something is definitely wrong, miss. Perhaps we should go to The Gilded Plume to be sure Mrs. Kane is all right."

"No, you had best stay here in case she comes home. I'll go and see what I can find out." Melody took up her shawl and draped it around her shoulders. Despite the autumn month the days and nights remained hot and humid, which made the streets dangerous this time of night because more men chose to roam about the streets rather than go inside where the air was close and dank.

It was madness to go dashing off into the night alone, Melody told herself, especially into the Patch. She could more or less hold her own among the roughs who came into O'Shea's saloon where she sang, but riding about alone in a carriage in the middle of the night was another matter entirely. One scream at Danny's place brought her protection; out here she could yell her head off and no one would much care. Decent people were supposed to be in bed where they belonged and if a girl got herself set upon, it was her own fault for gadding about at ungodly hours.

Melody often thought of the strange double standards she'd found when she first came to Chicago. Men could do whatever they pleased, illegal, criminal, whatever; women merely shrugged an indifferent shoulder, as if it was the man's right. Men were always right no matter what they did. Even the toughest madam down in the levee didn't do much when it came to having to stand up to the men, even when they took a notion to cut up one of the girls or pull the brothel into rubble if it pleased their tempers. In all the ruckuses in the whorehouses that Melody'd heard about, the madam always sided with the customer.

"The woman is always wrong," Melody said as she steered the horse and carriage toward DeKoven Street. If she had to go into the Patch, she'd have a man beside her. Besides, it would give her a chance to see just how upset Jeff would be when she told him Page was missing . . . if she was indeed missing.

Melody didn't want to rouse the O'Leary household so she pitched pebbles at Jeff's window until she'd attracted his attention.

"What in the devil do you mean, Page is missing?" he demanded hotly as he jumped into the carriage and took the reins.

Melody told him how she'd spent the last several hours and of Mrs. Chambers' concern.

"What in blazes did you want to talk to Page about?"

"That isn't important right now, Jeff. Let's find her first."

He grew sullen. "You know damned well where she is. Everybody knows. She's in my brother's bedroom over the Plume."

"We don't know that, Jeff, and the housekeeper

says she always sends word when she is going to be late getting home."

"So she fell asleep," he said with disgust.

"No," Melody said. "From all I've heard of Page Kane she never does anything without intending to." She watched him out of the corners of her eyes. He loved her. She could see the worry lines deeply rutted into his broad forehead, the creases of concern etched into the corners his mouth.

"She always was a deliberate kind of girl."

The way he said it, as if with pride, Melody knew she'd never make him forget Page Kane, not in a thousand years. Jeff was passionately in love with the woman; she saw that all too clearly now as he raced the horse toward Chicago Avenue and the Patch.

Jeff swatted the horse again. "She'd better be with Allan," he swore. "She'd just better be." He crouched over the reins, looking like a prizefighter jockeying for position, head down, shoulders hunched up, fists clenched. Melody had never seen him looking so angry, almost crazed.

Page was not with Allan. "She left here a good hour and a half ago," Allan told them.

"And you let her go home alone?" Jeff cried as he shook a fist at his brother.

"She insisted. She'd done it often enough and it's a safe enough distance from here to her house."

"Are you blind?" Jeff roared. "Nothing's safe in this damned city, especially a beautiful woman." He rubbed his hand across the back of his neck. "We've got to think."

"The Bengal Tigress," Melody suggested with hesitation.

Allan shook his head. "Page wouldn't be set upon by that big, soot-black woman. Besides, the

Tigress only trades in very young girls for sailors. No, it has to be a deliberate snatch. Page is too well known and too well liked. Even O'Shea's starting to keep her at arm's length."

"Danny O'Shea," Melody said as she snapped her fingers, remembering his yelling at Bull Ramsey. She hurriedly told Jeff and Allan what she'd overheard.

"Can't be. He certainly wouldn't refer to Page Kane as an old lady."

"But I kept an eye on Bull and he's all the time watching The Gilded Plume, and if he isn't watching then one of the other guys are. Maybe Danny wants someone Mrs. Kane can lead him to. Bull Ramsey seems very preoccupied with spying on the Plume lately."

"It's a start," Jeff said. "At least let's find Bull Ramsey and see if he knows anything." He looked at Melody. "Where does he usually hang out, do you know?"

"You mean which house?" After Jeff nodded, she thought for a minute. "Ramrod Hall."

Allan whistled. "He has tough tastes."

"He's a rough customer."

Melody amended her answer by adding, "But other times I've heard him bragging about how much the girls like him at The French Elm."

"The French Elm in the Levee?" Jeff questioned. "That's a pretty high-toned place for the likes of Bull Ramsey, but I guess the girls will do anything for a price." To Allan he said, "First off I'll check with Danny and make sure Bull's not with him. If he isn't, I'll check out Ramrod Hall. Kate Hawkins will tell me if she's seen him."

Allan said, "Okay, I'll check with the house-keeper and then take the long shot and see if anybody's seen him around the Levee. It's just the kind of place a goon like him would be attracted to."

Mrs. Chambers was in tears when Allan left the mansion and started toward The French Elm. He'd never been in the place but had heard of its reputation as being one of the better parlor-houses in the city. Being in the most disreputable neighborhood in Chicago, it offered the customers anything they wanted, including torture, bondage, all types of perversions; it might be just the kind of place Bull Ramsey would hang out.

The madam politely ushered him into a well-appointed room completely surrounded by mirrors, but when Allan told her of his reason for being there her cordiality fell away like melting snow.

"I'm here to give you pleasure, mister, not information," she said coldly as she walked him back to the front door. "Good night!"

With flagging steps Allan left the parlor-house and stood on the street wondering in which direction to turn. The Levee was a jumble of hundreds of whorehouses, some highbrow like The French Elm with gilt chamber pots and rare objects of art, but most of the places were low dives, where no man's wallet was safe. The hub of the Levee was Freiberg's Dance Hall, where Ike Bloom ran things the way he wanted them. Allan knew Ike casually and thought him to be a decent enough sort, giving hookers and reformers the same access to his dance hall, just as long as there was something in it for Ike Bloom.

"No, sorry, Allan," Ike said. "Bull Ramsey comes in now and again but not for a week or so. Ask Tom Scragger down at the oyster bar joint. He says he makes a week's income in a night when old Bull comes in hungry.

Page found herself bound hand and foot and stark naked. A slimy, penetrating dampness stung her skin as she tried to cover herself, tugging uselessly against the rough ropes that dug into her wrists and ankles, holding her flat and spread-eagled on the hard bare floor.

Stale foul air assailed her nostrils, making her breath labored as she struggled in vain against her restraints. In the glow of a candle she saw Bull Ramsey and two other men seated around a wooden crate playing cards. She had no way of knowing how long she'd been unconscious but she was pretty certain it hadn't been for very long.

"She's coming around," one of the thugs mumbled through the stump of cigar clenched between his teeth.

Bull Ramsey threw down his cards and came over to her.

"Please," Page pleaded, trying to ignore the lechery in his eyes as he stared at her naked body. "Let me go."

Bull chuckled deep in his throat. He reached into his belt and pulled out a switchblade, touching the button and clicking the long, shiny blade of steel into erection. Slowly he moved the blunt edge of the blade across her breasts, around each nipple, down over her bare skin.

Page strangled on a scream as she felt the blade touch the most intimate parts of her, traveling across and up one thigh, across and up the other thigh, prodding, almost cutting into the depths of her womanhood.

Bull touched the tip of the blade under her chin. "You don't think old Bull would take advantage of you in any way without you knowing about it, now would you, pretty miss? I'm a gent. I never do nothing without the lady knowing what's happening to her."

"Please, do whatever you want, but don't harm me."

"Too bad the boys here saw me duck in with you, missy. I wanted you all to myself. Never was one for crowds, if you know what I mean. Now that they had an eyeful of you and you've come around, I'll get rid of 'em and you and me can have us a time."

All Bull could think about was how this girl had cheated him out of bedding her in Abilene. Now the only thing on his mind was to even up that score. He knew Danny wanted some information out of the bitch, but he'd get that after he'd used her and maybe carved a couple of pretty patterns on her skin just so she'd always remember him.

He turned to the men sitting around the crate. Their cards were forgotten as the men's eyes roved covetously over Page's vulnerable body, lingering in the lush spread "V" where her thighs met.

She turned her head to the side so she would not see their evil stares, the wanton sexuality in their leers.

"Okay, boys, you've had your look-see, now beat it and let me and my lady friend have some time to get acquainted."

"We ain't in no hurry to go anyplace, Bull."

"Yes you are," the huge man insisted as he pointed his switchblade at the man's belly. "Out!"

The two hesitated, still staring lustfully at Page.

"Out!" Bull shouted. "Either of you yank out your dicks to get into this missy and I'll slice them off and stuff them down your throats. Now clear out if you want to leave here a stud and not a gelding."

The two muttered but knew better than to antagonize Bull Ramsey. It had been the knifing three of his own gang that forced O'Shea to send Bull to hide out in Abilene. "To hell with Bull," the one man said as they started down the alley. "Let's go have us some oysters and hot sauce at Scragger's. I'm hungrier than an overworked whore."

"Yeah. Dry, hot nights like this don't hardly make sex too exciting anyway," the other said as they rounded the building and headed for the oyster bar.

Allan had questioned Tom Scragger and was just leaving the oyster bar when Bull's two cohorts came in. As Allan passed them he chanced to hear something that made him turn back.

"Bull doesn't enjoy the sex. It's the fear in the girl's eyes that really turns him on."

"Bull," Allan said to himself as he went back toward the white marble counter and seated himself a couple of stools away from the two men.

"Decided I'm hungry, Tom," Allan said and asked for an order of oysters and lemon. "Too hot for the sauce tonight." He inched forward, keeping one ear cocked to the conversation of the two men seated nearby.

He heard one of them say, "That old Bull can think of the rottenest places to have his fun in." He sniffed the air. "The place smells bad enough in front without doing it back there in all the garbage."

Allan was off the stool and out the door before anyone knew he was gone. He skirted the building and started along the lonely alley. In the soft dirt he noticed buggy tracks that turned into doors that

259

were shut . . . and barred from the inside, he found when he cautiously tested them.

He studied the dry, wooden frame that leaned precariously to one side and wondered what was holding the two-story shack up. As he tried to find a way inside he thought he heard a sound and pressed his ear to the boards. He heard only two words, but it was Page's voice and she was terrified.

"No! Please!"

Allan tried to hold back the panic that grabbed him. He quickly felt the boards and was rewarded when two of them moved clumsily on their pegs, giving him just enough room to squeeze through.

Bull was kneeling beside her, digging his fingers into her very core. His other hand held a long-bladed knife poised against the nipple of her breast.

Allan heard Bull grunt as he moved and started to undo the front buttons of his britches. "What I'd really like is to slice off a tip of nipple just when I come."

Allan moved from behind the protection of Page's horse and buggy, moving carefully so as not to unsettle the horse and call attention to himself. There was little time in which to be cautious, he reminded himself, as he saw Bull position himself between Page's spread thighs and prepare to enter her.

Allan grabbed the first loose thing his hand touched, a short length of board which he didn't want to throw at Bull's head for fear of missing.

Page's scream moved him to action. With a flying lunge across the space separating them, Allan yelled Bull's name and at the same time brought the blunt side of the board flat across the side of Bull's head. The blow knocked him sideways, stunning him. Again and again Allan quickly brought the board down hard on Bull's head until the board split in his hand, but Bull was lying motionless.

Back in Scragger's Oyster Bar, Tom turned to bring Allan his order and looked at the empty stool. "Where'd O'Leary go?" he asked the only two other customers at the counter.

"Who?"

"Allan O'Leary. He was just sitting here a minute ago when I went in the back to shuck his oysters." Tom rubbed his chin and looked at the order of oysters and lemon.

"Here, I'll eat 'em," one of the men said.

"Come to think of it, it was you two O'Leary should have been talking to. He was looking for your friend Bull."

The two exchanged glances.

Tom said, "Seems O'Leary had to find Bull real bad."

The two were off their stools and out the door before Scragger knew what in blazes was going on. He rubbed his chin again and blamed it on the accursed hot, dry weather. The heat was turning everybody's brains to sawdust, he decided as he started to eat the oysters himself.

In the warehouse Allan quickly undid the ropes that held Page to the floor, then helped her get into her clothes and into the buggy. When he heard Bull groan and saw him try to sit up, Allan dashed for the doors and unbarred them. He grabbed the horse's harness and steered him backward out into the alley.

Page screamed when she saw the two thugs running toward them.

"Go! Go!" Allan yelled, slapping the horse hard on the rump, making him rear and kick out at the two men who were trying to grab the bridle.

"Allan!" Page screamed but the horse took off, galloping headlong down the alley, carrying her along in the buggy. "Allan!" She tried desperately to rein the animal but it was wild in its desire to be away.

"Allan!" His name tore from her throat as the buggy rocked and barreled around the corner, cutting him off from her sight.

The last glimpse she had was of Bull Ramsey coming up at Allan's back and the two thugs closing in on him.

Chapter Twenty-Two

Two days later Allan O'Leary's body was found floating among the sewage in Lake Michigan. When Jeff came to tell Page, she knew what had happened just by looking at Jeff's face. She knew all along that after that mad-dash escape from the Levee she would never see Allan alive.

And it had been on her account that he'd been killed. She knew his murderers only too well, but how could she tell anyone the real reason Bull Ramsey abducted her? What was she to do, tell everyone that she and her mother had murdered a man in Abilene? It was torture enough that she and Lily had to bear the terrible responsibility in silence, which is what Lily recommended when Page told her what had happened when they talked several days after Allan's funeral.

"Say nothing," Lily warned. "Hanging the both of us won't bring Allan back."

"What am I to tell Jeff?"

"What have you told him so far?"

"Just that Allan rescued me from my abductors and forced me to flee."

"And you mentioned no names?"

Page gave a quick shake of her head. "I was

afraid. Jeff said they suspected Bull Ramsey but I denied it. I had to," she said as she tried to hold back the tears.

"You did the right thing," her mother told her.

"The terrible part is that Danny O'Shea is behind Bull Ramsey. Bull Ramsey admitted to me that Mr. O'Shea was paying him to try to find you. I wanted to . . ." She couldn't finish, remembering too vividly those huge, thick hands tearing at her clothes, pinching her breasts, pawing between her thighs. "It was too horrible!" she cried and buried her face in her hands.

"Danny O'Shea," Lily said reflectively. "He's a very powerful man in his part of town and I'm sure with his running for mayor against Allan he has plenty of important people behind him. We can't afford to antagonize him. We must be careful, Page." Her mind began to click along sorting things out. "If Bull Ramsey told Mr. O'Shea what we did in Abilene, they are obviously trying to find me through you. They want something other than simply wanting to see justice done by turning us over to the authorities."

"The Gilded Plume," Page exclaimed. "Danny O'Shea's been telling me he'd get it one way or another."

"Give it to him," Lily said sternly.

Jeff walked into the kitchen. "Give who what?"

Page looked flustered. Lily got up and fussed with the coffeepot on the stove. "Just a promise we made to someone before we came to Chicago," Lily lied.

She needn't have made up any answer because Jeff's mind wasn't on anything but what was pestering him. "You say you can't be positive it was Bull Ramsey who's responsible for Allan's death, Page?"

"There were three of them," Page said lamely.

"I have a rotten feeling that O'Shea's in back of this whole thing. He didn't want Allan to run for mayor because he knew Allan had a damned good chance of winning."

Page gave her mother a furtive glance. Lily moved her head, warning Page to let Jeff draw whatever conclusions he wanted.

Jeff threw a small black ledger onto the table. "Do you know what this is, Page? I found it hidden in Allan's room when I was sorting out his things."

The book lay there, looking threatening, daring her to pick it up. Her hand was shaking as she reached for it. As she thumbed through the pages, each with a name, dates, amounts, she recognized the men who Allen often dealt with in his running of the Plume. When she looked up at Jeff he simply nodded and took the book out of her hands.

"I'm going to run for mayor in Allan's place," he announced. He shook the book at them. "With this little piece of work I should be able to keep Allan's supporters."

Lily took a step closer and stared at the ledger. "What is that book?"

He explained. "It lists all the big men who have been taking graft from The Gilded Plume."

Lily clutched her throat then quickly blessed herself. "Even in death that husband of yours passed the sinful stains of his life onto you," she said to her daughter.

Page paid her no heed. "So that's what Allan meant when he told me his association with the Plume was hurting his chances with voters in the other districts."

"I'd like to keep this if you don't mind, Page." He slipped the book into his pocket. "Danny

265

O'Shea bribes important men for their support; I'm not above doing the same if it in any way helps avenge my brother's death."

It had never occurred to Page how deeply fond Jeff was of his brother. His face was a mask of misery and more than once during the wake and funeral she saw Jeff's eyes glisten with tears which he forced back. And now he was picking up his brother's fight for what had been Allan's dream. Whether Jeff would accept her help or not she couldn't say but she had to let him know that she'd do anything for him.

"I have a lot of important connections, Jeff," she offered.

To her complete surprise he turned and glowered down at her. "Keep them! I want nothing from you. It was Allan's involvement with you that caused this whole mess," he stormed. "Why did Danny O'Shea send Bull Ramsey after you?"

"Who told you that?"

"Melody heard them talking."

"She heard wrong."

"You're lying."

"Please, Jeff, I . . ."

"You've caused enough trouble, Mrs. Kane," he said coldly. "You and your high-toned friends can go to blazes for all I care. If it hadn't been for you . . ."

"Jeff!" his mother cried as she came into the kitchen.

Jeff slapped his thigh in an effort to cool his anger and frustration. He turned sharply and walked out.

"He's very upset over this terrible thing," Catherine O'Leary said as she put a gentle hand on Page's shoulder. "He was more fond of Allan than anyone." She started to cry and let the tears run down her cheeks unchecked. "For all their squabblin' and their yappin' at one another, those two would give their lives for each other." She wiped her eyes on the corner of her apron. "Jeff didn't mean what he said, Page. He's just all torn up inside."

"I want to help."

"You can, love," Mrs. O'Leary said. "Do all you can to get Jeff elected mayor. He doesn't have to know about it. You and I can work together." She searched out a handkerchief and blew her nose. "Jeff's always been the independent one. I want to see my dear dead boy's dream for this city come true and so does Jeff, so we must all do what we can."

Before Page left the O'Leary house she caught her mother alone and quietly reminded Lily to keep a low profile. "Don't involve yourself in Jeff's campaign, Mother. Stay here and run the laundry, but keep out of sight. Danny O'Shea mustn't find you, especially now, or Jeff's chances will be zero. Mr. O'Shea will see to that."

"But what of you, Page?"

"Don't worry about me. Now that I know they are after us I'll be more careful. It's you Danny O'Shea wants to get his hands on and only Bull Ramsey knows what you look like. So as long as you keep here out of sight I'm sure everything will be all right."

For the first time in months Page felt her mother's arms around her. The overwhelming comfort it gave her made Page's eyes brim with tears.

"Be careful, dear."

Page kissed her. "After this is over and Jeff wins his election we'll go away somewhere together."

She saw her mother hesitate but then she nodded. "Yes," Lily said simply. "Perhaps we can go home again."

As Page wended her way home to the north shore mansion that she never managed to sell, her heart was heavy. She thought of what her mother had said about going back to where she was born, back to the lovely house and all the people they'd left behind. The more she thought of it, the greater the pain. She'd grown to love Chicago with its smelly stockyards and reeking slaughterhouses, its screeching locomotives, its bustling people, even its vice and corruption. There was something strong and solid about the city that commanded respect despite its undertone of decadence. It was like the beautiful serenity of the lake itself, calm and lovely to the eye but deadly if you swam too far.

Chicago was a rich, voluptuous city brimming with promise, thriving with industry, alive with progress. It would break her heart to leave it, but Lily was right. Now that their secret was known, there was no way Danny O'Shea would let them live here in peace, especially if Jeff O'Leary was elected mayor.

As the days followed, Page put her personal troubles aside and set out with Catherine O'Leary to work diligently in Jeff's behalf. No one of influence was overlooked, and one day she screwed up every inch of courage, put on her most sophisticated dress, and set out to pay a call on Carrie Watson at her parlor-house on South Clark Street.

The house was like something out of a wild dream with red flocked wallpaper, pink ball fringe, and white Austrian curtains of the sheerest material. Ferns and palms and rubber plants crowded the room and scattered about were china doves in gilded cages that chirped when wound up. The floors were covered from wall to wall in carpeting so thick it was an effort to walk. There was a profusion of tufted slipper chairs, oversized divans, and one couch covered in buffalo hide. A handsome Adams fireplace dominated one wall, looking rather out of place among the clutter of Victorian pieces.

"Lovely," Page commented, but the room was far too garish for her taste.

"It's home," Carrie said as she sprawled herself across the divan. "We go for only the top sporting crowd here, the well-established rich, the carriage gentry. I don't allow no walk-in traffic." She made a sweeping motion with her arms. "All first-class and very discreet."

Carrie patted the cushion beside her. "Take a load off your feet, Mrs. Kane." She gave a wicked wink. "Surely you're not here looking for work. I'd hire you in a minute, of course."

Page blushed. "No, but I have come asking a favor."

"Name it, honey. It was damned nice of that friend of yours—what was his name—oh, yeah, O'Leary . . . to bring me those papers. It was a great gesture on your part, handing over those mortgages and letters that Karl was holding. I owe you."

Page shook her head. "My friend, Jeff O'Leary, is running for mayor in his brother Allan's place."

"Oh yeah, the lawyer they found floating in the lake."

Page went on quickly. "I need all the help I can get to support Jeff for mayor."

"What do you want me to do?"

Page looked guilty and shrugged self-consciously. "You have a lot of connections with a variety of important men in Chicago as well as all over Illinois. If you were to . . ."

Carrie laughed and slapped the arm of the couch. "I'll get my people behind your candidate, Mrs. Kane, you can count on it. As I said before, I owe you."

"I'd consider it a favor."

"Sure, sure, a favor." Carrie laughed again.

Page had to be a little more forceful and direct with some of the other influential men whom she'd met through Karl, especially those so-called respectable businessmen who had their offices in the new brick and stone Union National Bank and kept suites at the Bigelow House with its marble façade, "an indestructible edifice of classic architecture," the newspapers called it.

One by one she made contact with just about everyone who could be of benefit, moving from district to district, soliciting votes wherever she could and boldly using threats if threats were leveled at her. Her success gave her the courage to approach one of the most powerful tycoons in Chicago, Charles Yerkes, who openly boasted that he bought aldermen, senators, and ward heelers the same way he bought his shirts . . . by the dozens. Karl had spoken often of Yerkes and she'd met the man once or twice.

Charles Yerkes growled the loudest about the size of the contribution Page exacted from him both by insinuation and flirtation, but he gave her an inspiration when he complained, "At least you could serve me a dinner for my promised favors."

Page smiled sweetly and a little seductively. "You shall have your dinner, Mr. Yerkes, if you deliver the support you say you can."

"I'll deliver."

Besides collecting crooked politicians, Charles Yerkes liked to collect women and art, and as he sat looking at Page he decided she'd make an excellent addition to his vast harem of American beauties.

Page rose to go. "Shall we say next Thursday? You can call for me at eight o'clock."

After receiving his assurance he'd be there, she hurried to the O'Learys and was glad to find Jeff wasn't there.

"We'll hold a dinner at the Palmer House next Thursday evening," she told Mrs. O'Leary. "I'll arrange everything; just make sure Jeff is there at eight o'clock. Leave the guest list to me. It will be an excellent opportunity to launch Jeff's campaign formally."

"A big fancy dinner in this hot weather?" Catherine complained. "Nobody'll be wantin' to dress up in evening clothes to crowd into the Palmer House ballroom. The nights are too hot and dry."

"They'll come," Page said. She laughed to herself. "At least I know that Charles Yerkes will be there."

The older woman's eyes widened. "Charles Yerkes? How in the name of all that's holy did you reach the likes of him? Why, he's as stuck-up as the English royalty."

"He'll be there and so will all the others. Just make sure Jeff doesn't know I'm arranging it or else he won't come."

Mrs. O'Leary shook her head sadly. "He's terribly down on you since Allan died, Page."

"He has every right to be. If it hadn't been for me, Allan would never . . ."

"Now stop that kind of talk. If you want to think like that, then the blame lies in that little blonde lass who started the whole thing."

"Blonde lass? Melody Sharp?"

"Aye, that's the one."

"What did Melody have to do with it?"

"She was the one who put Jeff and Allan on your trail that night."

"Jeff was also looking for me that night?"

"Of course. He took one direction and Allan the other." She heaved a sigh. "So you see, Page, if Allan wasn't in that grave today it might likely be Jeff."

"I didn't know."

Mrs. O'Leary brightened and gave Page a gentle slap. "And don't you be tellin' either. Jeff gets all riled whenever anybody says anything about you, good or bad."

Page threw herself into preparing for the dinner with renewed vigor. She even contacted the younger city pioneers who had a mad scheme to build a steel rail transport across Chicago which would be elevated over the existing streets. Insanity, of course, but they were finding a lot of impressive ears. Even Mr. Medill, the owner of the *Tribune*, was listening to these radicals with their progressive ideas.

When she contacted Joe Medill he couldn't give her a definite assurance that he'd be at her dinner party. "I'm thinking of running for the mayor's office myself," he told her.

"All the more reason you should be at the dinner." Her strategy was that Joseph Medill would come to check out Jeff, but all the others seeing Medill there would take it as an endorsement of Jeff.

The dinner, thanks to the help of Bertha Palmer and her friends with their staffs of servants, was a resounding success. Charles Yerkes had to laugh at the joke Page had played on him when they entered the ballroom late and found it filled.

"You're a sly one, Page Kane," he said as they took a table reserved for them in a separate alcove, curtained so that Page could see but not be seen by Jeff.

After the dinner was served a quiet fell over the room when Jeff stood up to speak. Page leaned forward in her chair, folding her hands on the table, absorbing every word. Just the sound of his voice made her tingle with memories and with anticipation. She loved him. The realization hit her with such force that a tiny gasp caught in her throat, a gasp audible enough to make Charles Yerkes turn and look at her.

It was true, she told herself as she tried to keep her mind focused on what Jeff was saying. She loved him and knew that it was useless for her to deny it any longer. Her mind flew into a torment of regrets when she remembered the hundreds of ways she'd hurt and abused him. Worse still, she knew how capable he was of hurting her, yet that didn't matter. She deserved his abuse, both physical as well as mental, for the things she'd said to him, the torments she made him suffer.

She was certain he didn't care for her one bit, she told herself as she looked at Melody Sharp sitting primly beside him at the head table. Even that didn't matter. Nothing mattered except her love for him, her love for a man who had raped her, commanded her, abused her; a man who was practically unknown to her except for carnal knowledge, a man she hated, yet a man she wanted more than anything in life.

There was a sudden commotion behind the backs of the French doors leading into the ballroom. Several glass panes shattered and the doors were flung open. Danny O'Shea and a dozen of his hoodlums stood menacingly scanning the elegant crowd. Danny was dressed in evening clothes.

"I must have mislaid my invitation so accept my apologies for being late, folks," he said as he strode cockily toward the dais. "You all know me," he told the crowd. "At least your husbands know who I am, ladies, and of course some of you ladies know me as well."

"Get out, O'Shea," Jeff ordered.

"Not till I say what I came to say and find what I'm looking for." He scanned the room again. Page pulled back behind the curtain.

Charles Yerkes saw her fear. "I'll put a stop to that imbecile."

Page put her hand on his arm but he left her and started toward Danny. Before he'd taken ten steps several of O'Shea's thugs strong-armed him and forced him out of the ballroom, ignoring Yerkes' threats of revenge.

Danny said, "All you swells had better remember the name O'Shea when you cast your ballots next month."

Joe Medill of the *Tribune* said, "How could we forget it?"

Several laughed, relieving a bit of the tension.

Danny jumped up on the dais, blocking Jeff's view of his audience. "Just remember that you know who I am, but more importantly, folks, that *I* know *you*." He made a sweeping gesture to include everyone in the room. "I remember all the faces

274

that sneak in and out of my back door so just don't forget my face come election day."

Danny's eyes moved from table to table. "I don't see Mrs. Kane," he said sarcastically. "Now surely the one behind this shindig would certainly be here."

"Here she is, boss," called one of the thugs Page recognized from that night in the Levee. She tried to fight free, but he held tight to her wrist and dragged her toward the doors leading outside.

Jeff made a grab for Danny. "Leave her alone," he yelled as he leapt over the table onto O'Shea's back. His sudden weight buckled Danny's knees and he went down.

Screams and yells went up from the diners as they made a mad scramble to get out of the way of the two men rolling about on the floor.

Jeff was young and muscular, but Danny had the advantage of being an experienced brawler, wiry and strong. He threw an uppercut that connected solidly with Jeff's jaw, throwing him backward. Jeff lay stunned, trying to get to his feet. Danny lashed out with his foot. Jeff saw it coming and grabbed the shoe, twisting it hard to the right, pitching Danny off balance.

In a flash Jeff was on top of him. He threw a chokehold around O'Shea's neck. Danny, with the expertise of a wrestler, reached up and locked his hands behind Jeff's neck and yanked forward, pulling Jeff over his shoulder. A moment later their positions were reversed as Danny caught Jeff in a hammerlock and began to apply pressure.

Jeff felt the strength in Danny's grip and knew his arm was going to be broken.

There was a sudden shattering of glass and Danny O'Shea toppled to the floor beside him. Jeff

275

looked up to see Melody Sharp standing over Danny's unconscious body, still holding the handle of the heavy water pitcher in her hand.

"Page!" Jeff yelled as he jumped to his feet and raced out of the room.

Chapter Twenty-Three

Page didn't know where the men were taking her, but it was obviously a well-planned abduction because they lost no time spiriting her into a closed carriage and galloped away from the Palmer House while onlookers were trying to figure out what was going on.

"O'Shea ain't leaving it up to Bull Ramsey this time," one of the men in the carriage said.

"You?" Page gasped when she saw his face clearly in the light of the carriage lamps. She turned and looked at the other man, the one holding her arms behind her. "Brock. Ziggy," she said, remembering Karl's two henchmen, the two men who'd rescued her from Danny O'Shea that first day in the Patch. "What are you doing? You don't work for Mr. O'Shea."

"We do now, Mrs. Kane. A guy's gotta eat," Brock answered.

"Where are you taking me?"

"Scrub Town. Danny has a shack out there."

Scrub Town, Page knew, was the most dangerous neighborhood on the western outskirts of the city, a bevy of shacks and lean-tos that served as saloons, dance halls, houses of prostitution and perversion. The brothels there weren't worthy of being called parlor-houses. Women openly paraded the streets with their legs and breasts exposed through transparent kimonas. Blacks and Orientals were crowded into the district like so much unwanted driftwood. And beyond was nothing but open hostile woods where the city folk seldom ventured, living under the premise that they at least were familiar with the crime and vice of the streets . . . one never knew what was outside the city. There were too many reports of scalpings by Indians and trappers alike, runaway slaves still afraid to believe themselves free, escaped convicts living in tent camps deep in the woods.

The only time anyone ventured into the wooded areas and empty stretches of prairie that bordered Chicago was to hunt game in a place they referred to as Lake Forest. Some of the rougher types went out to Driving Park to watch the horse race, a violent sport where the drivers were too often murdered before they reached the judge's stand if they weren't favored to win. Those clouds of dust at Driving Park hid many a deadly crime.

"Scrub Town," Page breathed as she tried to wrench herself free of Ziggy's hold. She'd heard it whispered about and those remembered whispers made her blood turn cold.

She had no way of knowing that a mile or two behind them Jeff was galloping after them. He'd caught a glimpse of the carriage lamps winking in the distance as the brougham dashed away from the Palmer House and turned down Monroe Street.

"They're heading for Scrub Town," Jeff said as he watched the carriage cross the river bridge and head west. He slowed his horse, not wanting to be spotted, and kept well back as he waited to see where the brougham stopped and where Page was being taken.

His instinct to rescue her blinded him to reason. Why was he so obsessed by this woman who seemed to do everything to irritate him, who was even responsible for his own brother's death? Of course he couldn't rightfully blame Page for what had happened to Allan. She'd been a pawn. But she knew who was responsible and refused to say. Why? What was she hiding, he wondered. And worst of all, if she did hold some dark, dangerous secret, surely she should know she could share it with him. Certainly she must know how he felt about her, how much he loved her in spite of everything.

He grinned without realizing it as he kept a close eye on the brougham. He and Page Kane were of a kind, both headstrong, self-indulgent, reckless, even indiscreet, he thought as he remembered how she'd clung to him so indelicately that evening in her husband's study with servants roaming about on the other side of the door. Then there was the other part of her, the smoldering eyes, the look of a wounded bird, the sensual movements of her hips, the delicate curve of her mouth when she was pleased.

As perverse as it seemed, he didn't envy Allan having been her lover. In fact he preferred that it had been his brother rather than some slick powder puff like that oily Karl Kane. God, how he'd despised that man and hated Page all the more for having married him. Why hadn't he told her how Kane had blackmailed him into doing those dirty jobs for him just because Kane played the philanthropist, the gracious benefactor, the giver of money to Jeff's mother when her husband needed to get out of town, out of the clutches of the law Danny O'Shea had sicked on him. God only knows how much Kane had gotten in exchange for his investment in Patrick O'Leary's trip to the California desert. And all Kane ever had to do was beckon to Jeff with his little finger and threaten to cut off the money he paid Jeff, money that kept his father safe, money that helped Allan through school and kept a roof over his mother's head.

"I did what I had to do," Jeff told himself as he rode after the carriage. "And no one need ever know, not even Page," he added. He'd been careful to hide all those records about the money Kane paid him when he went through Karl's safe. It had been difficult to ask Danny O'Shea for jobs, but his father's expenses had to be met.

Well, at least Allan had left some money when he died, Jeff thought, and after becoming mayor that would be the end to all the subterfuge and the lies.

"Who knows," Jeff said aloud to himself, "Perhaps I'll be able to send Ma off to that California desert to be with her beloved Patrick."

They had ridden through the well-populated area of Scrub Town and were heading toward the woods. When the carriage stopped in front of a low building, Jeff quickly dismounted and led the horse into some dry brush at the side of the dirt road. The heat of the horse only added to the dry heat of the night. He pulled loose his tie and stuffed it into a pocket, slipped out of his dinner jacket and draped it across the saddle. There was a slight breeze stirring but not enough to be cooling.

He watched two men take Page out of the carriage and hustle her into a shack without lights in any of its windows. He inched closer, being careful to stay hidden in the shadows. Far behind him he heard the echoes of Scrub Town, the laughter of the women, the drunken hoots from the saloons. This far away from the town's activity there was nothing but blackness and the quiet of a cemetery that stood off to his left, its straight, gray tombstones glinting ominously in the moonlight. To one side was a mound of dirt beside an open grave yawning for tomorrow's tenant. From the looks of the graveyard it had lots of tenants already and there would be lots more, Jeff knew.

One of the men came out of the shack, forcing Jeff back into his hiding place. He watched the man take something that looked like a coil of rope out of the carriage and then go back inside the shack.

Jeff waited. Somewhere in the north a forest was burning; he smelled the woody smoke and wiped his forehead free of sticky perspiration. He didn't have to wait long for the two men to come back out and by the way they moved they seemed anxious to be away, leaving their charge securely trussed up inside. Jeff supposed they'd been given orders to leave her fate in someone else's hands. From all Melody had told him he guessed that Page had some information that Danny dearly wanted.

The brougham pulled off, made a U-turn, and started back to the city. Jeff kept himself and his mount well hidden in the brush and shadows and waited until it was well out of sight.

He lost no time reaching the shack, scouting the place on the outside to make sure it wasn't guarded. He crept from window to window and in the only lighted room in the back he saw Page tied hand and foot to a rough wooden chair. A gag covered her mouth, her head was dropped forward and Jeff

281

could tell she was crying from the violent shaking of her shoulders.

He tapped on the window and when she looked up and saw him her eyes went wide with surprise. She gave no sign for him to be careful so Jeff assumed she was alone in the shack. He tried to raise the window but found it was framed permanently to the side boards. He hurried to the door, groping his way through the dark only to find it was locked. He lost no time in putting his shoulder to it, wrenching it from its hinges.

Entering the room, he worked fast and furiously, keeping both ears cocked for any approaching sounds as he removed the ropes and gag. As he pulled her from the chair she went naturally into his arms. He kissed her mouth and tasted the tears on her cheeks as he wrapped his arms more tightly around her.

"Darling," he whispered.

He looked deep into her eyes and stroked her hair as he again pressed his mouth to hers.

Page clung to him, savoring the strength of his body, the hardness of his desire for her.

"We must be away," he said.

"Danny O'Shea's coming here," Page told him. "I heard those two mention it."

Jeff grinned. "He'll come with a lump on his head. Melody conked him with an ice-water pitcher." He felt her draw away at the mention of Melody's name. "Darling," he said, tilting her face up to his. "She . . ."

Page put her fingers gently against his lips. "I don't want to think of the past, Jeff. None of it."

Jeff started to say something but the sound of an approaching horse stopped him. Without a word he snuffed out the single candle, opened the window

282

and lifted Page through it. A moment later they were crouched beside Jeff's horse well back in the woods, hidden by the tall bushes as a rider pulled up in front of the shack. The brightness of the moonlight made it easy to identify Danny O'Shea.

"Don't make a sound," Jeff warned as he put his arms around her and felt her snuggle tightly against him, pressing her cheek against his chest.

They heard Danny curse. "Those idiots didn't leave her a lamp. Damn."

Close to her ear Jeff chuckled. "At least he has your well-being in mind."

Page was trembling too badly to trust her voice.

They saw a match flare and heard Danny curse again as he found the empty room, the open window. He came out of the shack with a pistol in his hand and started to move stealthily around the clearing, peering into the darkness. He knew there were too many places where he could be ambushed if he moved into the overgrowth of bushes and trees, and decided that searching alone would be futile.

"Damn," he shouted, not caring who heard. Then he strode over to his horse, mounted, and galloped off.

"What in the devil is going on with you two?" Jeff asked as he helped Page to her feet. "What does Danny want from you?"

She still clung to him. "The Gilded Plume," she managed.

"Why abduct you?"

"Please, Jeff. I can't tell you. Trust me, dearest. It is something that happened before Mother and I came to Chicago. Something Danny O'Shea found out about."

"Surely it can't be so monstrous that you can't confide in me."

"That isn't for me to tell," Page said and when Jeff started to object she asked that he please leave it at that. "One day it can all be told, darling, but not now."

He shrugged off his frustrations. "All right, then let's get out of here before O'Shea comes back with his army of goons. They'll burn the place down if they have to."

They skirted Scrub Town and traveled north, entering the city around Division Street, close to Page's house. As they headed toward Lake Shore, Jeff smelled smoke again but this time it wasn't from a forest fire. An alarm was heard from the watchtower on the courthouse and in the distance there was the clang and clatter of the fire steamers, a horse-drawn, gleaming brass-plated wood-burning boiler, whose steam drove water through a force-pump.

"Another fire," Page commented, more weary than concerned.

"There's been an awful lot of them this summer. That's one of the things I want improved in this city," Jeff said. "We need more and better fire equipment."

She snuggled closer. "No politics tonight, Jeff darling."

He laughed, lifted her hand and touched it to his lips. "I promise. No politics."

The house was still, the hour not late. Twin lamps were burning in the foyer as they entered the mansion. Mrs. Chambers came out from below stairs and smiled. "I trust the dinner was a grand success," she said, seeing them together.

For the first time Page and Jeff realized they were still in evening clothes, albeit Jeff's tie was gone and his jacket off, but by all appearances they looked as if the dangers of the night had never happened. They looked at one another and started to laugh.

Later, while sipping their coffee in the sitting room, Jeff stood up and picked up his jacket.

Page said but one word. "Stay."

In her eyes he saw the passion, the longing, the need for him. Hand in hand they went out of the room and up the curved stairway to Page's bedroom.

"You're beautiful," he whispered as he took her in his arms and kissed her.

"Dearest."

Jeff slowly undid the back of her gown and eased it down over the layers of petticoats, stripping her layer by layer, like taking the petals from a rose. At last she stood before him, naked and trembling with desire. He eased her onto the bed and quickly undressed.

Page opened her arms as he lowered himself, wrapping them around him as he settled on top of her. She reveled in the heat and strength of his body as she felt herself being pressed deeper into the mattress.

He lost no time in entering her, but the entry was delicate as velvet, hard and strong as the smoothest ivory. Page rose up to meet his thrusts. She wanted what he wanted: release. Afterward, there would be time for the caresses, the tender lovemaking. Right now they both felt the urgency of release and worked swiftly to achieve it.

They were one; that's all that mattered. Words and promises weren't necessary, even wanted. Page ran her hands down his muscled back and over the curves of his buttocks, urging him on, throwing herself with wanton abandon up against his pounding flesh. He moved faster and faster, filling her completely as waves of delicious sensations overpowered her. She felt herself being lifted, rising higher and higher as Jeff assaulted her more mercilessly, driving into her with the force of devils.

Great, crashing waves pounded down over them as they writhed and twisted and pounded, welding themselves so tightly together no human force could ever separate them.

For one long, unbelievable moment the two of them hung suspended in the throes of ecstatic pleasure . . . reality shattered into nothingness as they clung to each other with desperate desire. A common shuddering wracked their bodies as the heavens opened and the stars exploded into a kaleidoscope of color as they went hurtling off into space.

In Danny O'Shea's office Bull Ramsey looked up when his boss stormed in and slammed the door. He saw Danny's rage. "What's wrong, boss?"

"Those two numbskulls are as stupid as you are. They let Page Kane get away. O'Leary obviously followed them to the shack and those fools weren't smart enough to stand guard over her until I got there."

"No sweat," Bull said with a self-satisfied grin. He snapped shut the switchblade he was using to scrape the dirt from under his fingernails. "I know where we can get our hands on her old lady."

Danny gawked. "How? Where?"

"I ain't so dumb as you think."

"Damn it, where is she?"

"At the O'Leary's place on DeKoven."

"How do you know?"

"Because I saw her." He put his feet up on the

286

desk. "You all went to that fancy dinner and I got to thinking how close, like peas in a pod, that Mrs. Kane is with the O'Learys. Just on a hunch I rode out to the O'Learys and there was the old lady sitting in the kitchen."

"And you didn't snatch her?"

"I couldn't. She was with some other woman and a man. There would have been a fuss. You want me to go get her now?"

"No," Danny said as he started to think. "Just so long as we know where to find her. I'll wait until close to election time before I show my hand to Page Kane. I'm sure I will be able to get her not only to turn over the Plume to me but to get Jeff O'Leary to pull out of the election."

As the thoughts germinated inside his head he saw all too clearly that he at last held the winning hand. He threw back his head and started to laugh.

Bull looked annoyed. "But you promised me the Kane doll."

"You can have her, Bull. You can have anything you want, come election time. Just be patient for a couple of weeks."

Chapter Twenty-Four

By the end of the first week in October, Page was deliriously in love. Jeff's campaign was going extremely well, though it consumed most of his time, time which she would have liked for him to spend with her.

"I can't be with you every evening, darling," he said. "There are a million and one people I have to see and meet . . . men who want to talk freely without a woman being around."

She understood, of course, but there were many nights when she was so lonely for his company that she was tempted to go to wherever he said he was going. She knew, however, that that would anger him, so she waited and took whatever time he could give her.

It bothered her also that Jeff wouldn't allow her to do anything for him financially. She wanted to provide a spacious office headquarters for him in the downtown district but Jeff flatly refused.

"I've already arranged for a little place over on the southwest," he told her. "I know it's far from a fashionable part of town but it's where I came from and I want the voters to know that. I won't put on a front and pretend to be what I'm not."

Page visited his so-called headquarters one afternoon and was horrified. It was no more than a shabby tarpaper shed near the stockyards.

"But the smell of those pigs and sheep and steers?" Page argued, touching a scented handkerchief to her nose.

"That smell is what gives jobs to over a thousand voters and puts meat on the tables in every city and town in this country. Besides, both Mr. Armour and Mr. Swift have promised to endorse me for mayor, which is a big surprise to everybody because those two hate each other and never agree on anything."

"Slaughterhouse operators?" Page sneered.

"People don't eat live animals," he said patiently. "Now get out of here and let me get back to work."

"But . . ."

"Out!"

It had almost started a serious quarrel but Page wisely told herself to keep still, to say nothing. It was Jeff's campaign, not hers.

Like so many other people, Page didn't want to think about the realities of living; she closed her mind to the thousands of pigs and sheep and cattle as well as horses that arrived by box car after box car at the long unloading platforms, where double shutes were fitted to the top and bottom compartments of the cars and the animals freed into pens. While they lived, the poor beasts ate the finest of feed and drank water purer than that drunk by the people in the city.

The railroads didn't like the slaughterhouses pole-axing the animals, cutting them up and shipping them out, because packed meat took up less freight space than a whole animal. So there was a running battle between the rail lines and the slaughterhouses. The railroads usually won because barreled meat and sides of beef didn't stay fresh very long on long trips in box cars where the ice blocks melted quickly, especially in long hot, dry spells like this one.

Page gave her head a little shake and refused to even glance at the animals in their pens as she drove away from Jeff's office. There were so many other more pleasant things to think about, especially now that she was hopelessly in love. The future looked absolutely perfect.

The only thing that puzzled her was that Danny O'Shea had ceased to show any interest in either her or Jeff's campaign. He made no big show of himself; if it wasn't for his ads in the *Tribune* she'd have thought he'd withdrawn from the race.

Thankfully Bull Ramsey had left town, or so it appeared because there wasn't a sign of him anywhere. The boys at the Plume said they thought he'd gone back to Abilene. Still, Page couldn't break the habit of looking back over her shoulder whenever she was out walking and never went anywhere without her small derringer.

She didn't know it, of course, but Bull Ramsey was closer than she thought. On O'Shea's orders he stayed holed up on the second floor of The Scarlet Lady, where O'Shea kept him pacified by supplying a continuing string of doxies who enjoyed the kind of games Bull liked to play.

It was on Saturday that Danny decided the election was getting close and he'd better make his move. He called Bull into his office and closed the door. "All right, Bull, you've been lolling on your ass long enough. It's time you went to work. And this time," Danny warned, "I don't want any screw-ups."

Bull shifted uncomfortably.

"First things first," Danny said. "Now tomorrow is Sunday and I know for a fact a herd's coming up from Kansas, due in the yards first thing Monday morning. The drovers are pasturing them outside the west side Sunday night and bringing them in at dawn. What we're going to do is get rid of Jeff O'Leary first and then take what we want from the Kane doll and her old lady. I don't trust that woman. Besides, I don't think it will be enough just to force O'Leary out of the mayor's race; he'll always be trouble, so I've decided to get rid of him permanently."

"What do you want me to do?"

"Snatch the old lady."

"But you said you wanted O'Leary first."

"I'll take care of O'Leary. He works in his shack most of the time. I'll see to it that he's there Sunday night." A sly grin crept across his mouth. "A cattle stampede would trample that headquarters of his into splinters." He shrugged. "If Jeff's inside when they charge through—and he will be—too bad for O'Leary."

"Cattle stampede," Bull said, frowning. "How do you want me to cause a cattle stampede?"

"Don't bother about that. I don't want this bungled so I'll do it myself with some of the boys to help. All I want from you is, tomorrow pick up the old lady at the O'Leary house. If anyone gets in the way, get rid of them, but make sure you grab Page's mother and bring her back here to me. And for Christ's sake, Bull, don't get too rough with the old woman. I don't want her having a heart attack or something. She's no good to me dead."

Sunday was another hot, close day, dust clogged

and dry as dead leaves. The entire city of Chicago seemed restless, bored with the monotonous weather, the absence of rain. Everybody drank more; liquor sales boomed, men cursed and got drunk, women sweltered and lost their tempers. The only excitement seemed to be the many fires which were constantly springing up all over the city, keeping the fire department exhausted from overwork.

Melody was both glad and sad to be leaving Chicago on the six o'clock train for New York. It was the kind of chance that wouldn't come again and she knew her love for Jeff was wasted. He thought of nothing but his campaign and Page Kane.

"Oh, well," Melody said to herself as she snapped closed her portmanteau and looked at herself in the mirror. "A whole new life is opening up for you in New York, kid. A new nightclub, a new city, a new start."

As she started out of her room she saw Danny going down the stairs. He was the flashiest dresser in the Patch and he looked odd in his broad-brimmed western hat, cowhide pants, spurs and boots. She wondered where he could possibly be going dressed like some drover up from Texas. Curiosity made her look out the window in time to see Danny ride off with Brock and Ziggy who were dressed for herding steers, certainly not for a Sunday afternoon picnic.

When she turned from the window she walked unaware into Bull Ramsey's arms. "Can't keep your hands off me, right, Melody," he kidded.

She slapped his hands away, then thought better of it when she saw he too was on his way out. She smiled sweetly at Bull. "All us girls find you irresistible, don't you know that, Bull, honey?"

"Yeah," he said oafishly. "Women know what a real man is when they get me."

She flirted with him, fluttering her eyelashes and toying with the buttons on the front of his shirt. "I took that job in New York," she said as she played up to him. "I'll be leaving on the six o'clock train. Maybe you and I should say a proper good-bye. We never did get around to knowing each other real well."

"Gee, Melody. I got a job to do for Danny. He'll skin me alive if I screw up."

"He's gone out. I saw him ride off with Brock and Ziggy."

"They're going to stampede a herd of cattle," he blurted out without realizing what he said. He felt torn between having to leave and wanting to stay. "How's about taking a later train?"

She let him pull her into his arms and plant a wet, slobbery kiss on her neck. Tactfully she eased herself away. "Maybe I will. Hurry back," she said as she gave him a playful shove toward the stairs leading down.

A stampede, she wondered as she slowly came down the stairs and watched Bull hurry out the front door. "Hey, Mike," she called to the bartender. "How about one for the road?"

"Sure, Melody." As he poured her a drink he said, "I'm going to miss you around here, kid."

"Yeah, thanks, Mike. I'll miss you too." She sipped the whiskey and ginger ale. "Why are Danny and the boys stampeding a herd of cattle?" she asked, looking disinterested.

"Who said they were?"

"Bull."

"Bull has a loose mouth."

She leaned forward. "What's going on?" She saw

294

him hesitate and moved back. "I really don't care. I'll be on the six o'clock to New York; I just thought I'd be missing out on some fun Danny was planning, something to break up the boring routine around this hot, damned town."

Mike laughed. "It has something to do with the election. That's all I know."

"The election for mayor?"

Mike nodded. "I guess Danny plans on calling attention to himself by driving a stampede into the stockyards. The packing house guys are against him so I guess it's his way of showing them where the muscle is."

Melody pretended to be bored. "Yeah, that's just like old Danny . . . always with the muscle, never with the brains."

The bartender laughed. "I doubt if he realizes those cows will rip up everything standing on the southwest side."

She finished her drink and got off the stool. "Well, thanks for the drink, Mike. See you in church."

He thought that funny and started to laugh as Melody went back upstairs to collect her portmanteau.

The southwest side was where Jeff's headquarters were, she told herself, wondering if Danny's stampede had anything to do with that. She bet her life it did and as she picked up her suitcase and started back out of the place she thought she'd better warn Jeff, just in case. She glanced at her lapel watch.

"Jeff will be at the headquarters now," she said as she hurried off.

Lily was just finishing the ironing. She emptied

the boiling water out of the flat iron, then set to rubbing its hot surface with pumice until it cooled, after which she'd put on a coat of paraffin to keep it from rusting.

She heard a noise at the front of the house and thought it was Catherine coming back for something she'd forgotten.

"Catherine?"

There was no answer but that wasn't unusual; Catherine O'Leary never heard anything when her mind was preoccupied, especially lately, what with the election day getting so close.

She heard the footsteps behind her and turned, still holding the heavy flat iron. When she saw Bull Ramsey she staggered, the backs of her knees banging into the chair behind her, forcing her to sit down.

"You remember me?" Bull said as he leered down at her. "I see you do by the way you're looking at me."

"What do you want?" Lily stammered.

"I ain't going to hurt you, lady." He reached for her. "You and me is going for a little ride, that's all."

"No," Lily said, pressing hard into the chair as she unconsciously lifted the flat iron onto her lap. It was still very warm, which she felt through her skirt, but she wasn't aware of anything but Bull's menacing face. "I'll scream," Lily threatened as he came closer.

"Nobody here to hear you, lady. I've checked on that before I barged in. You're all by yourself. I saw the other old lady leave. Now you come along nice and peaceful-like and I won't have to hurt you none."

Again he reached for her, this time with a deter-

296

mined grab. Lily pushed sideways out of the chair and out of his grip. Unfortunately she moved the wrong way and found herself backed into the corner.

Bull rushed at her. She had never known real violence and thought herself incapable of it, but when she felt his strong, brutish hands tighten on her arm, she lifted the flat iron and slammed it into the side of his head. A loud roar of pain and rage tore out of him as he grabbed his face and fell backward.

Lily lost no time scrambling around him and rushing into the front room of the house, still holding tight to her only weapon of defense.

He caught her before she could reach the door leading out, where she thought she would find some place to hide in the boxes and piles of old lumber and other ever-present discards that always find their way into poorer neighborhoods.

"I told you not to make me mad," Bull said as he raised his hand to strike her.

Again she lifted the flat iron, but this time he anticipated it and wrenched it out of her hand. He slapped her hard across the face with the flat of his hand, sending her reeling across the room and up against the far wall.

When she saw him closing in on her, Lily grabbed for whatever was within reach. The oil lamp only grazed his shoulder and shattered on the floor, its easily ignited fluid soaking deep into the faded pattern of the carpet.

Bull lifted her easily and crushed her tight in his massive, hairy arms as he carried her toward the door. Lily kicked and screamed and clawed at him, but her strength was beginning to fail and she knew she had to do something desperate or she was lost.

With a vicious kick she sent the toe of her pointed boot into his groin. Bull howled and threw her aside to cup the agonizing pain in his testicles.

Almost senseless, Lily started to crawl toward the flat iron that lay across the room. Inch by inch she strained and reached, fighting and praying for time. Her fingers touched the still warm metal. Her hand curled around the wooden handle.

Bull's heavy boot came down hard on her wrist. Lily screamed as the bones snapped. His rage was too great to be held in. The blinding pain in his groin, the mere thought that an old woman could have gotten the better of him, put him into a blind fury. He grabbed her by the hair of her head and yanked Lily to her feet.

Lily's eyes rolled in her head as he struck her again and again until she felt the last of her strength leave her. Her lids dropped and she passed into unconsciousness. Bull continued to slap and beat her limp body. When he saw she'd passed out, it only fueled his anger. He threw her onto the floor, picked up the flat iron and slammed it deep into her skull. Time and again he brought the heavy iron crashing into bone and hair and blood until the sweat was pouring into his eyes, blinding him, sapping his rage.

He knelt over her for several minutes, breathing hard, trying to bring the room into focus as the glaze moved slowly from across his eyes and his temper cooled.

The old woman was dead, he knew. The blood was staining the carpet, mingling with the lamp oil that had soaked it minutes before. For a while he couldn't decide what to do. He just stood there breathing hard, sweating heavily as he stared stupidly at Lily's dead body.

"What in hell do I do now?" he asked himself as his senses started to settle. Danny had warned him not to hurt the old lady and now she was dead.

The daughter! "Sure," he said, rubbing the side of his head. "Kane's widow would do just as good as the old lady," he reasoned, knowing she believed herself to be an accessory to the murder.

It was the noise of a youngster with a wagon that brought him back to the present. He got to his feet and peered out through the lace curtains and saw a boy of about nine or ten walking toward the front of the house, pulling a wagon of rattling milk cans and dragging a stick against the broken pickets of the fence.

"Mrs. O'Leary," the boy called as he stopped at the gate.

Bull pulled back, still watching. The boy called again then started toward the porch.

"Shit!" Bull cursed when he noticed that the front door to the house was still open. He cursed himself for not having closed it when he'd crept in, but the heat made it more sensible to leave it open for any stray cool breeze.

"Mrs. O'Leary!" The boy was almost to the porch.

With one swift kick, Bull yanked up the edge of the carpet and threw it over Lily's dead body. To all outward appearances he was rolling up a rug when the boy appeared in the doorway.

"Oh. Hey, who are you?" the boy asked.

"Never mind. I'm moving stuff for the old lady."

"Mrs. O'Leary?" The boy watched him for a minute. "Does she have any empty milk cans she wants picked up?"

"She ain't here. Come back later, kid."

The boy hesitated, still watching Bull fooling with the rug, then he turned to leave.

Bull looked at the lump in the carpet and tried to think what he should do. "Hey, kid, wait a minute."

The boy came back to the door.

"You know The Gilded Plume in the Patch?"

"Sure. The classy joint."

"That's the one." Bull fished in his pocket for a half-dollar. "Go there and find Mrs. Kane. Tell her her old lady's real sick and to come here right away." He flipped him the coin.

The boy's eyes bugged. "Gee, sure thing, mister." He ran off down the dusty street leaving his wagon and milk cans sitting near O'Leary's gate.

Bull looked down at the rug. "Now all I gotta do is wait." He dropped into a chair. "Danny won't be back till after dark so I'm in no big rush."

He yawned, leaned back and closed his eyes, propping his feet up on the lump in the rug.

Chapter Twenty-Five

The sun was starting to go down when Page rose from her Sunday afternoon nap. It was a little after four o'clock and still as hot and sticky as it had been when she'd laid down at two. It had to be the hottest, driest October 8th ever, she thought as she wet a towel and dabbed her face, wrists, and neck.

Another unbearable evening without Jeff lay ahead. Perhaps she'd visit her mother because she wasn't in any mood to go to the club. The new man she'd hired to manage the place seemed capable enough and it was time she began thinking seriously about selling the place. After she and Jeff were married she'd want to concentrate on his career and on raising a family.

Page frowned suddenly as she realized that Jeff never mentioned marriage. Not once in all the weeks of passionate lovemaking had he even suggested the idea. He professed his love most ardently but never the desire to make her his wife.

She shrugged. Jeff had plenty of things on his mind these days. After the election, he would have the time to think about his personal future.

As she slipped into a yellow linen dress she again tried to think of a way to pass the evening. Certainly not by going to another lecture, she told herself. George Train's talk in Farwell Hall last night had so unnerved her she never wanted to hear the man's voice again. She could still hear him saying: "This is the last public address that will be delivered within these walls! A terrible calamity is impending over the city of Chicago. More I cannot say; more I dare not utter."

A shiver ran through her as she remembered those chilling words. She had always hated hell, damnation and doom prophets but Bertha Palmer had insisted they go and hear the world-famous traveler, author and lecturer. Afterward even Bertha apologized. It had been a depressing experience for everyone and Page was determined that tonight would not be a repeat.

She tried to remember with whom Jeff was spending his evening. Another politician from one of the districts; it was always some politician. For a man without political interests a month ago Jeff certainly had found something he truly loved, she thought. There were times, however, like right now, when she was downright jealous of Jeff's sudden obsession.

"It isn't healthy," she said as she came down the stairs. Jeff was too involved lately. Page decided that tonight she'd see to it that he forgot about politics for one entire evening. Whoever he had appointments with would have to see him tomorrow. Tonight, she told herself with a determined squaring of her shoulders, she and Jeff would go out and have fun, just the two of them.

The clock on the mantel told her that Jeff would still be at his headquarters. She'd go and drag him away by force if necessary. The idea cheered her and when Mrs. Chambers came in and asked about supper Page was humming gaily to herself.

"I'm going out with Mr. O'Leary," Page told her. "You may visit your sister if you like, Mrs. Chambers. She still has her little place up on the shore, doesn't she? It should be cooler there."

The housekeeper thanked her and Page, now looking forward to the evening, resumed humming the little tune as she put on her prettiest hat and started for the carriage house.

The city felt scorching, she thought as she rode along the street, the bordering trees drooping in the relentless heat, their leaves powdered with dust. It was as if she were riding through a make-believe place that had been baked too long and was now slowly turning brown. Everything, even the tall sturdy buildings of limestone and brick, looked vulnerable with their frames and sills and trim of wood and roofs of tar-covered paper over square beams.

Page decided that after she picked up Jeff they would drive farther north along the shore and as the smell of the stockyards reached her nostrils she said, "And get as far away from that odor as possible."

Melody sat anxiously leafing through the Sunday *Tribune* as Jeff finished talking with the man in the white ducks and striped cotton blazer. She got up when Jeff returned after walking the man to his carriage.

"Now," Jeff said, taking both her hands in his. "What's so all-fired important and why are you wearing that worried little frown?"

"Jeff. Danny's up to something awful."

"Danny's always up to something awful."

"It's about you." She hurried through what she

knew about the planned stampede. "I'm sure he expects to trample this office to splinters."

Jeff rubbed his finger along the line of his jaw. "With me in it," he said.

"What?"

Jeff thought for a moment. "Danny got word to me that he wants me to meet him here later tonight. He said he didn't want to take the chance of anyone seeing him coming here to me and asked that we meet real late, close to midnight in fact."

"Oh, Jeff. Be careful!"

Jeff grinned. "That bastard! He knows he doesn't have a chance with me in the race so he's planning on taking me out of it." He smiled down at her. "Hey, don't look so frightened. Thanks to you, my sweet, I will be miles away from this office tonight." When she returned his smile he added, "And I owe you a great debt of gratitude, Melody. I hope someday I'll be able to repay it."

"Next time you come to New York, come as the mayor of Chicago. That's all the thanks I want."

"That's a promise." He glanced at the clock. "What time's your train?"

"Six."

"You'd better hustle that pretty bustle of yours. We can't afford for you to miss it."

Melody turned toward the open doorway feeling a terrible heaviness in her breast. She would have given her life for him to have said, *Miss the train, Melody. Stay here with me.* But as she looked up into his eyes she knew the telltale gleam of love would never be there for her. She'd seen the way he looked at Page Kane; it was as though his eyes changed color and texture and luster.

At the door she paused. "Jeff," she said in a faltering little voice.

"Yes, Melody?"

She bit down on her lower lip and fixed her eyes on the floor as her cheeks began to burn. "I do have one favor to ask before I leave."

"Ask it. You have my solemn word I'll grant it if I can."

She steeled her courage and raised her eyes to him. "Kiss me," she said. "I mean, really kiss me, as if you meant it." She saw him hesitate. "Please. It's all I'll ever ask of you."

"Of course, Melody, my dear," he said as he took her into his arms.

It was a long, lingering kiss. Melody clung to him knowing that this would be the last time she'd be in his arms. She savored the taste of his mouth, the feel of his body pressed hard against her own.

Her hands toyed with the hair at the back of his neck as she closed her eyes, trying to make herself believe that the kiss was what she wanted it to be.

Page's buggy rounded the corner just as Jeff took Melody into his arms and kissed her lovingly, passionately on the mouth.

Page began to shake so violently every part of her seemed to be coming apart. A dark ugly hate started to form deep down in the dark places of her heart.

"Liar! Betrayer!" she wanted to scream but they were so engrossed in one another she was certain they would not have heard her, nor would have cared. She pulled the buggy to a halt and sat staring at them locked in embrace, oblivious to everything and everyone around them.

Page watched, etching his deceit well into her memory then turned the buggy and started back the way she'd come. So this was how he'd been filling his crowded schedule? While she pined and languished in her loneliness, he was spending every free hour in that other woman's arms.

You fool! Page swore.

The pain began slowly, like a dull ache in her soul, gradually growing, devouring the hate, the shame, the loathing until there was nothing left inside her but a terrible suffering. The thought that she'd lost him was almost too much for her to bear. She'd given herself so completely to him that all she had now was a dreadful emptiness.

She let the tears run down her cheeks unchecked as the crushing hurt of his deception blinded her. Page wanted her life to end. She never wanted to see another day, hear another voice. Grabbing the buggy whip, she snapped it again and again on the horse's rump sending him galloping over the pine-block paving, careening around corners at break-neck speed.

The horse reared when it raced toward the bridge and found it raised. Its front hooves pawed the air as if trying to climb the barrier and hurl himself and his mistress down into the black waters of the river. He stopped, digging his hooves into the paving, skittering, almost upsetting the buggy.

Two men, thinking Page in distress, ran over and grabbed the harness, settling the horse.

"Are you all right, miss?"

Through her hurt and her anger she found her voice gone. She gave her head a quick nod and kept her face averted, hiding her tears.

"Mrs. Kane?" one of the men asked, straining to identify her in the dwindling light.

"Yes," she managed.

"There's a boy at The Gilded Plume waiting for you. He says he has an important message. Something about your ma."

"My mother?" she said, sobering.

"That's what he said."

Feeling exhausted, numbed by the ache in her heart she backed the horse away from the upturned bridge and started toward the Patch. A deep heavy sigh escaped her as she closed her eyes and once again saw Jeff take Melody in his arms.

He had used her! Her first impression of him had been the right one. She should have known from that first day in the O'Leary barn what kind of a man he was. Selfish, cruel, conceited, she swore. She never wanted to see him again. She had money now. She knew people. She and her mother could leave Chicago. There was nothing to tie them here now, she told herself as she rode through the dingy, littered streets and looked at the leaning shacks and drooping fences. The place could burn in hell for all she cared, she thought as she pulled the buggy to the hitching rail in front of the Plume and got down.

"Sorry, boy," she said as she smoothed the brow of the horse, then leaned her head lovingly against his snout. "I've overheated you, I'm afraid."

The horse snorted as if to say he understood and nuzzled her. She patted him again and went into the club.

"Hey, Mrs. Kane," the manager called. "We've been looking all over for you."

"I've been riding."

The man looked more closely into her face. "Are you all right? You don't look too good."

"I'm all right, Jake. It's the heat, that's all."

"Here," he said handing her a glass of ice water.

She drank and seated herself in a chair. "Now what's the trouble?"

"Some kid said he had an important message for

307

you. It seems your ma's taken sick. She's asking for you. I sent the boy over to your house looking for you but you'd gone so he's out combing the streets trying to find you."

She'd only heard part of it. "My mother's ill?" She stood up.

"That's what the kid said. Somebody from the O'Leary house sent the boy to fetch you. A neighbor, I think it was."

"Oh, dear." Page breathed as she hurried out.

"Want I should send a doctor or something?"

"Thanks, Jake, but if it's serious I'm sure there's someone there already," she called back over her shoulder.

Though her heart was breaking at Jeff's treachery, she climbed into the buggy once more and started off toward the O'Learys'. Hiding her face in the dark of the fast-falling night, she let the tears come. In the distance she heard the whistle of the eastbound train as it pulled into the depot. One day very soon she and her mother would be on that train, she vowed.

Danny O'Shea and his two henchmen crouched in the shadows of the trees and watched the drovers sitting around a small fire, drinking coffee.

"When are we going to start shooting, boss?" Brock asked as he continued to polish his six-shooter.

"It's too early. I want that herd to hit the southwest side about midnight so we'll start them moving in about three hours. The timing's got to be just right, so relax. It should take the herd about an hour to stampede the distance from here to the stockyards."

"What about those drovers?" Ziggy asked.

"When we start shootin', they'll start shootin' too, but at us."

"No, not at us," Danny assured him. "They know about the planned stampede. They've been well paid off."

"So why in blazes are we sitting here in the dark when we could be drinking coffee with those boys?"

"Because they don't know who paid them off and I don't want any of those cowboys to see our faces. Men sometimes get greedy and try to hold out for more than the bargain called for." He nodded toward the herd. "We'll mingle with the steers, get them kinda skittish, then start blazing away. The drovers will shoot too and help us make sure the cattle are stampeded toward the city. We'll keep on the herd's tail until we reach the southwest, where we'll turn them back over to the drovers who will tell everybody how the herd got spooked and couldn't be handled."

"You think of everything, boss."

"That I do. Absolutely nothing can go wrong." He laughed and slapped Brock on the back. "And when I'm mayor of Chicago, boys, I'll give both of you the keys to the city."

Chapter Twenty-Six

There were no lights on in the O'Leary house when Page arrived. She thought that odd as she tied the horse to the gatepost and went around back to the kitchen and her mother's room beside it.

"Mother?"

The place was black and still as the night outside and twice as stuffy. Page fumbled for the lamp that was always kept on the kitchen table. She almost knocked it over in the dark.

"Mother!"

The lamp showed the kitchen empty. Her mother's room beyond was empty as well. She stood in the kitchen looking around, remembering suddenly the first time she'd seen the room. Jeff had ushered her in after . . . Her flesh began to tingle as she remembered the familiar feel of his naked, muscled body, the firmness of his arms, the hardness of his passion.

There was a sudden stinging of tears again as she lowered herself into one of the straight-backed chairs and put her hands over her face. How could he be so deceitful, so horrid? It had all been a game to him. She had laid bare her heart and he had trampled on it, had kicked at it until he'd had everything it offered, then he had turned to another.

Her fists clenched, the nails digging into the palms. Someday, somehow she'd have her revenge on Jeff O'Leary. Her original need to run away dissolved. She would stay in Chicago and do everything she could to destroy him, to hurt him as much as he had hurt her.

A moment later the tears were back and she was crying out her love. Deep inside she knew he was the only man she would ever love, could ever love. Perhaps it would be best after all to turn him out of her life by taking Lily and moving away some place where she'd never see a single reminder of him.

A noise interrupted her reverie. She looked up sharply but saw nothing. She hadn't been mistaken, however. There had been a noise, like something heavy moving on the other side of the door leading to the front room of the house.

She stared at the bare door and strained to listen. Slowly she got up from the table and stood in the dull light of the oil lamp.

"Mother?" she called out but only silence answered.

Her hands gripped the back of the chair, steadying herself, trying to take strength from the strong, sturdy wood. After a moment of fortifying herself she picked up the kitchen lamp and moved toward the door. The china knob felt surprisingly cold to her touch.

The lamp she held above her head showed the front room as she'd never seen it. The rug was rolled into an ungainly shape, the lamp was smashed, the furniture overturned.

Page choked back a strangled scream when she saw Bull's face pale and white in the moonlight. His eyes, yellow and narrow, peered back at her. Fear paralyzed her. She found herself unable to move as Bull Ramsey got to his feet.

"Took your time getting here," he said. He yawned.

"My mother?" Page asked anxiously.

Bull leered, then lowered his eyes to the rug and gave it a kick. "She had a little accident."

"No!" Page screamed as she stared at the bulky rug and slowly, with terror clutching at her, began to back away.

"Not leaving without your ma, are you, missy?" Bull laughed.

When she turned to run Bull let out a roar and thundered after her. As she ran through the kitchen toward the back door she turned and hurled the lamp at his face, but he ducked aside and the lamp smashed against the cast-iron stove, setting the wooden floor afire.

Page screamed again and dashed out the back door. Bull smothered the flame with the oilcloth table cover then took off after Page.

She fumbled with the double knot she'd foolishly tied in the horse's reins. It wouldn't untangle and Bull would be on her before she could get it undone, she told herself. She saw the barn door ajar and darted inside, hoping to find an avenue for escape or a place in which to hide herself until someone came.

The animals started to move restlessly in their pens and stalls as Page searched in the blackness for some way out. This was where she'd been deflowered and now it may well be where she died, she told herself as she saw no windows, no way out except by the doors through which she'd entered.

She started back out but Bull was lumbering toward her. Quickly she slammed shut the double

313

doors and barred them. Bull used every ounce of his strength and he crashed into the doors, snapping the bar as if it were a twig.

"You can't hide from me, missy, so come along quiet-like. I don't mean you no harm," Bull called. He took down the lantern from the nail beside the door and lit it. When it flared up he saw her looking frightened and helpless in her yellow linen dress. Slowly, moving forward, favoring the bruised shoulder he'd used to force the barn doors, Bull backed Page toward a corner.

The animals, sensing danger, moved nervously, wanting to get away from whatever had broken the door and was threatening them.

"Stay away from me!" Page snatched up a hay fork and held it before her.

Bull put down the lantern and laughed. He swatted the pitchfork aside as easily as one would a cobweb. Before him stood the girl he'd been deprived of for too long and now, by God, he intended having her, regardless of what Danny O'Shea had to say about it.

Slowly Bull undid the buttons on the front of his baggy pants and pulled out his huge member, letting it hang grotesquely from the opened fly as he came menacingly toward her.

Her eyes were riveted, yet she was repulsed by what she saw.

"I'm going to have you, missy, so make up your mind to it," Bull said as he fondled himself and his manhood began to stiffen.

He circled her, undressing her with his eyes as he started to undo the front of his shirt. The barn was hot . . . oppressively so, yet it only seemed to add to his need to feel her sweat mingle with his own.

314

"I'll kill you!" Page snarled as she tried to see some way to escape him.

Bull laughed. Her fear only added to his desire. When he pulled the shirt from his belt he unconsciously touched the switchblade that was tucked there in its case. He let his fingers play over the handle as his brutish mind moved in another direction.

No, he told himself. He'd killed the old woman. Danny would have his skin if he didn't deliver this one in one piece.

When he reached for her, Page bolted backward but her foot caught in the straw and she fell in a heap. She lay there shuddering with fear, pressing herself deep into the dry, brittle hay as Bull loomed over her.

Give yourself to him, a little voice told her. Let him satisfy himself quickly and have it done with.

And then what? she asked herself. He was a killer, a man obsessed with maiming and sadism. But perhaps this was to be her fate. Jeff was gone from her life. She had lost her only love and her mother as well; if a life without them was all that lay ahead, then better she die.

Bull started to pull off his pants. Page stared at his hardness, the tense thick thighs, the hairy brown of his body, like an oak, gnarled and coarse and mighty. She cringed back into the loose hay as she watched him step out of his trousers and advance toward her, his rigid member cleaving the air like a saber.

His breathing was labored and sweat was trickling down over his chest as he closed in on her. Page searched around but saw nothing with which to defend herself. When he stood over her, naked and grotesque, she tried not to look at his ugliness.

315

He pounced on her like a huge brown bear on a trapped fawn. Page rolled swiftly to one side and threw straw into his face as she desperately scrambled to her feet. Bull grabbed her ankle and pulled her back. Page kicked hard and the heel of her shoe struck the side of his head, weakening his grip long enough for her to pull free and dash headlong for the doors.

He was on her before she'd covered half the distance and dragged her back into the circle of light from the lamp. His huge, burly arms wrapped themselves around her as he slobbered kisses on her throat and neck. He tore aside the top of her lovely yellow linen frock, exposing her creamy breasts. As he tore the dress from her shoulders he began kissing and sucking the nipples.

Page tried to push his head away, to wriggle free of his embrace, but it was useless. He was far too strong and her own strength was giving out. She felt the thick hard-set muscles of his legs as he pried apart her thighs and tried to impale her on his rigid member, holding her tight against his naked, hairy chest.

"No!" she screamed as she felt him prod and poke at her. She squirmed and twisted but to no avail. In desperation she sank her teeth into his ear and heard him yell out in pain. He dropped her into the straw and grabbed his ear, feeling the blood streaming into his palm. Again Page rolled to one side and scrambled to her feet, holding the shreds of her dress up over her exposed breasts as she ran toward the doors that stood askew.

Just as she was about to slip through to freedom Bull's hand tightened on her wrist and yanked her back inside. He swung out at her, hitting her with such force that he sent her sprawling against the side of the barn, almost knocking her unconscious. He looked at the doors that he'd broken through.

"You'll not get away from me until I've had my fill of you." Using all his strength he wedged the doors shut so there was no way for Page to escape, then he turned back on her and bellowed like the angered bull that he was.

He threw himself on her, pinning her to the floor. Again he pried apart her thighs and started to fit himself into her. Gradually she came out of her stupor and grew conscious of what he was doing. Somewhere she found strength to lash out, dragging her fingernails down his cheeks, clawing at his eyes, kicking, kneeing, bucking. He tried to hold her hands, her arms, but she'd become a wildcat as she bit and tore and scratched.

Bull was forced to the side as Page continued to scream and fight for her life with every ounce of her resistance. Her hands flailed the air and scraped the wall she'd been knocked against. Her fingers touched something hard and cold. Whatever it was didn't matter; it was something to wield. She brought the metal bar down on Bull's skull. In an instant she was on her feet and racing toward the doors. They were too heavy to move aside to allow her to slip through. As Page labored to push down the door she heard Bull grunt as he started toward her. She looked around for somewhere to hide and fled to the darkest side of the barn, hiding herself in the far stall in which the brown cow was housed.

"You can't get away from me, damn you," Bull yelled as he picked up the lantern and started to search her out.

As the light hit each stall in turn the animals started to move more uneasily, shuffling and snorting, shifting their bulks from side to side. Page steadied the brown cow as she tried to hide herself with its body. The animal's eyes were large and staring and·Page saw the same fear and terror that must be reflected in her own eyes.

"There you be," Bull snarled as hc held high the lamp and saw Page cringing at the front of the animal.

The brown cow gave a low, guttural bellow, a sound of terror as her stall was suddenly lighted by the lamp. She kicked out, sinking her hooves squarely into Bull's middle.

A loud, long groan rushed from him as he was pitched up off his feet and knocked backward, sprawling flat on the floor. The lamp smashed against the wall and immediately a yellow line of fire began licking its way toward the loose straw that floored the cows' stalls.

Page screamed when she saw the fire. Bull, clutching his stomach, staggered to his feet. In his dazed state Page saw that he had not yet noticed the flames.

"The fire," she yelled, but he didn't pay her any mind. He staggered toward her, intent upon having what she was fighting so hard to deny him.

"Bitch!" he snarled as he slapped the cow aside. Instead of moving, the animal kicked again and this time connected solidly with Bull's hip. He fell back, banging his head on a joist supporting the partition.

Page saw the flames moving quickly along the floor, eating their way in two directions, toward the wall and toward where she and the cow huddled in terror.

Keeping her eyes glued for any sign of movement from Bull, Page used the animal as a buffer between them, backing the cow out of the stall, leading it away from the flames that were gradually getting higher and hungrier.

Bull didn't move; he lay sprawled on his stomach as the fire began up the side of the barn, sending billows of thick smoke into the hot, stuffy air.

The other animals in the barn smelled the smoke and began to panic, bumping and kicking at the sides of their stalls. Page wrestled with the heavy doors but Bull had wedged them too tightly together for her to budge them. Her eyes stared as the fire crept higher and higher up the wall, lapping its way to the rafters, filling the barn with hot, thick, black smoke.

As she tugged and pushed in vain, she suddenly realized that the only person who could save her was the man who was tormenting her. Without hesitating she rushed over and knelt beside him, trying to shake him into consciousness.

"Please," she cried, "wake up. We've got to get out of here. Oh, please," she pleaded as the flames touched the dry straw of the far stall and the entire corner of the barn exploded like a bomb. Page tried to pull the heavy naked man toward the doors. The animals were bellowing hysterically as the flames rose higher, filling the barn with intense heat, sucking out all the breathable air.

Somewhere overhead she heard a crackling sound and just as she looked up she saw the flames touch the edge of the hay bales stored in the loft. One bale blew up like a powder keg, igniting the others, and as she stared up at the fire racing along overhead she heard something crack and saw the blazing support of the loft start to give way.

A scream tore from her throat as the flaming inferno started to fall toward them.

Chapter Twenty-Seven

Jeff waited until Melody's train was out of sight before turning out of the station. The hot orange sun was setting and Jeff felt too sluggish to bother with any kind of business tonight.

He shrugged uncomfortably under his light jacket and looked up and down the dry dusty street. An entire evening alone with Page suited him. He'd send a note to that alderman cancelling their appointment. He could always see him tomorrow. He smiled to himself knowing how pleased Page would be when he showed up to take her out someplace cool for dinner. A happy little tune bounced about inside his head as he stepped into his surrey and started away from the ornate train depot.

He suddenly remembered the thousand dollars he'd gotten from Charles Yerkes earlier when Melody came to warn him. He'd locked the cash in his desk but it should be put in Page's safe until tomorrow when the banks opened, especially since Danny O'Shea intended stampeding a herd of cattle through the headquarters.

Noticing the time, he decided Page would be at The Gilded Plume and turned the horse toward the Patch. He'd call for her there, then pick up the money. They could make a quick stop at the mansion on their way to dinner on the north shore.

The streets were crowded with people out for a ride, trying to catch a breeze, on their way for some refreshment, and Jeff made slow progress. By the time he reached the club he was hot and rather irritable.

"She ain't here, Mr. O'Leary," Jake told him. "She was here but there was a message that her old lady was sick or something. I guess she went there." He squinted at Jeff. "I don't mean to pry, Mr. O'Leary, but are you two fighting or something? You look as mad as she did . . . and Mrs. Kane had been crying. She didn't want anybody to see but I could tell right off. Her eyes were all red and puffy."

Jeff frowned. "Crying?"

"No question about it and she looked real mad about something. She was all shook up, even before she heard about her ma."

"Most likely this damned weather. It's making everybody edgy and then maybe she had some kind of quarrel with her housekeeper or someone."

Jake shook his head. "She didn't come from home. I sent a boy there with the message about her old lady. The housekeeper told the kid Mrs. Kane had gone out with you."

"With me?"

"Her buggy came from the direction of your place when she rode up here all in a huff."

"Oh, no," Jeff said as he slapped his forehead. He remembered kissing Melody; Page must have seen it. "Oh, no," he said again as he ran out of the club and jumped into the surrey.

He saw the smoke rising up into the air when he turned down DeKoven Street. Several neighbors were trying to pry open the barn doors. Jeff pulled up and raced to help.

"There's a girl or somebody inside," one of the men said. "I heard a scream."

"Page? Page!"

There was a roaring sound overhead and suddenly flames burst through the far corner of the roof carrying burning tufts of hay and straw up into the air, across the yard and onto the roof of the house. The dry tar paper caught like a match and within seconds the entire top of the house was ablaze. The men scattered, looking for water and buckets, leaving Jeff to tussle with trying to pry the doors loose.

Smoke was seeping through the cracks and crevices of the barn as he desperately called her name and struggled with the doors. Inside he heard the frantic bellowing of the animals as the flames worked their way steadily closer to them.

Straining with all his might, Jeff finally managed to move one of the heavy doors. Smoke stung his eyes and burned his throat as he went inside. Page was lying in a heap beside the door; the animals were huddled together near the wall farthest from the flames.

As he lifted her in his arms and carried her outside he saw her eyelids flicker as she started gulping fresh air into her lungs.

He saw her naked breasts as he laid her on the ground and propped her up against the fence. He took off his jacket and fitted her arms into the sleeves, then buttoned up the front.

Page opened her eyes. "The animals," she mumbled. "I untethered them."

"I'll get them out," Jeff promised as he rushed back into the barn.

The smoke and flames were thicker. He lost no time chasing the animals toward the opening in the doors. Attracted by the current of clean air coming from the opening, the beasts almost stumbled over each other in their dash to get out.

When he came back to Page she was sitting in a daze staring at the house as the men tried in vain to put out the fire.

"Your mother!" Jeff cried. He started away but Page clutched his sleeve. When he looked at her she simply shook her head. In her half stupor she murmured, "It's too late, Jeff. Mother is dead." She started to cough, gasping for air.

"Dead! Dear God!" he said as he gathered her in his arms and felt her collapse against him in a dead faint.

When she opened her eyes again the entire O'Leary house was on fire, flames shooting out through the windows, fire balls rocketing up into the air. A terrifying scream ripped from Page's throat as she stared, horrified, at the blazing building, knowing her mother lay dead inside.

"I'm getting you out of here," Jeff said as he felt the heat on their skin. "There's no way they're going to save the house and the barn is going to fall in any second." Again he lifted her in his arms and carried her toward her buggy. He unhitched his mare from the surrey and tied her on behind, then climbed in beside Page.

The brown cow was leading her charges nonchalantly down DeKoven Street, away from the heat, stopping now and again to munch on tufts of dry grass and dandelions.

"What happened, Page?" he asked as they started away.

"Bull Ramsey," Page groaned through her

coughing. She gulped more air and felt her lungs begin to clear. "He killed my mother. He almost killed me as well. He's still in the barn." She could still see the flaming corner of the loft collapse on him as she rolled clear of the fiery terror; she could still hear Bull's agonizing screams as he found himself pinned beneath the blazing beams and hay bales.

"Page, for God's sake, tell me what is going on!"

With her mother dead none of it seemed important any more. Speaking in a trancelike voice she told him about the murder in Abilene. "But the man was alive when we left that alley, Jeff, I'd swear to it."

"He was," Jeff assured her, piecing together bits and pieces of what Melody had told him over the past weeks, snatches of conversation she'd overheard between Danny and Bull. "The old woman Melody heard them speak of was your mother. Melody heard Bull distinctly say he killed the man and let the woman believe she did it." He touched Page's hand. "Oh, darling, why didn't you tell me right at the beginning?"

She pulled away from him. The mention of Melody's name brought back the pain.

Jeff gave her a curious look when she moved to the corner of the seat. "What did I say?" When he saw her anger he added, "You should be pleased Melody is an eavesdropper."

"And you're a skunk!"

He slowed the horse and turned toward her. "What?"

"How dare you, Jeff O'Leary! I saw you . . ." She could not finish. Her heart broke and she collapsed in tears.

"You saw me kissing Melody," he finished.

325

"You admit it!" she sobbed, unbelieving. "How can you be so dastardly?"

"I was kissing her good-bye." He quickly explained about Melody coming to say good-bye and the final favor she had asked of him. "She knew I loved you and that there was no place in my heart for her. That's why she took that job in New York and went away. She was a darned good kid, Page. I'm not sorry I granted her that favor."

She wanted to believe him and there was something in the way he was looking at her that told her he spoke the truth. Page hid her face again, this time in shame for having doubted him and for all the terrible things she'd thought of him. After a moment she raised her tear-stained face to his. "I'm sorry, Jeff. It's . . ."

"I know, darling. You've had a rotten time of it lately. I can't blame you for what you thought. But you're wrong in thinking I don't love you. I could never love anyone else, hard as I tried," he admitted with a sly grin. He pulled her close to him. "Let's get you home," he said as she rested her head on his shoulder and closed her eyes to the terror from which he was taking her away.

Seeing her collapsed with exhaustion, Jeff looked back at the blazing house and barn. A fire ball shot up and set fire to the roof of the house across the narrow street. He couldn't understand why the watchman on the courthouse fire tower hadn't seen the blaze and sounded an alarm.

He remembered the fire alarm box at Grant's drugstore on the next street and decided the bucket brigade of neighbors would need help.

"Thank God Ma wasn't home with Mrs. Carver," he said to himself. "Damn it, why didn't Lily go with her to Evanston?"

The new fire alarm box was attached securely to the outside wall of the store but it was locked and the store was closed. Jeff pounded on the door, trying to raise Mr. Grant, but a neighbor came out of the shanty next door and told him the Grants had gone to the lake to cool off.

"There's a fire!" Jeff said pointing toward the flames on DeKoven Street. "We've got to sound the alarm."

The woman looked unconcerned. "There's always a fire someplace it seems," she said.

"The key to the alarm box?" Jeff asked impatiently, glancing to make sure Page was still comfortably asleep.

"Mr. Grant keeps it on his key ring," the woman's husband said as he came up behind her, hiking up his suspenders.

"Damn!"

"The fire watchman surely has it spotted," the man said as he watched the smoke and flames. "Wouldn't worry, mister. They'll take care of it."

The watchman on the cupola of the courthouse turned to the southwest and saw the flames leaping against the dark sky. He studied the blaze for several minutes, trying to pinpoint the exact location. He decided it must be at Canalport and Halstead, which would be Fire Station Box 342. He called down the speaking tube and told the night duty fireman to strike Box 342, little realizing that he was alerting a fire brigade several miles away from the O'Learys' house.

Jeff looked back at the flames that were lighting the sky. He got back into the buggy and drove slowly toward Page's mansion, trying to convince himself there was nothing to worry about, that the fire brigade would take care of things.

Page was still in a faint when he pulled the buggy under the west portico. He carried her gently into the house and up the stairs to her bedroom. He lay her on the bed and drew a light sheet over her. Even with her disheveled hair, her dirty face, she was the most beautiful woman he'd ever seen. Jeff stooped and lightly kissed her mouth then went to the writing desk. On a sheet of her stationery he wrote:

"Went to my headquarters to pick up cash from my desk drawer. I want to put it in your safe till tomorrow. Will be back as soon as I can. Marry Me!
Jeff."

He propped the note on the nightstand and after kissing her again, tiptoed out of the room. Sleep was what she needed most, he told himself as he unhitched his horse from the buggy and went toward the carriage house to find a bridle and saddle. On horseback he'd make better time getting to the south end and back, especially with the crowds of sightseers who inevitably would stream in that direction to watch the fire brigade put out the flames.

By the time he reached State Street he was thankful for having decided to ride the horse. People were clogging the streets and boardwalks all moving toward DeKoven Street to get a closer look at the spectacle. Jeff's horse whinnied and skittered when a steamer with its hose wagon raced by, their horses snorting, nostrils flared, galloping like demons toward the flames and smoke.

As Jeff watched the crowds he decided to turn east and skirt around the congestion. It took quite a while for him to reach the shabby little office near the stockyards. It was almost eleven o'clock, he noticed, when he stuffed the thousand dollars securely into his boot and got back on his horse.

A wind had suddenly come up from the southwest and as he looked in the direction of DeKoven Street he thought the flames were higher and wider, moving more rapidly toward the north.

By the looks of it, he told himself, if the fire was getting bigger there'd be a greater number of sightseers. Remembering Page lying sound asleep in her room, Jeff decided to take the longer route back to the mansion and headed his horse toward the lakeshore. There was no hurry, he decided, figuring sleep was what Page needed most. And besides the ride along the shoreline would be cooler.

Chapter Twenty-Eight

By the time the crews of the *Little Giant* and *America* steamers reached the scene, the entire neighborhood was an inferno, the heat and smoke so intense they could do little but try to keep the fire confined. Reinforcements began arriving but the flames were overpowering. When a large brown house to the west of DeKoven Street exploded like a torpedo, the fire crews were forced back as the sparks ignited the adjacent barns and shacks along the alley.

Other steamers began arriving, trying to throw a circle of water around the fast-spreading flames which were fanned by a gale of hot, dry wind driving across the plains from the southwest.

The heat was unbearable as the firemen fought gallantly but futilely to hold back both the spreading fire and the crowds of spectators who'd come to gawk at the brilliant display.

All the houses on the north side of Taylor Street went up like one huge torch as the fire wagons were forced back. Still, the firemen were convinced, despite the ferocity of the fire, that they had the upper hand and that it would be only a matter of time before they had it completely contained.

The situation suddenly worsened as old hoses, long in need of repair, began to split and the water pressure dropped to a trickle. The wind picked up, creating a growing updraft, sending armies of sparks, embers and debris flying high over the heads of the firefighters. The spectators were too busy marveling at the towering flames to even think about the dangerous tiny torches that were being carried by the wind to the other houses and buildings all around them.

Page opened her eyes and looked around the dark bedroom. Outside she heard the clatter and clang of the fire wagons, but the sound had become so familiar during the past hot, dry weeks she paid it little mind.

As she lay there listening she could again feel the heat inside the barn and her throat ached from the sting of the smoke. She sat up quickly, wanting to rid herself of the nightmare she'd been through. She didn't want to think of her poor mother, of Bull Ramsey's death screams as the flames ate his flesh.

She reached for the matches to light the lamp and as the wick flared she saw Jeff's note. Her heart leapt at his words.

"Yes, oh yes, Jeff," she said as she clasped the note to her bosom. "Of course I'll marry you."

She reread the note then noticed the time; it was just a little after eleven. She got out of bed, took off Jeff's jacket and sponge-bathed. After changing her dress she paced the room, wondering what was keeping Jeff. She stood at the windows overlooking the lake and thought she saw an orange glow reflecting in the water. There was an overpowering smell of smoke in the air, which made her go to the south windows where she saw the threatening flames.

"Good heavens!" she gasped as she watched the

fire eating its way gradually toward the Patch. She stood staring at it, wondering if Jake and the others at The Gilded Plume knew of the impending danger. From her vantage point she could easily see that it would only be a short while before the fire reached the Patch. They had to be warned.

She snatched a light shawl as she raced out of the house and climbed into the buggy still hitched under the portico. At Taylor and Ewing she saw the flames mounting around the sightseers as a clutter of wooden buildings burst into flames, spewing blazing fire balls up into the gust of wind which carried them north toward Page's buggy, igniting more houses along Ewing.

The mob, suddenly finding themselves almost encircled by fire, let out horrible terrified screams as they began pushing and shoving away from the flames and toward Page's oncoming buggy.

Page saw the panic and quickly turned the horse east toward the lake and after several blocks headed south toward the Patch. Clouds of dense smoke were drifting over the area when Page arrived at The Gilded Plume.

"Jake!" she yelled. "The fire's coming this way." She rushed into the office and began twirling the dial on the safe. "Put the books and records in here," she told him. "And take all of the cash out of the registers. Stash it in here as well. The safe makers guarantee this thing to be fireproof."

"From what I hear about this fire, it'll be a good test of that guarantee, Mrs. Kane. I hear it's hotter than the one down below," Jake said with a grin.

A moment later Jake was handing her all the money from the tills. "What else do you want saved, Mrs. Kane?"

Page looked at the little stage, the room where

she'd had so much pleasure. She let out a sigh. "Let it burn if it must," she said as she turned to leave. "Take whatever you like, Jake."

"I think we should save the stock, Mrs. Kane. There's the wagon out back. We could load it up long before the fire reaches here, if it ever does."

"Do whatever you want, but mark me, Jake, that fire is moving fast in this direction."

When Page went out into the street, she saw that the flames had already spread to the roof of one of the saloons several buildings away. Suddenly another building burst into flames and a second later it seemed the entire south side of the street was on fire. Danny O'Shea's Scarlet Lady was the last to catch fire and its flames were starting to grow higher, threatening The Gilded Plume and the buildings on the north side of the street.

"Get out of here, Jake," Page screamed as she got into the buggy and switched the horse.

Streaming from the saloons and brothels, doxies and gamblers and drunks ran into the street. One woman, half naked, ran out of one of the parlor-houses, then apparently having forgotten something, ran back inside. A moment later she came out screaming, her hair ablaze. A drunk, carrying a bottle of expensive brandy, thinking he could douse the flames, poured the liquor over the doxy's head.

Page screamed as the woman was entirely engulfed in fire. The horror of it sent Page galloping toward the lakeshore but the mobs were all around her, screaming of the danger chasing them. At every corner the mob was joined by people rushing from their beds carrying whatever they could carry as the flames leapt from shanty to shack to barn to house. Though it was night the streets were bright

334

as day as the flames rose up in searing, scorching waves of every conceivable color.

More and more fire wagons tried to battle their way to the threatening fire only to be hampered by the mob-clogged streets, the people screaming and clamoring toward the safety of the lake waters. Some drays loaded with household belongings that blocked the way were overturned by both the mob and the fire brigades. Fights started, which only added to the bedlam.

One staggering drunk tried to grab Page's horse and buggy but she beat him unmercifully with the whip and galloped down a deserted alley only to emerge confronted by a solid wall of fire. The horse reared and turned left, taking Page toward the stockyards.

"Jeff," she breathed when she realized where she was headed. She remembered his note saying he'd come here. Perhaps he'd still be in his office. The wind, she noticed with relief, was pushing the fire north, away from where she'd found herself. She slowed the frightened animal and rode between the pens toward Jeff's office.

Danny O'Shea fired the first shot; a second later the quiet night was blasted away. As the guns set up a horrific racket, the herd stampeded across the flat prairie land. The cowboys blazed away, keeping the herd moving toward Chicago.

No one seemed especially concerned about the orange glow in the sky directly ahead of them and as they raced toward it, it seemed to add an element of excitement to the fun of it all. Danny rode with the others at the tail of the galloping herd, all of the men laughing and shouting and shooting.

Thousands of hooves pounded the dry open plain, thundering across the night like an angry storm.

Page didn't hear the sound of the oncoming stampede as she stepped from the buggy and went into the little office. She called Jeff's name but knew immediately that he wasn't there.

The office was empty and through the brightness of the night outside Page noticed that the desk drawer was open. Again remembering Jeff's note with a smile she knew he'd been here and had gone. Most likely on his way back to the mansion, she decided as she went back outside.

The fire had worsened. Then to her horror she watched as the fire turned back and began eating its way both against the wind as well as along with it, bringing the flames directly toward where Page stood screaming.

There was no direction she could turn except west, out into the prairie. The fire was forming a complete horseshoe about her and was rapidly closing the opening in the circle.

She climbed into the buggy and swatted the horse with the whip, sending it galloping away from the flames. She'd gone only a short distance when she saw before her the billowing clouds of dust and the stampeding cattle.

Page reined the horse, gasping with terror. She made a quick turn back but the fire towered before her in a solid wall. She knew there was no chance of escape unless she outraced the front of that thundering herd and reached their flank before they trampled her to death.

"Giddap!" she yelled as she lashed out with the whip. The horse bolted off in a mad dash across the face of the oncoming cattle.

At the rear of the herd Ziggy galloped alongside Danny O'Shea and pointed to the city in flames.

"Fire!"

Danny saw the flames but was too taken up with the excitement of the moment to think of the fire as anything but another group of burning shacks that the firemen could easily extinguish. The frightened cattle thrilled him as he watched them race blindly forward, trampling everything into pulp.

Up ahead Danny and the others saw the buggy careening across the face of the herd and watched with diabolical delight, yelling bets at each other, setting odds on the chances of the buggy making it safely across.

The wind grew more fierce, carrying the heat and smoke out over the plain. The lead steers raised their heads and sniffed the air as they felt the approaching heat. Then they veered off, turning sharply away from the danger.

"They're turning!" Ziggy yelled to Danny. "They're turning back!"

Page saw the cattle make a sweeping arc, still heading directly at her. There was no way she could reach their flank now. The arc was widening, like the current of some wild river, destroying everything in its path.

The cattle galloped smoothly along turning, turning until Page saw them veer off and start back over the way they'd come.

"Back! Back!" one of the cowboys yelled as he saw the herd start toward them.

Danny reined his horse, forcing its high hooves to dig into the dry dusty ground. He jerked the rein and swiftly turned his horse, then dug his spurs sharply into the animal's haunches. The horse reared, kicking its front legs up into the air, then bolted, pitching Danny backward out of his saddle.

"Danny!" Brock yelled as he started toward his boss who was lying flat on his back, the wind having been knocked out of him.

But the herd was too close.

Ziggy and Brock both started to yell for Danny to watch out for the stampeding cattle. Danny staggered to his feet, dazed and unaware. The ground under his feet started to shake and tremble. As he turned he saw the line of cattle thundering down on him.

He let out a terrified scream and held his hands over his eyes as the herd raged over him, tearing, slashing, ripping his body to shreds beneath their sharp, pounding hooves.

Chapter Twenty-Nine

By midnight the firemen manning the steamers were dropping from exhaustion as the flames grew more voracious. Glowing embers were falling like drops of rain over the dry wooden structures of the west side and carrying the flames into the business district.

The fire jumped the Chicago River and devoured everything in its path. A solid wall of flames towered skyward along Dearborn, where the tall so-called fireproof buildings fell in heaps of rubble.

Page sat, feeling safe, watching the flames leap higher and higher. She turned to see the herd vanish like ghosts back from where they'd come but as she looked she saw a new danger. The fire was eating its way into the prairie grass and across the plain. She had planned on riding south, skirting the city and going toward the lakeshore, but that route was now cut off to her. There was nowhere she could go except out into the prairie itself or northward where the grasses had not yet been set afire. But it was to the north that the fire was moving.

She was tempted to seek safety in the prairie, but she knew she could never run away when Jeff was in the city waiting for her. She had to reach him and let him know she was safe.

Again Page switched the horse and started looking for some way home. She raced along the burning city's edge until she reached the north side, outrunning the prairie fire that was chasing her.

At Division Street she turned toward home. The fire was still to the south but she knew it was only a matter of time before the entire city would be reduced to rubble. She shuddered, remembering the story Allan had told her of Black Hawk's prophecy and his bones that were burned to ashes.

Fighting the streets clogged with people and wagons carrying household possessions, she finally reached the mansion on the north shore. It was empty and somber as a tomb. Here was where Jeff would come for her—if he were still alive, she reminded herself as she looked toward the flames.

Slowly Page mounted the stairs and went to the very top of the house. She climbed out onto the widow's walk with its wrought-iron railing and looked toward the fire.

The city was in a total panic. The telegraph wires to St. Louis and Cincinnati pleaded for all possible fire fighting equipment.

CHICAGO IS BURNING!

Long lines of flatcars were hooked to locomotives and steamed toward Chicago, but the fire was now completely out of control and spreading out in all directions.

The temperatures melted cast-iron columns two feet thick, turning steel streetcar wheels into molten heaps. Fireproof safes lasted only minutes, bank vaults were reduced to lumps of smoldering lead. Barrels of paint and oil exploded like firecrackers. Looters ransacked whatever buildings they could, private or public. Saloon keepers, rather than see their stock in trade be wasted feeding the fire, rolled kegs of their most expensive liquors and wines out onto the sidewalks and let whoever wanted take whatever they wished. The drunkenness increased and only added more to the chaos.

It seemed everyone in the city was drunk or had gone mad as women and children were trampled under the feet of the mobs that rushed toward the west side bridges and through the tunnels under the river.

Wabash Avenue was completely clogged with people and precious abandoned possessions. The wealthy fought their way toward the lake, running shoulder to shoulder with the poor. Rich women had their jewelry snatched from their necks and wrists as they clawed their way to safety. Every inch of the grassy space between Michigan Avenue and the lake was filled with every conceivable kind of salvage and homeless terrified citizens.

For hours Page watched the ever-growing carnage. As morning came Page saw a flock of pigeons swoop high into the sky, riding a current of air that lured them above the flames. She watched them hover there like halos of white over a devastated city, then choosing death the flock dipped and disappeared down into the flames.

A scream caught in Page's throat as she watched where the birds had vanished. Then her scream became a cry of joy as she saw Jeff galloping along the shore road, his clothing torn, his face bloodied, his horse near exhaustion.

She rushed from the rooftop tripping, almost falling down the stairs and into his arms.

"My darling," she sobbed as he kissed her eyes, her mouth, her throat, her hair.

"I thought I'd lost you. I came back. You were gone. I went into the city to search for you."

"Jeff, my darling," Page said as she clung to him. "Never, never leave me again."

"I promise," he said as he gathered her tight in his arms and kissed her passionately.

Breathlessly she gasped, "The fire?"

"Completely out of control. The people have all gone insane. General Sheridan is putting the city under martial law with orders to shoot all looters. I had a terrible time fighting my way through the mobs. It's complete bedlam. Nobody knows what to do. Even the governor, I was told, is refusing to let Mayor Mason call out the army, insisting that that is the state's right and not the city's. I tell you, it's insanity."

"Oh, Jeff, will we be safe here?" she asked, looking at the mansion.

"For a while at least. They're planning on blowing up the Union National Bank and the Grand Pacific Hotel along with a line of other buildings in order to make a fire break. That should hold the flames back."

It didn't.

One blazing missile soared several hundred feet and fell on the cupola of St. Paul's. The church steeple went up in flames, spreading new firebrands out over the city. Entire blocks were torched as churches, stores, plants, houses, bridges, lumberyards, railroad, everything succumbed to the hungry flames.

Late Monday night the fire was still out of control and moving ever nearer to the mansion.

"Jeff!" Page gasped as they stood together on the widow's walk. "It's getting closer!"

"Yes. We should move north, but that mob down

there," he said, shaking his head and looking doubtful. "They had to set all the prisoners free from the jail house and they're more deadly than the fire. Still," he said, "we can't stay here. We'd better get together whatever you want to take."

By midnight they had a carriage loaded. Just as they climbed aboard and started out from under the portico a light rain began to fall. A moment later it grew heavier. An eerie hush fell over the city as people turned their faces up to the black heavens.

"Thank God," Page said as she threw herself into Jeff's arms.

"Yes," he said softly. "But the miracle came too late."

"Oh, Jeff," Page cried as she looked toward the dwindling flames. "Chicago . . . it's gone . . . it's all gone."

"No, my darling, not all of it. Chicago will be rebuilt and this time nothing will ever destroy it." He kissed her softly on the mouth. "Besides," he said with a grin, "how am I going to be mayor if there isn't a city?"

Page smiled, then laughed. It felt so wonderful to laugh.

She knew now that this city and this man—they were her future.

The Windhaven Saga
by Marie de Jourlet

Over seven million copies in print!